The Six Rules of Maybe

ALSO BY DEB CALETTI

The Six Rules of Maybe

DEB CALETTI

Simon Pulse
New York   London   Toronto   Sydney

SIMON PULSE

An imprint of Simon & Schuster Children's Publishing Division

1230 Avenue of the Americas, New York, NY 10020

First Simon Pulse hardcover edition April 2010

Copyright © 2010 by Deb Caletti

For information about special discounts for bulk purchases, please contact Simon & Schuster Special Sales at 1-866-506-1949 or business@simonandschuster.com. The Simon & Schuster Speakers Bureau can bring authors to your live event. For more information or to book an event contact the Simon & Schuster Speakers Bureau at 1-866-248-3049 or visit our website at www.simonspeakers.com.

Designed by Mike Rosamilia

The text of this book was set in Scala.

Manufactured in the United States of America

2 4 6 8 10 9 7 5 3 1

Library of Congress Cataloging-in-Publication Data

Caletti, Deb.

The six rules of maybe / by Deb Caletti. — 1st Simon Pulse hardcover ed.

p. cm.

Summary: Scarlet, an introverted high school junior surrounded by outcasts who find her a good listener, learns to break old patterns and reach for hope when her pregnant sister moves home with her new husband, with whom Scarlet feels an instant connection.

ISBN 978-1-4169-7969-2

[1. Interpersonal relations—Fiction. 2. Sisters—Fiction. 3. Pregnancy—Fiction. 4. Mothers and daughters—Fiction. 5. Family life—Oregon—Fiction. 6. High schools—Fiction. 7. Schools—Fiction. 8. Oregon—Fiction.] I. Title.

PZ7.C127437Six 2010

[Fic]—dc22

2009022232

ISBN 978-1-4169-8545-7 (eBook)

To Ben Camardi,
with deepest gratitude for your many years
of friendship, guidance, and great humor.
Your belief made it possible.

Acknowledgments

My most repeated phrase these days is, "Oh, I'm a lucky woman," due in good part to the people named here.

First, huge thanks to my editor and friend, Jen Klonsky, who makes every book better, and my life, too, by being in it. Gratitude to all of the fine people at Simon & Schuster: Paul Crichton, Molly McLeod, Emilia Rhodes, Laura Antonacci, Michelle Fadlalla, Bess Braswell, and the fabulous sales reps who stand behind my work, particularly my dear Leah Hays. Thanks, too, to the other "family" in my and my books' life—Vulcan Productions and Foundation Features. Michael Caldwell, Richard Hutton, Rob Merilees, Amber Ripley—I'm thankful for the good hands in which you hold my work.

My family has always been my most solid ground—Evie Caletti, Paul and Jan Caletti, Sue Rath, Mitch, Ty, and Hunter Rath, and Jupiter, too—big thanks, and bigger love to you all. Love and appreciation as well to our great extended gang: Ann Harder, Irma Lazzarini, Joanne Wishart, Dea Belrose, and Carolyn and Lee Harper and family. They will groan at my corniness, but will also know it is true—Sam and Nick, you continue to be the light of my life. God, I'm proud of you guys. You are such good people.

And, finally, to John Yurich, my husband—you are proof that one should never stop believing in the right and happy ending. With you in my life, I'm permanently and perpetually blessed. Gratitude, gratitude, and more love than this writer could ever have words for.

The Six Rules of Maybe

Chapter One

 ou could tell something was different about Juliet the moment she stepped out of that truck. She was wearing a yellow summer dress and her hair was pulled back so that you could see her cheekbones and her straight nose and the blazing eyes that used to make all the boys crazy in high school. I don't know how to explain it, but she seemed smug in some way I'd never seen before. Like she had this satisfying little secret. Like something had been decided by her and her alone. She held her head as if she were the period at the end of her own sentence.

We knew Juliet was coming home; we just didn't know she'd be bringing someone else with her, or several someone elses, depending on how you counted. Hayden's dog, Zeus—he was one of those people-like dogs; he listened hard and looked at you with knowing in his eyes, even if two minutes later he'd decide to zip around the living room, slightly crazed, ears pinned back, taking the corners around the furniture like he was in his own private race with lesser dogs.

When the truck door slammed outside, Mom looked out the window and gave a little *It's her!* squeal and we hurried outside. The afternoon was just right warm—a May day that could have been a role model for all May days, and the air smelled wet and grassy because Mrs. Saint George across the street had turned her sprinkler on. The truck was one of those old kinds with the big wide front that could slam into a tree and still come out smiling its chrome smile. Juliet stepped out and she was all sunbeams in that dress. She was wet grass, and summer, and sunbeams, same as that day was. The thing about sunbeams, though . . . Well, it might sound unkind. You've got to know that I loved my sister very much even if our relationship was complicated (and, anyway, aren't *love* and *complications* basically words partnered forever, like *salt* and *pepper* and *husband* and *wife*?). But a straight shot of sun directed at a mirror can set things on fire. Juliet and I had learned this ourselves when we were kids one August day on the sidewalk in front of our house. When I was seven (and, honestly, nine and twelve and fourteen), I'd have held that mirror toward the sun for days even if nothing had happened, just because she'd told me to.

Mom ran across the lawn to hug Juliet like she hadn't seen her in years even though it had only been five months since she'd been home last, three since Mom and I had gone down to Portland, Oregon, where Juliet had gotten her big break singing four nights a week at the Fireside Room at the Grosvenor Hotel. When you saw her onstage in that sapphire gown, her head tilted back to show her long throat, smoke from some man's cigarette circling around her like a thin wisp of fog in some old detective movie, you'd never have thought she'd come from tiny Parrish Island. Tiny and *inconsequential* Parrish Island, where the only important visitors were the pods of Orca whales that came every summer. You'd never have thought Juliet was a regular girl who had graduated from Parrish Island High School only the year before. Barely graduated, I might add, almost flunking Algebra II had it not been for the tutoring of her younger sister, thank you, although Mom would say Juliet had never been a regular girl.

The driver's side door opened, and that's when Hayden got out. I thought he was having a nice stretch before he got back in and went home, a friend doing a friend-favor, maybe. He was about twenty-three or -four, tall, with easy, tousled brown hair. He wore Levi's with a tucked-in white T-shirt, and his jeans had a big wet spot on the leg, spilled coffee was my guess, which he was blotting with napkins.

And then he looked up at us. Or at me, because Mom didn't even notice him. Usually I was the invisible one in any group, but he was invisible along with me then. Mom was clutching Juliet to her and then holding her away again so that Juliet's fiery eyes could meet Mom's blazing ones. So his eyes met only mine, and mine his, and right then my heart shifted, the way it does when something unexpected begins. There are those moments, probably few in a life, where *before* and *after* split off from each other forevermore in your mind. That was one of those moments, although I wouldn't realize it for a long time afterward. I saw something very simple and clear there, in his eyes—that was the thing. Honesty. But with the kind of hope that was just this side of heartbreak.

He smiled at me, went around to the back of the truck. I guess anyone would have noticed the way he looked in those jeans. Of course I did. In the open pickup bed there was a big dog waiting to be let out. He was the sort of large, energetic dog that made Mom nervous. A sudden dog, and Mom didn't like sudden things. She mistrusted squirrels and birds and men and anything that had the capacity to surprise. If she ever got a dog, she'd say, it was going to be one of those white and fluffy ones, like Ginger, the Martinellis' dog, who looked the same as the slippers Mrs. Martinelli wore when she went to get the mail. You could put a dog like that into your purse like a lipstick and take it anywhere you wanted it to go, like women did in New York or Paris. A lipstick with a heartbeat that might pee on your checkbook, in my opinion, but this was Mom's dream, not mine. I liked a dog you could lean against.

The dog jumped down and made a galloping leap toward Mom, and the guy in the Levi's lunged for his collar and said, "Zeus!" in a way that was both emphatic and desperate. Zeus, it would turn out, was actually a very well-trained dog—he'd do anything for Hayden. Zeus would look at Hayden in the complete and adoring way you privately wished and wished and wished that someone, someday, might look at you. But Hayden was a good dog father and knew his boy's limits—meeting new people turned Zeus into a toddler in the toy aisle, with the kind of joy and want that turned into manic jumping. Zeus leaped up on Mom, who was horrified to be suddenly looking at him eye to eye, and she held him off with a palm to his tan furry chest. She looked down at her clothes as if he might have made her muddy, although the ground was dry and she was only in her old cargo pants and a tank top, her hair in a sort-of bun stuck up with a pair of chopsticks.

It was then that Mom realized that Juliet had not descended alone from the heavens. She looked surprised at the unexpected

·   Deb Caletti

visitors and the facts in front of her: this truck, not Juliet's ancient Fiat convertible; this lanky, excited dog; this lanky, somewhat tousled and tangled guy grabbing his collar . . .

And that's when we saw it. We both did, at the same moment. It caught the sun, so shiny and new was the gold. A wedding band. On the guy's finger. We both did the same thing next, Mom and me. We looked at Juliet's left hand. And, yes, there was one there, too. That same gold band.

My mother put her hand to her chest. I heard her gasp. And then she breathed out those two words, the ones I was feeling right then too, that multipurpose, universal expression of shock and despair.

"Oh fuck," my mother said.

Chapter Two

efore Juliet came home married to Hayden Renfrew, I had other problems. Clive Weaver, the retired mailman across the street, was losing his mind, and Fiona Saint George who lived next to him (she was a senior at Parrish High, where I was a junior) had fallen into some deep depression, judging by the dark designs she drew in chalk on our sidewalk. Mr. and Mrs. Martinelli, who lived next door to us, were on the cusp of dangerous involvement with scam artists who sent them Urgent Business Propositions by e-mail. And then there was my best friend, Nicole, and her parents' divorce, which so far involved one breaking-and-entering, one restraining order, various personal items thrown onto the street (a television, too), and an impending trial to decide the custody of two kids almost old enough to vote. Nicole was in a constant state of turmoil, which had meant bouts of sobbing, endless phone conversations, and a brief fling with her parents' liquor cabinet.

But my sister's sudden marriage to someone she'd never before even *mentioned*—a someone, *that* someone, who was now heading inside our house carrying a backpack and Juliet's old purple suitcase—it was a three-car pileup right in our very own driveway.

Juliet spilled her purse while leaning into the car to retrieve a bunch of daffodils that Hayden had brought for Mom, and we chased an eyeliner and a roll of mints making an escape down the driveway. Finally, we'd gathered everything and went into the house and stood awkwardly in the kitchen. Hayden introduced himself and Mom folded her arms and looked at him as if he'd managed to marry Juliet without her permission. I got a mixing bowl for Zeus and filled it with water and let him into the backyard; he seemed to be embracing this new experience better than anyone else. He sniffed the garbage can and the Weedwacker. He trotted around the willow tree and the rosebushes. He put his paws up on the fence and tried to peer at the Neilsons' cat through the slats of wood.

I went back in through the screen door and let it slam shut behind me. I wanted to make some kind of noise, because Juliet had gone off to pee and Hayden just stood there in the kitchen with Mom, his hands clasped in front of him. I felt sorry for him—those clasped hands made it look like he was praying.

"I really love your daughter, Mrs. Ellis," he said. "I'm crazy about her, actually." One thing was becoming very quickly clear: Hayden was not Juliet's usual type. Not at all. He seemed solid and grounded the way a tree is, and he was kind, you could tell. He had the sort of kindness that announces itself. Already it was obvious he was nothing like Adam Christ or Evan Giordi or, especially, Buddy Wilkes. Buddy Wilkes gave you the shivers.

Me, the bad kind of shivers; my sister, the good kind. If Juliet was going to run off and marry anyone, I'd have guessed it would have been him. Buddy Wilkes III was the one my sister had given her heart (and everything else) to on and off for all four years of high school. Who was named Buddy anymore? No one. And he still did all those things guys named Buddy did years ago: smoked cigarettes, worked at a gas station, gave girls a "reputation." He wasn't a tree, but a high voltage power line, thin and electric and dangerous.

"I'm not a 'Mrs.,'" Mom said. "Unlike my *daughter*. What did you say your name was?"

"Hayden," I offered.

"Scarlet. Go upstairs. I have more than I can handle here already."

I made a *can you believe this?* face to Hayden to convey that Mom had obviously and suddenly lost her mind. I didn't want him to think I was someone who could be "sent upstairs," which was something parents did in TV movies, anyway, not Mom. She was going a little nuts, and he looked stunned and helpless. Juliet appeared again. You could hear the gurgling sound of the toilet tank filling up from the open door of the bathroom. "I know this is a surprise," she said.

"Surprise? Surprise? You're kidding, right? Let me just think a minute, here," Mom said. She rubbed her forehead with her fingertips as if a plan might appear to undo what had been done. Mom was always a little frazzled on a regular day. I figured it was what happened when the way things were and the way you wished they would be were not quite the same thing.

"Did you go to Vegas?" I asked. I was suddenly interested in the details, mostly because I was suddenly only realizing there *were* details. My sister had gotten married. My sister, whom I had grown up next to, who sat beside me in the car and at the dinner table, whom I used to take baths with, who taught me how to use makeup and shared her friends with me like she used to share her white-and-pink animal cookies because she always seemed to have more of everything—she'd gotten *married*. We both used to hide the zucchini we hated in our napkins and test Mom's patience and fight about who had what and now she'd joined hands with this particular guy and pledged her long life to his, and maybe she'd worn a white dress or maybe her jeans and maybe there was music or maybe there wasn't and maybe they'd been in a long hall with big windows or barefoot on a beach or gazing into each other's eyes at a Chapel of Love. How could we not have been there?

"Portland courthouse," Juliet said. "Five minutes, and the deal was done."

"It was the happiest moment of my life," Hayden said. "Even if it was all a little . . . unplanned." He reached for Juliet's hand, but she was taking her hair down and putting it back up again. His ring—it sat solid and permanent on his finger. He was the kind of guy who would want love everlasting and silver anniversaries and Thanksgivings at big tables. The things you *would* want. *I* would want. Juliet's ring—it seemed small and light. I could see that. Juliet's ring had wings.

"Jesus Christ," Juliet said, although I doubted He'd come if she called. The two of them didn't know each other very well. "I can't believe it but I have to pee again."

Mom stopped her forehead rubbing and stood wide-eyed, her face frozen. A freight train might have just come through the living room, its single light barreling straight toward her.

"No," she said.

"What?" I asked.

"No," she said again.

Hayden looked desperate. He was pacing while he was standing still; that's what he was doing.

"What?" I said again.

"Scarlet, I told you to go upstairs!" Mom shrieked.

I didn't have much choice, then, and as I left the room, I felt the shame and embarrassment of having a mother, which followed me the entire way up the stairs. Banishing me wouldn't do much good anyway. I was someone who liked to stay toward the background, and when you're that kind of person you have a way of finding things out no matter where you are. Sometimes, you don't even have to try—information seeks you out and clings, same as the smell of cigarette smoke to clothes. I knew from a very young age, for example, that our father, Steven Ellis, moved to Vancouver Island around the time I was three, even though I had no memory of it or of him, and even though our mother never spoke of it. Fatherhood was too much for him, from what I understood, the way rich foods are too much for some people's stomachs.

I knew various facts about other things too. My mother's subsequent boyfriends: Vic was a cheapskate and Tony's ex wife took everything he had and Mark thought he was so hot but he couldn't figure out how much to tip a waiter without counting on his fingers. I also knew that my sister lost her virginity with Buddy Wilkes on her fifteenth birthday, in his parents' rec room, under a mounted deer head that Buddy and his father killed on a hunting trip. The day after Juliet's fifteenth birthday, she became a vegetarian for one year; until then, that was the longest she'd been dedicated to anything. And somehow she'd also become just as dedicated to Buddy, as attached as that deer head was to the *faux* pine paneling of the rec room wall.

From my place upstairs, then, I did something I was very good at. I watched and I listened. From the landing I could see Mom's feet—painted toenails, brown sandals—which were facing Hayden's—a pair of guy's feet in sturdy well-worn Birkenstocks. Can toes look angry? Because Mom's did. It was a foot face-off. I wished I had my camera with me, because it would have been a good shot. Feet versus feet, the moment in the animal shows just before one creature gets ripped to shreds.

"I know this is a shock," Hayden said. These were the words being used—*shock, surprise*—words of sudden ambush. "It's a surprise to me, too," Hayden said.

"You must have realized there was this *possibili*—"

"Can we go outside or something? The heat is killing me." Juliet's feet joined theirs. White sandals with fragile, thin straps and the narrowest of heels. That summer, I would come to understand something about fragility—how powerful it was, how other people's need could draw you in, bully and force sure as an arm twisted behind your back. But right then I saw only shoes, no big metaphor, two sets of reliable, dedicated feet following those delicate heels outside.

The feet exited stage left. I heard the screen door open, and Hayden called out something to Zeus. Ice cubes were freed from a tray, clinked into glasses. The screen door shut again. Everyone was likely sitting at the umbrella table outside, which meant I'd have a good enough view from the bathroom. I crossed the hall, lifted myself up onto the countertop. The bathroom was still all new starts and shiny surfaces, smelling the blue-brightness of

Windex, cleaned only an hour ago by me. Since Juliet had left home, her returns had reached the status of Company Coming, meaning the bathrooms were cleaned for her and Mom had made a dessert, and Mom never made dessert.

"It's just Juliet," I had said as Mom spread the pink peppermint-chip ice cream into a chocolate-cookie pie shell, swirling it with the edge of her spatula.

"Juliet's doing big things in the world," Mom had said. Mom respected "big things in the world." Ever since we were kids, we'd hear her talk about *Following Your Dreams* and *Aiming High* and *Seeing the World* as she packed our lunch or drove us home from swimming lessons or carried our tri-fold boards into the cafeteria where the science fair was being held. She'd sing her favorite song "Be" by her favorite singer Neil Diamond as she pasted photographs of places she'd never been into the scrapbooks she made with the scrapbook club Allison, her best friend, started. She'd belt out *"Sing as a song in search of a voice that is silent"* as she glued bits of feathers or shells or other found things to the borders of images of vineyards and castles and ancient cities and other faraway places. The song was her personal big dream anthem—she thought it was about embracing life and finding your true love, but if you listen closely, it's really a song about God. Big *Him*, not little *him*. I pointed this out once, but she didn't seem to care. She told me she went through her entire high school years thinking "I Don't Know How to Love Him" from *Jesus Christ Superstar* described her boyfriend, Roger, perfectly.

I opened the window, put my face close to the sneezy mesh of the screen. In the window ledge was one long-expired potato bug, who had apparently set off on a journey across the wide plain of the south side of our house, traveling the endless distance up and over each dangerous stretch of siding, all in order to die in the gutter ledge of our second-story bathroom window. He had had big dreams, too, and look where that had gotten him.

The umbrella of the table hid their faces, but I could see Hayden's back, and Juliet's tan arms, and Mom's profile. Juliet poked at her ice with the tip of her finger.

"I told Hank I quit," Juliet said.

"Oh, honey," Mom said. "I just can't believe this." She shook her head. One of the chopsticks in her hair was sliding loose and about to fall.

"I suggested maybe just some time off . . . ," Hayden said.

"They're not exactly going to want a pregnant woman crooning to middle-age men on business," Juliet said.

I sat away from the window. I may have actually gasped. I leaned my slow and clueless self against the just-cleaned mirror. *Pregnant?* As in, having a *baby?* *Juliet?* I think my heart might have stopped for a second then. At least, the moment had a shutter click of stop action. My stomach did the elevator drop stomachs do when something is utterly and completely wrong. This was not our life. Juliet as a *mother?* Juliet had had a cactus once, given to her by some boy just back from a vacation in Arizona, and that cactus had sat on her bookshelf until it turned a despairing yellow and then shriveled up and died. She could kill a *cactus.* She'd be one of those parents who left a kid behind at a rest stop, driving for miles before she noticed. We'd hear about her on the evening news.

And how did this happen? I mean, I know how, but *how?* It was just after Buddy Wilkes when I first saw the round pink package of pills in a protective oval appear in our bathroom drawer, hidden under the box of tampons. Maybe my cluelessness was understandable, given that pregnant was the last thing you'd expect from Juliet. You'd expect that she'd be telling us she'd just gotten a record deal and was about to become world famous. Maybe that she was moving to a foreign country and taking us all with her, which was, in a way, what was happening. If anything was a foreign country, marriage was. A baby, too.

Hayden leaned back in his chair. There was a sigh in his shoulders.

"So you don't have your room at the hotel anymore," Mom said. She sounded crushed. Juliet's job at the Grovesnor came with room and board, meaning a great big suite and room service whenever she wanted. The room was a strange mix of past and present—a quilt from home on the shiny gold hotel bedspread. A photo album in the drawer next to the bed with pictures of Juliet's friends from high school, keeping company with the room service menu and the *Portland Attractions Guide*. When it was time for a meal, though, a little table would be wheeled in, with a white tablecloth and elegant food under silver domes and tiny salt and pepper shakers. During our first visit there, my mother, who is as honest as anyone I know, wrapped those tiny salt and pepper shakers in a napkin and snuck them into her purse. The next time we visited, we had a new bath towel at home, with a big, embroidered *G* across the bottom. Mom loved that hotel.

"I didn't think quitting was necessary—we could stay in married student housing. I could finish my degree. . . ." Hayden was appealing to Mom, but when Juliet sighed, Mom reached out and took Juliet's hands. I more than anyone could have told him that no one came before Juliet. You could feel the truckload of loneliness heading his way, as he just stood there, blinking in the bright light of his new marriage.

"I just want to have my baby at home," Juliet said.

There was the weight of silence, the clasped hands. The chopstick finally slid free from Mom's hair and clinked to the floor. She bent down and picked it up, stabbed it back decisively in her hair. Zeus, maybe sensing that his beloved Man was outnumbered, came over and set his chin on Hayden's lap.

"Of course you do," Mom said. The words were a whisper. Gentle as falling snow. As quiet and powerful, too. "Of course."

Chapter Three

I've been told a million times that when I was only three years old, I gave my beloved blankie to my mother because she was crying. It was when my father left, I'm sure, though that isn't the part of the story that gets told. I covered her knees with it. I still have that blanket, though I won't go around admitting it.

From that moment on, being kind and caring was what I was known for, same as some people are known for being smart or beautiful or for playing the piano, a quality as much a part of me as the scar on my hand from when I picked up broken glass when I was two. In the first grade, I was the one who invited Sylvia Unger to my birthday party (nine years before her first suicide attempt), and from the second grade on, the weird and friendless sat with me at lunch. You ate your tuna and Fritos and tried not to stare at their misguided clothing choices or the way they'd chopped their bangs or the red scratches on their wrists.

The truth was, though, I had never really had a golden heart; that's not why I did any of those things. Not really. It sounds awful, but, honestly, I didn't even really want to be friends with those people. Gillian Tooley, for example, was weird to the point of obnoxiousness, Kevin Frink was almost scary, and Sarah Volley had a disturbing tendency to grasp my arm with both hands while we walked, as if she were Helen Keller and I was Anne Sullivan. When Renee Wilters started hanging around Jackie Tilsdey instead of me, I felt the giddy relief you feel when you pass off the joker to someone else when you're playing Go Fish.

The real reason I was so supposedly "kind"—well, it was just less painful to put up with a weird person's company than to feel the horrible weight of their loneliness. I had a low tolerance for other people's pain; that's what it was. And a low tolerance for other people's pain guarantees that you win the booby prize of hangers-on and clinging, irritating oddballs. You're probably destined to grow up to be the sort of person who's nice to telemarketers and who gives money to starving children in Africa while everyone else buys some great new pair of shoes instead. You're definitely the one the dog stares at during dinner.

But on the other hand, Gillian Tooley had alcoholic parents, and Kevin Frink's mom drove a hearse, and Renee Wilters lived in that creepy house with all the cats, and you could see they were hurting inside. I guess I also had the old-fashioned beliefs that if everyone turned their back on hurting people, the world would not be a very nice place. And that *nice* was a great word, even if it was a stepped-on and shoved-aside word, and even if nice people were stepped on and shoved aside too. That's what I told myself anyway, every time I felt hollowed out by someone's need, the kind of hollow that makes your insides feel like the wind is rushing through and that sends in the loneliest of lonely thoughts: *How did I get* HERE? You tell yourself that what you're doing is good, because *nice* is sort of the reward for your efforts. A limp reward, a forever bronze medal, but still a reward. Helping people becomes who you are and what you do. It's your job in the universe, and no one likes their job all the time. Still, you do it.

When I went to my room later that day, then, the day Juliet and Hayden came home married and pregnant, I shut the door and pulled out the boxes of books under my bed. It was clear that *something* should be done, although I had no idea what or for whom, which was probably a lie I was already telling myself. I saw those eyes, his eyes, again in my mind and the helplessness in those shoulders and I felt a true want, the urge to help maybe for the first time out of actual desire and not out of a painful sort of pity. I hunted through a few of the books—*Principles of Psychology, Behavior Understood, Casebook of Abnormal Psychology, Personality Disorders of Our Age*—looking for the right kind of advice. All of the psychology books I read said that too much information was bad for kids, but if you wanted too much information, they were a great place to start.

Personally, I loved information. The more, the better. Knowledge was a personal life preserver you could always count on when you were swimming in the deep end. I ran my finger down the glossaries. Teen pregnancy wasn't exactly accurate—Juliet was twenty. I didn't know how to define the problem. I couldn't exactly find Nonmaternal Sisters Suspected of Getting Pregnant on Purpose. Or even, Nice Guys About to Be Destroyed.

I gave up on the books for the moment. I ignored a call from Nicole, who was likely only going to tell me about her father's recent legal maneuver, or her mother's, or a sighting of Jesse

Waters from our American Government class whom we nicknamed Shy, because that's what he was. Jesse was cute and quiet and never said a word to anyone, and Nicole loved him madly and was convinced he loved her back only he couldn't express it. She'd use her camera phone to sneak-take pictures of him, or even better, herself with him in the background. She could study those pictures for hours. She'd give his elbow or ear or jacket sleeve fine qualities, like sensitivity or generosity.

I was at a loss about what to do with myself and my thoughts. I tried to do my biology homework for a while, but the pictures of the swimming organisms in a marine biome only made me think of one thing. Right then at that moment, a creature was growing inside my sister—*creature* was the word I thought of first. Cells dividing and forming. *Baby.* I tried to make this more than a word. More than science or a Fisher-Price commercial, with chubby-cheeked toddlers and sturdy dump trucks; more than the pink, soft smell in the baby aisle at the grocery store. This would be a real person, with real toes and real lips and real things it needed from us. But no matter what I did, baby just seemed like an idea, an unreachable concept like *Paris* or *Mardi Gras* or *husband.*

After a while, the smell of lasagna came up the stairs—warm cheese and tomato sauce, a *dinner's ready* smell that would have ordinarily meant I'd be called to set the table. But I heard Mom down there, opening drawers and cupboards and doing it herself, and when she finally called us to eat, the daffodils had been set in a vase in the middle of the table.

"Your sister is having a baby," she said, as we sat around the table and she edged out a fat piece of lasagna and slid it toward Hayden's plate which he'd held up at her request. Most people could manage only a single tone in their voice—disappointment, or sarcasm, or joy. But my mother could play an orchestra of emotion in hers. In six words, she conveyed that she had been disappointed, gotten through it, and was now trying to view things in a positive light.

Juliet shouldn't be trusted with a baby, I imagined myself saying. But I didn't want to say what I was really thinking in front of Hayden, who might get the wrong idea of me or, rather, the right idea of me. Instead, I ran the words through the nice and polite filter and out they came in their revised form, sort of like a doughnut going through the icing machine. "So I heard," I said. "That's great."

"You're going to be an *auntie,*" Juliet said.

There was something about this that made me feel sud denly sick. Maybe because she made the word cute, and Juliet never made words cute. Juliet was a lot of things—beautiful and aloof and strong, feminine enough that men seemed to want to rescue her. But she was never artificially adorable. Maybe being pregnant had done it—something about hormones and maternal instinct. Maybe after the baby, she'd turn into Ally Pete-Robbins, our neighbor with the rotten twin boys, who hung those holiday banners up in her yard, in case we might forget it was Christmas.

"Wow," I said. I remembered suddenly the time Juliet was supposed to watch Ginger, the Martinellis' dog, when they took their new RV, the Pleasure Way, out for its maiden voyage to Montana. She'd forgotten to feed the little dog for a full day and a half until I had reminded her. Maybe it was a good idea that she'd come home to have the baby after all. Maybe it would have to stay in my room so that I could keep an eye on it.

"You going out to the game or something tonight?" Juliet asked me. And just like that, we were transported to some sort of normal life. Or we were using my normal life to pretend every-thing else was normal. Juliet was inhaling her lasagna like one of those superpowerful vacuums you see on TV, the ones that can suck up nails.

"It's May. Football season was over a long time ago." This was a stupidity of hers I was comfortable pointing out.

Hayden laughed, covered Juliet's hand with his. It was a sweet laugh. The sort of laugh that meant he thought everything she did was fabulous. She probably could have robbed a bank teller at gunpoint and he would have thought it charming.

"Game. Any game. Not just football," she said. "I didn't just mean *football*."

"Football games are a singles bar with an ASB card," I said. Hayden grinned at me across the table and I grinned back.

"Scarlet would never go to a singles bar," Juliet said to Hayden. "She's the good one in the family. She's never done a wrong thing in her life."

"No," I said. "That's not true." She was right, though.

"Okay, she cut her own hair when she was three," Juliet said.

"It was a *lot* of hair," Mom said.

"After that, her days of wild living were over."

"Ah, you don't know. You don't know that at all. Everyone has their secrets," Hayden said.

He looked at me and grinned and I had one of those flashes of irrational thoughts you get sometimes, like when you're sure a song on the radio has been played as a message to you, or when you think a certain star can bring you particular luck. When he said that, I felt like he might know things about me. Things I didn't even know about myself yet. Things that might happen or would happen. "I'll never tell," I said.

"Okay, there's no football. There are still spring sports to go to," Mom said.

"Track meet . . . The student production of *The Music Man*. Whatever." Juliet had gone to all those things when she was at Parrish High. Some people are high school people and some people are not high school people, and that's just a fact of life. Juliet was one, and I wasn't. She could do high school because she didn't care about it in the least, whereas I couldn't because I cared too much.

"*Oklahoma*," I said.

"Again?" Juliet said.

"Mrs. Phipps, the drama teacher, lacks imagination," I said to Hayden.

"Well, it *is* Friday night," Mom said.

Sometimes you've been lectured on a topic so often that all a person has to do is say a few words and all of their former lectures come pouring out of your brain like people from a crowded elevator. It's a good time-saving trick for the person doing the lecturing. My mom, Annabeth Ellis, assistant manager of Quill Stationers, was under the impression that my life was lacking things—things like more friends, places to go, stuff to do, a *passion*, a boyfriend, maybe. I had held back from pointing out that these were precisely the things her own life was lacking— she had her job, sure, and her oldest friend, Allison Bond, and the women in Allison's scrapbook club. She had her boyfriend, Dean Neuhaus, too. But when she came home from work, she'd flop on her bed, claiming exhaustion, and she complained often that she had nothing in common with the women in that club, who actually went on all the trips they were so decoratively remembering. And Dean—sure, he had a great job and a fancy car, but he was always pointing out how she could do things better. He had once taken out our own silverware tray from our own drawer and reorganized it so that only spoons were with spoons and knives with knives and he had cleaned it so that not a single bread crumb remained. Dean was more a promise of rejection than a boyfriend.

"Friday night. Why does everyone make such a big deal about Friday night," I said.

"And New Year's Eve, too," Hayden pointed out. "Hate that."

I smiled. "If you don't have plans, you're a loser."

"If you don't want to get drunk and wear those stupid hats," he said.

"Those hats show disrespect for eons of evolution. We came out of the sea for *that*?"

He chuckled and stared back down at his lasagna because he knew, the same as me, that Mom's level of irritation was rising. You could feel the silence being turned up as sure as if it were sound. I felt a surge of something. Happiness. It was that joy you feel when someone's suddenly on your team when you were used to playing alone.

Mom's lips were thin and tight. For some reason, she was being very motherly with me right then, probably because she wished she could do it with Juliet, but it was too late. She was never really much like that—even her lectures were more strong suggestions, darts thrown with best effort, with no expectation of actually hitting the bull's eye. Honestly, how much could she actually care about my social life right at that minute? It felt a little like a mother performance. Displaying her authority to Hayden, the way teachers did on the first day of class to set the general tone.

"I used to love Friday night," Juliet said.

"Scarlet, you have to make things happen for yourself. You can't just wait around for the doorbell to ring," Mom said, which, by the way, was exactly how she had met Dean Neuhaus. His Lexus had broken down on our street and his cell phone battery was used up, so he had asked to use our phone.

I rolled my eyes in Hayden's direction, to let him know that public humiliation had no effect on me, and then used the favorite line of social losers: "I've got a ton of homework anyway," I said.

"Well, it's your decision," my mother said with that uphill warning-rise in her voice. A person who says *It's your decision* is informing you that your decision sucks, but I pretended not to know this. Instead, I smiled and changed the subject back to where it belonged. Someone needed to.

"When's the baby due?"

"October tenth," Juliet said.

"She's four and a half months along." My mother's fork *tinked* against the plate in a way that seemed either angry or heartbroken. It was a long time to keep a secret. Juliet probably even had known last time we'd come to visit. I wondered what it would be like to keep that big a secret for so long. That could change you, maybe. The press of it day in and day out. Pretending everything was the same when we all sat in her hotel room and ate room-service meals. But Juliet looked just the same as she always did, except for maybe a small mound under her sundress if you looked closely. She was plucking off a crunchy corner of Hayden's lasagna with her fork. I hated when she did that. You never wanted to sit by her at dinner because her fork would come visiting your plate uninvited.

Deb Caletti

"You thought of names?" I asked.

"Scarlet," Mom said. Maybe she thought if we ignored this, it would go away. But I didn't think that baby was going to stay inside Juliet forever.

"We haven't talked about that yet," Juliet said. You got the feeling they hadn't talked about most things. "Hayden calls it Jitter, as in Jitterbug."

I felt his embarrassment before I saw it, saw his neck flushing red. We didn't know who he was or where he even came from, and this small bit of information seemed too suddenly personal. Maybe you should hear that someone is softhearted only after you at least know if they came from Saint Louis or Michigan. There's an order to those things.

He braved our eyes, looked up. "It seemed wrong . . . you know. To keep calling it *it*."

Juliet didn't seem to notice his embarrassment. In fact, she didn't seem to notice him much at all. When she looked at him, it was with the flat and uncommitted gaze one gives to boring television.

"Jitterbug . . . ," my mother said slowly, as if this were taking a long time to reach the understanding part of her brain.

"It was just one of those things that comes into your head. . . ." Hayden said.

"I like it," I said. "It's very friendly."

"Scarlet's the generous one too," Juliet said.

"Last time I heard, that was a good thing," Hayden said.

Right then, one of the neighborhood dogs barked, Corky maybe or Ginger, and Zeus leaped to his feet and barked a loud and strong reply. He was doing his job, as far as I saw it. They communicated, and you communicated back, or you were rude.

But Mom put her hand to her heart as if she'd just heard a cannon explode.

"Oh my God," she said. "Jesus."

If you judged by the mess we were all in then, it didn't much look like He came when she called, either.

After dinner, Mom cut the pie and brought it into the backyard and she and Juliet had some hushed conversation that involved living arrangements and Juliet's room versus the basement, while Hayden threw a tennis ball over and over for Zeus. There was the sort of tension that made you feel like someone had left the gas on in an enclosed room, even though we were outside.

My head felt too busy, as if it were an old room being moved into or out of—boxes about to be opened or shut, things being shifted around, movers bringing in new furniture there wasn't a place for yet. I decided to surprise my mother and Juliet by not being such a loser introvert and by going over to Nicole's after all. Her parents' restraining orders sounded kind of peaceful. I left Mom a note, grabbed my backpack, and headed out.

As I walked down the drive, my eye caught on something over by the tire of Hayden's truck—a sheet of paper folded and folded again until it was a fat chunk. When I leaned down to pick it up, I also saw the sticker on his back bumper: *The only good clown is a dead clown.* Ha. Another person with clown fear who was actually *doing* something about it.

Before I could open the paper to see what it was, I noticed old Clive Weaver across the street, on his hands and knees in his driveway. I liked Clive Weaver. I maybe even loved him. Even if he was always doing some loud, industrious thing like chainsawing tree branches or vacuuming his car at annoying hours on

Saturday mornings, he made me feel happy when I saw him. He always gave a hearty wave and said hearty things to me like "Go give 'em hell today!" When he walked his dog, Corky, he let Corky lead, which sometimes meant that you'd find Clive Weaver in your hedges or up other people's driveways. Right then, he was crouched next to his boxy white Jeep with no backseat, (which he'd bought when the postal service sold its old fleet), peering underneath. He was wearing his usual attire—blue shorts, blue shirt, and knee socks, as close as you could get to the mail carrier outfit he'd worn for thirty-five years without actually being the mail carrier outfit he'd worn for forty-five years.

"Mr. Weaver?" I called.

"I had them a minute ago," he said.

"Did you lose something?" I asked.

He looked over at me, startled.

"My keys. I had them right here," he said. His white hair stood out in an alarmed fashion. It was usually combed straight across.

"There." I pointed. "In your hand."

He looked down, his mouth gaping at the surprise appearance of the keys. He was really worrying me lately. His old-guy vigor and capability seemed to be seeping from him daily, turning into something confused and feeble.

"That happens to me all the time," I lied.

"Goddamn," he muttered.

"See you, then," I said.

"See you," he said to his keys.

Clive Weaver went to his mailbox next and opened it with a tiny key on his key ring. I hoped something was in there. He loved it when he got mail. You could tell. Even if it was some Domino's Pizza ad or one of the endless notepads or calendars or letters from Yvonne Yolanda, Your Friend in the Real Estate Business, he seemed pleased. He'd walk off looking at the envelope with a smile and a bounce in his step, as if he were walking on promises. Most of all, I think, he loved to hate getting his electrical bill. He'd shake his fist at the envelope. "Roscoe Oil!" he'd say. "Those bastards!" But today, nothing. I heard the sad metal door shut against the sad metal box.

I held the clump of paper in my hand and unfolded it as I stood there on the grass. It was a letter. Black ink and small block letters. Hayden's handwriting. I had no proof of it, but I knew it inside, down deep and clear as day, the way you know all of the most truthful things. It said:

> *A little evidence of God . . .*
> *Stars.*
> *Raspberries.*
> *Sand dollars.*
> *The need to make music and art.*
> *Sight. Insight.*
> *Tree rings.*
> *Evolution, yes.*
> *Genius, invention, and the brain itself.*
> *Repetition of design, and on the flip side, variety of*
> *design.*
> *The sea.*
> *Color.*
> *Language.*
> *Babies.*
> *And most of all . . . you, my beautiful Juliet.*

Deb Caletti

For a moment, I could barely breathe. I held the note in my hand as Mr. Weaver shuffled inside; as Fiona Saint George shuffled outside, wearing all black and grasping a box of chalk; as the Martinellis' dog, Ginger, squatted by the juniper bush; and as Ally Pete-Robbins's banner blew in the breeze, reminding anyone who might forget such a thing that it was spring.

Some place opened in me that I didn't know could open. I felt a rip, a thing being torn, and underneath, something laid bare that I'd never felt before, some sort of longing. The words on the page were as beautiful as any I had ever seen. They were an offering, a gift held out in careful, cupped hands. They were the shining silver tips of a wave at sea, in contrast to the deep, gray watery depths of those other words in my head. *My* baby, Juliet had said. *My.*

Chapter Four

*I*n the morning, the smell of burned toast climbed the
stairs, drifted into my room, and woke me up. Someone
was burning toast in the kitchen, and usually Saturday
mornings just smelled like the same old dusty-vent smell of the
furnace going on or last night's baked-chicken odor that couldn't
bear to leave us. No one cooked breakfast anymore—Mom would
eat a bowl of Total (I once caught Dean Neuhaus grabbing a pinch
of her side as if it were excess flab even though Mom had a thin,
careful body), and I would have a bowl of Life, but the days of weekend breakfasts of French toast or scrambled eggs appeared to be
over, disappearing right around Juliet's senior year, when Mom
basically decided her cooking days were done. After Juliet left, the
two of us ate like bachelors, quick dinners sometimes downed
while standing at the counter, take-out eaten with plastic forks out
of white Styrofoam containers. So the burning-toast smell made
me feel happy. I actually hurried out of bed with the kind of child-

hood excitement brought about by simple things like Otter Pops and a new lunch box and hot chocolate with marshmallows.

I pulled my hair up and made sure I didn't look entirely stupid and was pleased when I saw that what I had imagined was true—Hayden stood at the kitchen sink in his jeans and a soft green T-shirt that looked a million years old. He was rumpled in a way that made you think of sex and sheets and Sunday morning and the bed he'd just risen out of next to my sister. His face was scrubbly and unshaven, and he held a piece of toast in one hand, scraping the black off with the edge of a knife. There was something about that scraping sound and the black dust falling into the kitchen sink, though, that made me feel bad for him again. Black toast was plain old good intentions gone awry.

"Toast fiasco," he said when he saw me. A bowl on the counter was filled with the wet, wobbly yellow of cracked eggs. Zeus sat at Hayden's feet, hoping for the jackpot of dropped food.

"Need some help?" I asked.

"Sure," he said. "Maybe start the bacon?"

"We have bacon?" I said. I didn't remember bacon since Mom still felt motherly.

"I went to the store this morning," Hayden said.

"Already? It's only"—I checked the microwave clock—"nine thirty."

"Couldn't sleep," he said. "I had the scariest dream." He held out the still-sort-of-black toast out to me. "Pre-breakfast snack?" he said. I shook my head, so he bit the corner off himself.

"What was the dream?"

"Don't laugh," he said, crunching.

I made a very solemn face. "Promise."

"I was in the ocean. The waves were really high. You know,

over my head?" One of his cheeks was a round ball of toast. "All I had was this little dumb-ass toy to hold on to—a rooster. Those inflatable things you wear around your waist when you're a kid. I actually had one in real life."

"A rooster? Not exactly a water animal."

"I know. Ask my mother. Maybe a whale or something, right? It was probably on sale. Anyway, forget my twisted childhood for a second, okay? I was gulping water and flailing around and then suddenly there was this shark."

"A shark."

He swallowed. Took another bite. Hayden was a vigorous eater. "But he was this . . ." He hesitated. "Very light white-red color."

"You mean pink," I said.

Silence. "Well. Yeah."

"A pink shark." I laughed. I stopped. "I said I wouldn't laugh."

"I believe you promised," he said. I found the bacon in the fridge, opened the package. I laid out the flat slabs in a pan.

"A pink shark, though," I said. "You can't exactly blame me."

"It was a *horrible* pink. Okay, shit." He sighed. He ran his fingers through the loose curls of his hair. "I give up. I knew it would sound stupid. Nightmares sound so pathetic in the morning. 'And then I was in the jaws of a giant hawk who turned into a can opener.'" Hayden held our own can opener, which he was aiming to use on the lid of a can of peaches.

"Supposedly they're your subconscious talking."

"My subconscious speaks in a foreign language," he said.

I tried to think what a pink shark might mean, but came up with nothing. I didn't always believe much in the subconscious anyway. I knew pretty well what was going on inside my head,

I thought, just maybe I didn't always *want* to know. You can shield your eyes from an accident and still know the accident is there. Zeus was sitting right in front of the utensil drawer. I nudged him and he scooted to the side. "Sorry, boy."

Hayden pointed at me with the can of peaches. "Hey. You're a person who apologizes to dogs."

"I probably apologize to everything."

"I'm positive that the world is made up of those who apologize to dogs and those who don't."

"I apologize to this azalea in the front yard every time I run over it backing out of the driveway."

He laughed. "Hmm. A plant apologizer. This might blow my theory all to hell. Spatula?" I pointed, and he took one out of the drawer.

"Can you imagine if you one day apologized to Zeus and he said, 'Hey man, no problem'?" I said. The idea pleased me, dogs talking.

"I wonder what his voice would sound like," Hayden said. The bacon was beginning to sizzle nicely and the orange juice sat ready in our old pitcher and new toast had been pushed down into the toaster. Hayden cut a hunk of butter and plopped it into a second pan for eggs. The kitchen was humming with a nice busy importance.

"Wouldn't it be great, though, if you could have an actual conversation with him?"

Hayden and I looked over at Zeus. Sometimes you were sure dogs had some secret, superior intelligence, and other times, like right then, you knew they were only their simple, goofy selves. Zeus looked back at us, a bit blank but hopeful, wondering if something was going to happen that involved him.

"I'm not sure we'd want that," Hayden said. He gave Zeus a long look. "Nah. He'd start doing all the things you hate in people. Bitching, complaining . . ."

"Get me off of this leash! Who do you think I am?" I said.

"This food tastes like *shit*," Hayden said.

We were laughing when Mom came downstairs. Her brown hair was wet from a shower and she was already dressed in capris and a T-shirt. She gave me a look that said she didn't approve of me liking Hayden when she hadn't figured out yet whether she liked him or not herself. Mom was what you'd call *fiercely protective*. I know this was supposed to be a good thing and I appreciated some of its positive qualities, but it didn't always feel like a good thing. It was hard to do "big things" in the world when she was on the other side of the street, wringing her hands.

Mom fluffed her hair with her fingers to get it to dry and looked around at the breakfast taking shape.

"Well, this was awfully nice of you," she said to him.

"I hope you're hungry," he said.

She cruised around the kitchen looking at some mail on the counter and then at a cellophane bag of overripe bananas. She tossed them into the trash. "I was going to make banana bread," she said. "I don't even like banana bread."

"No one really likes banana bread," Hayden said. "You know who makes banana bread? The few people in the world who feel guilty about black bananas."

I watched the corner of Mom's mouth go up in a little smile. For the record, the only time I ever saw my mother smile at Buddy Wilkes was the time we saw him pulled over to the side of the rode by Officer Beaker, the red light on the patrol car spinning slowly, telling everyone who passed that Buddy had finally been caught at something.

It seemed like Hayden was just going to be one of those *few, few, few* people who just kept getting better the more you saw of him. And even Mom, who could see danger in an unwashed apple, could tell that.

I had to wake up Juliet for breakfast. She was the same lump in her bed I remembered from when she lived at home and had stayed out late the night before. And when I called her name and threw one of her stuffed animals at her butt, I heard a muffled "Goddamnit, Scarlet" from way down in the covers, just like the old days too. But when she sighed and sat up, she looked different to me. It felt like the past but not the past, because she looked like a woman, somehow. Maybe because I expected her to be a woman now, but maybe not just that. Her face looked older, like she'd been somewhere and back, and not just to Oregon, either. She rubbed one eye with her hand and said, "Oh yeah," as if her life had just returned to her, the way it does sometimes when you first wake up. I wasn't sure, though, if it was her old life that was returning or her new one.

I was aware that there were two sides of the bed, now, too, and that Hayden had slept in that bed, with his head on that pillow. It was very husbandly-wifely. There was a small pile of loose change on the end table, a paper clip, a beat-up peppermint candy wrapped in cellophane, as if he'd emptied his pockets before bed. His backpack was on the floor, unzipped, and I could see some of the contents inside. The blue stripes of a pair of boxers, the open zipper of Levi's, the cotton of a dress shirt stuffed way down inside.

"Hurry up," I said. "Hayden made breakfast."

Juliet sighed. "Hand me that, I can't reach," she said to me, gesturing to her bag on the floor by the bed. I handed it to her and she sorted through it, pulling on a pair of underpants and then her jeans. I wondered if Hayden slept naked too.

"Eggs are getting cold." Mom popped her head in the door. She probably felt uncomfortable down there alone with Hayden.

"Look at this," Juliet said. She showed Mom her gaping zipper—the impossible space between the jeans' button and the buttonhole. "Look."

"It's still mostly water, not baby," Mom said.

"Hurry up, people," I said. No one seemed to be very considerate of the fact that this great guy had just made all this nice warm food. Besides that, I felt weird talking about the odd things my sister's body was now doing. *Mostly water . . .* I wanted that talk to stop right there. I'd put endless sun lotion on that back, braided that hair, handed those arms a towel, but her body seemed unknown to me then, capable of private and unimaginable things.

As we finally left Juliet's room, I noticed something else there too, on Juliet's side of the bed. On the small round table that held her old CD player and that candleholder shaped like a butterfly that Buddy Wilkes had given her one birthday, there was another fat chunk of paper—a note, folded and folded once more. From Hayden again, I knew. It seemed to hold possibilities right there where it lay.

I made a silent promise to myself—I would come back when no one was here, and I would read those words. Maybe at that moment I knew what a thief must feel, a jewel thief. The way his heart would quicken with need and envy and want when he gazed down at the promise of diamonds and rubies. The way he knew he would soon hold them in his hands, pretending they were his even if they could never be.

Chapter Five

During the spring and summer of that year, and all of the years previous, too, I had a secret, and that secret was that I lied a lot. It felt like a lot—I did it more than truly necessary, anyway. Sometimes there was no good reason for it. At school, I would lie about what I did on the weekend. If I stayed home and read I would say I went into the city or visited my cousins, when I don't even really have cousins, or none that we actually ever visited. I would say I went to Hair Apparent to get my hair cut when I trimmed it myself with Mom's kitchen scissors (probably a lie people saw right through), or that I had a salad when all I ate was fries. I told people I wanted to be a photographer, when I didn't know what I really wanted to be, and I didn't say that I'd never been on an airplane. I'd say I went to Hawaii once or to California, because everyone had been to California. I never admitted to liking horror movies, when I actually loved them. The gory ones. The true crime books too, where some clean-cut suburban type, someone you'd never expect, kills someone in their own garage.

I lied partly out of insecurity, I knew that. I read all about insecurity in my books. Insecurity was a colorless sense of not being good enough that could sit upon your spirit the same as a filmy layer of dirt on a window; something you might not know was even there until the sun tried to shine through. Insecurity, too, was probably part of why I preferred to be alone, and why I was not always brave enough to show who I was, but it was more than that, the lying. I also did it to make people more comfortable. I'd say I was nervous for the AP U.S. History test when I wasn't, or that something cost less than it did if a person was poor, or that I was bad at sports too when there were some I was honestly pretty good at.

I guess for me, lying evened things out. Smoothed the rocky spaces between people. It could settle a million possible tiny upsets before they actually happened, though I have to say, the thought of speaking the truth all of the time seemed like it would be the greatest thing in the world. The greatest. I couldn't even imagine how great that would be and how freeing. But I didn't think that would ever happen, because speaking your own truth on a fairly consistent basis seemed like one of the hardest jobs a human being could take on. A giant and endless wall to get over and one of those walls that are spiked with cut glass at the top. People were often in the greatest crisis just because they couldn't speak the truth—*I don't love you. I'm gay. I don't want to go to that college. I don't really want to be friends with you. I hate the way things are.* With lying, you walked a wide circle around it all. It kept things simple and running smoothly, even if that meant you held hard to your own secrets.

Deb Caletti

I didn't know if other people did this too, the way I did. Lying wasn't exactly something you told the truth about.

So that's what I did when Mom asked me to show Hayden around town while she went with Juliet to buy maternity clothes. I lied. I moaned and protested when the thought actually made me happy. Really happy. Too happy. I think I even said, "Can't you guys take him later?" when right at that moment I was figuring out in my head what to show him. I guess when you lied, you were trying to be a better person than the creep you actually thought you were.

I waited for Hayden to be ready. I sang, "It's a Big Dog," to Zeus, to the tune of "It's a Small World." Dogs are patient about those things. Finally, when Hayden was ready, I wasn't. I forgot my camera and had to go back upstairs to get it. Not taking my camera was the same as going shopping when you don't have money. You go shopping without money and you see a ton of things you can't live without. You have money, and . . . nothing. Going somewhere without my camera meant I was sure to see a hundred things I wanted to capture but that would be forever lost.

"Anyplace we can get Zeus's nails clipped?" Hayden asked as we finally headed out. "He's looking like Howard Hughes."

"Sure," I said, but I didn't really know where. We'd never had a dog ourselves, or any pet for that matter, except the class guinea pigs I used to bring home on school vacations. Harold, for example. Juliet had put a tiny cowboy hat on him that had belonged to her Ken doll. I'd gotten mad at her and made her take it off. Probably guinea pigs didn't get humiliated, but he looked like it anyway.

"Sidewalk artist?" Hayden gestured one thumb across the street, where Fiona Saint George was already sitting cross-legged on the cement, filling in a new disciple with yellow chalk. For the last few days, she'd been making a vampire version of Leonardo da Vinci's *Last Supper*. All the characters around the table had fangs and white faces—some bald, some with wild, flowing snakelike hair. Fiona's own long hair was black and shiny as the crows that watched her draw from the branches of nearby evergreen trees. When I saw her at school, I would smile at her, even though she'd only look back with her face as still as stone. Both of her parents, Mr. and Mrs. Saint George, had gone to Yale. They had Yale window stickers in both of their cars so that you would be sure to know it when they drove off to work at the Marine Science Center. Fiona's brother, Robert, had left home to go to Yale two years ago. Probably their dog, Buster, had gone to Yale too.

"Goth Girl," I said when we got into his truck. "That's what they call her at school. She's depressed."

"She's also really good," he said.

It pleased me that he could see beyond Fiona Saint George's white face and black eyeliner, to who she really was. I'd seen her eyes up close once or twice. And even though Fiona Saint George never said much, her eyes wanted things badly.

Hayden backed out of the driveway. "Watch out, azalea," he said, looking over one shoulder.

"You get run over enough, you're immune to all pain," I said.

"Same way I went this morning?" he asked. "Turn right at the sign that says WHISTLING FIRS?"

I nodded. "They don't exactly whistle," I said. We started down the street, drove past the Martinellis' house with their big RV parked by the curb (*The Pleasure Way* was written in green script across its broad side) and continued past Ally Pete-Robbins, who was already in gardening shorts and a sun hat, kneeling on one of those cushy weeding mats you didn't think anyone a used. Jeffrey and Jacob, her twins, ran around on the lawn w. squirt guns. They held them low, below their waists, and pulled the triggers to look like they were peeing. They screamed with laughter, raising the guns again the minute Ally Pete-Robbins turned her head to see what was so funny.

"Huh," I said.

"What?" Hayden said. He looked in his rearview mirror to check on Zeus, who sat straight in the truck's back bed, prim as an old lady waiting for her bus.

Huh was Shy, the boy Nicole was so crazy about, on his bike on our street. He was riding really slowly and looking at what I guessed were house numbers. He turned a long full circle in front of the house on the corner to get a better look, then cruised by Ally Pete-Robbins.

"Someone from school," I said to Hayden. "I didn't know he lived around here." We drove right past him then, and I caught his eye. He looked shocked, caught. I wondered what he was doing. He seemed guilty and lost. I'd have to tell Nicole that he had even more of a secret life than we thought.

"He just ran into that parked Acura," Hayden said as we turned the corner.

"You're kidding." I turned to look, but he was too far out of sight.

"Right into the side."

"Oh man. Ally Pete-Robbins will lose it if she sees a scratch. She's one of those people, you know—tight smile plus phony cheer equals utter control freak."

"I know the ones," he said.

"Her boys fake-belch instead of using actual words."

manhood," he said. He flicked on his turn signal.
t of his big hands on the steering wheel. He still
liked that, too, the way it sat sturdily on his wrist.
hat guy all shook up."
e was probably looking for my friend Nicole." The
only time I ever shook a boy up was in the sixth grade when I ran
smack into Gregor Ybinsky while he was carrying his cafeteria
tray. It was his first day of school in the United States, and after
we collided, his dress shirt was splotched with mashed potatoes
and school gravy. Okay, maybe I shook up Reilly Ogden, too. I
went to a dance with him once just to be nice and now I couldn't
get rid of him. I had shaken up Kevin Frink a few weeks ago, but
that was only because I caught him lighting a firecracker out by
the school Dumpsters. He calmed right down when I promised
him I wouldn't tell anyone.

"You shook him u-up," Hayden said, his voice doing that
teasing dance. "I know it. You're a heartbreaker, just like Juliet."

He seemed to love saying her name. It was as if her name
was made out of rose petals or soft rain or the sound a seashell
makes. The way he said it—it made me wish what he said
were true, and I had never before wished to be a heartbreaker.
Breaking hearts was Juliet's department, not mine—we were
different in that way and in every other one. I had the long dark
hair and wide brown eyes that our mother had, while Juliet had
the golden-white hair and blue-ice eyes that must have been our
father's. I was too tall, too thin; I had too much of what there
should be less of and too little of what there should be more of.
And most of the time, I was only a visitor in a land that Juliet
ruled, Gregor Ybinsky on a forever first day in a forever foreign
country, where I didn't speak the language and had school gravy

Deb Caletti

on my shirt. Nothing happened to people like me and Gregor except occasional unfortunate accidents.

I wasn't used to wanting things badly, except maybe for other people. I wanted my mother to ditch that creep Dean Neuhaus and I wanted Clive Weaver to be well, and Goth Girl to be happy, and the Martinellis to be safe. But as I looked at Hayden's strong hands on the steering wheel, his wrists, the smile crinkle beside his eyes, I felt some want in me grow, the way a snowball grows when you roll it. I prayed to the God in Mom's Dream Big song, "Be." Please, let me be a heartbreaker. God, if you're up there, I wouldn't mind being a heartbreaker just once.

By the end of the afternoon, there was a small stack of job applications on the seat between us. We'd gathered one for the Hotel Delgado, the old ivy-covered building by the marina where Teddy Roosevelt supposedly had once stayed; one for Johnny's Market; one for the ferry terminal. The Franciscan nuns used to run the terminal, guiding the ferries into port wearing orange vests over their long brown habits, but they had gotten too old. One day they themselves had just slipped quietly away on a ferry, moving to the Franciscan Center in Bridal Veil, Oregon. Now Joe and Jim Nevins ushered the cars on and off the boats, and they were always looking for extra hands.

Hayden didn't want to "sit idle" all summer. That's what he said. *Sitting idle* made me think of that car in front of Buddy Wilkes's house, his El Camino. Practically anytime you drove past his street, you could see its hood up and the back of Buddy in his baggy-ass Levi's as he leaned into the open hood, a beer bottle sitting on the curb. Juliet used to sit there too, on the curb, watching him. I saw her there many times, and later her breath would smell the sour yellow tang of Coronas.

I'd liked riding in that truck in Hayden's passenger seat. I'd liked standing beside him, both of us making reassuring sounds to Zeus as Big Bill held Zeus firmly and clipped his nails. We'd gotten back into the car and imitated Big Bill's drawl, laughing at a dog groomer with a cowboy hat and big cowboy buckle that said *USA* on it.

I'd liked hearing Hayden talk about school, too—graduate school, architecture. He wanted to make beautiful buildings with steel curves and angles of light. I'd also liked waiting outside the Hotel Delgado on that bench by the roses that looked out over the marina. I'd waited with Zeus sitting at my feet and my camera in my lap until Hayden came back out, the application in his hand. *Front desk or waiter?* he'd said. He had a big grin and his tousled hair was going all directions like it was up for anything. *Front desk,* I'd said. *King-size bed, no smoking room, here's your key,* he'd said, shaking his car key at me, and we strode happily back to the car with Zeus running ahead, and it felt like we'd done it every day for years.

There was so much liking that I convinced Hayden to buy Juliet some chocolates. It was probably one of those furtive moves your guilty conscience makes, even if you've been as innocent as everyone knows you to always be. Still, if Juliet didn't really love Hayden, and if her love was what he wanted, chocolates were a smart move on his part. Juliet liked presents. Daniel Chris had given her that necklace one time and she hadn't taken it off even after she had dumped him and moved on to Harrison-something, who had given her roses and more roses. Our house looked like the funeral parlor where Kevin Frink's mom worked. But Buddy Wilkes had given chocolates at first, before he had given neck-

Deb Caletti

laces and roses and butterfly candleholders and everything all the other boys had given but more. Some people get adoration mixed up with love, and Juliet was one of them.

I brought Hayden into Sweet Violet's, across the street from Randall and Stein Booksellers and Mom's store, Quill. Sweet Violet's wrapped their boxes in thick purple paper and gold ribbon, and even Buddy Wilkes, who reeked of sweat and foul language, understood the importance of this.

"I don't even know if Juliet likes chocolates," Hayden said. We stood in the chilled store air, which smelled thick and rich with dark cocoa and sugar. Hayden peered through the shiny glass cases at the truffles set gently in gold ruffled paper. "She's always talking about her weight."

I could tell he might not understand the first thing about Juliet. Getting chocolates wasn't about *chocolates*—it was about unwrapping the box and lifting up the lid and seeing what was inside. Chocolates were an invitation, a selection of possibilities, *hope*, the chance for something great, same as a letter, same as Christmas, same as car keys dangling from a finger or a passport with your picture inside. Maybe *expensive* chocolates meant too that someone was willing to sacrifice for you, and sacrifice seemed somehow tied to devotion. But it was too complicated to explain to Hayden, who pulled out dollar bills from his wallet; crumpled, jammed-in dollar bills which meant he didn't have a lot of money. People with money—like Dean Neuhaus and Mom's boss, Allen—they kept their bills flat and orderly. It wasn't necessary to fluff and stuff in some act of monetary self-deception.

"Trust me," I said, as we left the cold of the store and went back outside into the glad sun. "She likes to be given things. Presents. Compliments. To feel special."

He looked at me and laughed a little like he thought I was joking. "Chocolate. Check," he said. I could tell he still thought he was doing something for me, not for himself. He probably thought that ring on his left hand and on hers meant that he and Juliet would sit on some porch watching their children play on some lawn for years to come. But Juliet didn't stick with things too long. I'd played the flute all through middle school and had been taking pictures forever, but Juliet went from flute to guitar to pottery to boys. Her speed wasn't porch so much as highway. And a ring, anyway—a ring was a declaration of hope, not a mission accomplished.

Zeus waited in the back of the truck parked at the curb in the shade, his tongue hanging out the side of his mouth like a drunk in a bad cartoon. I swear, dog tongues doubled in length on a hot day. Zeus's toes had their new manicure from Pet Palace, which we had found all the way out of the main part of town, next door to the Rufaro School of Marimba. Zeus had walked out of there all careful and proud as if he knew he was different and more beautiful. But now he looked as if his enthusiasm was wearing thin.

"Gotta give him some water, pronto," Hayden said. He retrieved a large, full plastic jug behind his seat and a pale, old Tupperware bowl, used just for that purpose.

"I'm going to pop in there a sec," I said, as he unscrewed the water bottle lid and poured. I gestured to Randall and Stein Booksellers across the street, next to Mom's store, Quill.

"Sure."

They knew me well in there. Bonnie Randall raised her eyebrows when I set *What to Expect When You're Expecting* on the counter.

"For my sister," I said.

I dashed across the street with my green bag, hopped back in the truck. We were done with our errands; probably Hayden wanted to get home. But I didn't want the time to be over yet. The day had been the kind of comfortable good fun you just wanted more of. I didn't know when I'd had that much comfortable good fun, maybe way back when I was a kid.

"Do you have time to see one more thing?" I said.

"I'm not in any hurry," he said. "I'm having a great time."

I took a big breath, and the day smelled especially good. "Remember Deception Loop that took us to the hotel? We get back on there." The Horseshoe Highway was the island's inner main road, and Deception Loop circled its outer edge, giving glimpses of the Strait of Juan de Fuca between the tall firs and evergreens that lined the road. I directed Hayden around the island, toward Point Perpetua Park. There was a preschool class having lunch at the picnic tables and an old lady with one leg in the air doing tai chi on the grass, but we passed all of them and walked down the trail toward the lighthouse. Zeus ran ahead but kept running back again to make sure we weren't far behind him. We emerged from the trail onto a wide beach, and I led Hayden over driftwood and around rocks toward my favorite huge boulder just before the lighthouse itself. It took some climbing, but the rock was high and flat and from up on top, the view over the sound went on forever. This was one of my favorite places to take my camera. I'd come out here alone, on my own, just to watch and see what might appear. It was a great big peaceful movie that was running all the time.

"Wow. This is some view." Hayden sat right down, dangled his legs over the side. I lifted my camera, took quick aim, called his name. "Oh great, I'm sure my eyes were closed," he said.

I sat beside him. Zeus was down below, happily sniffing sea-weed and exploring the mysterious crevices between driftwood logs. It was the kind of windy that makes you feel pleased and alive. "In a few weeks, the orcas will be here. This place will be packed with people. The island gets nuts. When all the tourists leave, there's an annual 'Thank God They're Gone' celebration."

"Invasion, huh?" Hayden said. "Well, it's fantastic right now." The sound gleamed, sunlight on sea, a thousand glimmery water stars. It was cool there by the water, but I knew the sun was secretly intense. I tilted my chin up, breathed the salty air that always seemed to me delicious enough to drink up.

"No great silver steel buildings, though," I said.

"God architecture," he said.

"He knew what he was doing."

"And no Urban Studies final for Him either."

"It makes you think about all the big words," I said.

"I was just thinking that," he said.

We were sitting close. Our legs were almost touching. I could feel Hayden's, I don't know, presence, self, Hayden-ness, right there next to me. His watch on his wrist, the strength of his square shoulders. I was just being myself then. This seemed shocking. Even talking to boys at school made me feel I was on some swinging rope bridge high above a raging river, where the lines just ahead looked fuzzy and frayed. Myself wasn't some-thing I was all that often. Not without all the inner and outer monitoring systems working, the ones that looked out on the horizon for oncoming disasters. But I was just being myself, and you wouldn't believe what a relief it was.

"I like your places, Scarlet Ellis," he said.

"Yeah?"

"I do."

"Everyone likes the beach," I teased. "Who doesn't like the beach?"

"I like *this* beach."

We sat in that ease in the sun before a sparkling sea. It was one of those few right moments in your life that you might always remember. When something was as still and true as a blade of grass, when you wished you could hold your breath and make time stop for a good long while. On and on, it would go. On and on, and it would just keep being right.

Mrs. Martinelli barreled in our direction the second we pulled into the driveway. She stepped over the junipers between our yards like an army recruit in a row of tires.

"Who is this young man? I've seen his truck," she said, but you could tell she couldn't care less if she got an answer. Bits of juniper now clung frantically to her white tennis shoes. She was wearing her favorite sweatshirt—the one with a pair of frogs sharing a single umbrella, sheltered from sequined raindrops.

I made an uh-oh face toward Hayden so he'd be ready. You need advanced warning for some people, and, as much as I loved her, Mrs. Martinelli was one of them.

She thrust a paper into my hands. "I've been waiting all day to see you. We have received a New Communication." She was beginning to sound like the scam letters themselves—those Business Propositions written by criminals who were very fond of Capital Letters.

I'd felt a little generational responsibility for her and Mr. Martinelli, ever since she first told me about getting the e-mails.

Our elders had tried to warn us about the risks of drug use, something they knew about from personal experience. Maybe we needed to return the favor about technology use, something *we* knew about. They had no idea of the dangers involved. Rose Marie and Herb Martinelli had gotten their first computer about five months ago, and somehow word had gotten out that two new suckers were driving full speed along the Information Highway without their seat belts buckled.

"This arrived via Electronic Mail," Mrs. Martinelli said. Her eyes were big behind her glasses. "Mr. Martinelli experienced a Printer Jam. He had to dismantle the machine with a kitchen knife. You may notice a few words missing."

God, he'd killed that printer. There were long white spaces between some of the words, which Mrs. Martinelli had filled in with a pen, her handwriting as thin and fragile as the veins you could see all over her legs when she wore shorts.

> Dearest One,
>
> Permit me to inform you of my desire of going into business relationship with you. I must not hesitate to confide in you for this simple and sincere Business.
> I am MORIN JUDE the only daughter of late Mr. and Mrs. Boni JUDE. My father was a very wealth cocoa merchant in Abidjan, the economic capital of Ivory coast. My father was Poisoned to death by his business Partners on one of their outings on a business trip to France. My mother died when I was a baby and since then my father took me so special.
>
> Before the death of my father in a private hospital here in Abidjan he secretly called me on his bed

side and told me that he has the sum of Five million,
Five hundred thousand United State Dollars. USD
($5,500,000) left in one of the prime Banks here in
Abidjan. He asked that I should seek for a foreign
partner in a country of my choice so that they might
continue his cocoa plantation. . . .

"Mrs. Martinelli, just click the REPORT SPAM button on your e-mail page and don't open up mail from people you don't know. I told you, remember?" This was my version of the "Just Say No to Drugs" speech.

"Scarlet. This sounds like a wonderful opportunity." Her cheeks were flushed.

"Millions of people received this same letter, Mrs. Martinelli. Millions. Some guy with a creepy mustache and no job wrote it in his mother's basement."

"Mr. Martinelli and I love cocoa in the evenings," she said.

"Trust me," I said.

She stared hard at me with those big eyes. "The Ivory Coast," she said. The words managed to be both wistful and full of adventure.

"His mother's basement," I said.

She sighed dramatically as if there were things I'd never understand. She made her way back into her own yard, but not before she snatched the letter back with a little bit of nastiness. Her butt was big and bumpy in those stretchy pants, but still she held that paper as if it were somehow breakable. The way you hold precious things, or should hold precious things.

"Uh-oh," Hayden said as he locked the door of the truck.

"I know."

"I always wondered how those guys actually made any money," he said.

"There you go."

He came around the other side of the truck and stopped for a second, set his hand on my arm. "Scarlet."

Some things had the right amount of weight. A quilt as you slept, carefully chosen words, fingertips.

"I really want to thank you. It's a little weird for me here. You know—all of it. What's going on, a new place, the whole deal. But you made it great today, and I really appreciate that."

His eyes were warm and brown as coffee. I looked at them for a long while and he looked back. I felt something from him that you don't feel very often. I guess it was sincerity.

"No problem, Hayden," I said.

He let my arm go. He went inside to find Juliet. But I could still feel his touch there on my skin, lingering for a moment before fleeing, the way a good dream does, just as you wake.

Chapter Six

*Y*ou two got sunburned," Juliet said at dinner. Juliet was in a bad mood, and I remembered then what Juliet in a bad mood looked like. Her temper rolled in, clouds over sky, first hazy and meandering and then dark and full and fixed. Juliet's bad moods were irritation and dissatisfaction looking for a purpose. In other people, in me, irritation needed something to grab on to or else it just faded away with a cold drink or a nap or someone else's patience. But Juliet seemed to like the thrilling ride from irritation to anger; she searched around for a reason to lose her temper until she found one.

It might have even felt a little good if our mutual sunburn had been what had made her mad. But I could never be a threat to Juliet. I was sure of that. Juliet held men in the palm of her hand. I had no magic tricks or power; I was only my plain old self and didn't know how to be different than that.

I knew Juliet, anyway. The accumulation of small things that together make you momentarily hate your life and everyone in it could send her fuming—not finding pants that fit and then spilling her lemonade, or a long, hot day in the car with Mom who never seemed to notice when the light turned green. Juliet had a way too of putting things and people in the space between herself and what was true. If she'd had a fight with Buddy Wilkes, it was me whom she yelled at, and if our mother had upset her, Buddy himself might be the one to get her frosty words. I wondered if Hayden knew this about her yet. It was something a husband ought to know.

"It was a sunny day," Hayden said. It sounded like an apology, and Hayden shouldn't have given that. Not just for the obvious reasons but for a bigger one—Buddy Wilkes never took her crap.

"Must be nice to have a day off work," Dean Neuhaus said. Mom had invited him for dinner. He sat at the end of the table in his pressed pants and pressed shirt, his tie still tight against his throat, his brown hair cut straight across the back of his neck. It was the kind of hair that said you followed the rules.

Dean had sort of been forgotten down there at the end of the table, with his prim, righteous mouth and expensive watch and leather shoes, and Dean Neuhaus didn't like to be forgotten. One of the things I hated most about Dean was how he'd hint at his moral superiority while at the same time pointing out how humble he was. To Dean Neuhaus, *everything* was a sign of his moral superiority, from the way he loaded the dishwasher to how manicured his fingernails were. Dean Neuhaus had come here from London, and he managed to make our entire country inferior to his too—our grossly abundant restaurant meals, our bad-mannered children, our sloppy and distasteful use of the English language. He was even morally superior about our leftovers—he would never waste food like we did. I located him in my psychology books, the way a bird-watcher finds the exact bird he's seen: Obsessive Compulsive Personality Disorder. King of Order was disordered.

"You always spend so much time at your job, it'd be good for you to have some time off," my mother said to OCD Dean Neuhaus.

"I don't take time off when my company needs me. Do you know how hard it is for me to take time off? I have six months of vacation time accrued," he said. Dean Neuhaus did something with computers at Microsoft, something that obviously made him money. He had an ex wife and two kids, Brenda and Kevin, but we hadn't met them yet. His real past seemed to be the Volvo he had had before his Lexus, and a Rolex he had once owned that had been stolen.

"I'm so happy that you two had such a great time while I was off being pregnant," Juliet said.

"Did you like your present Hayden got you?" I asked. My own gift, *What to Expect When You're Expecting*, sat near her plate, the cover glossy and uncracked.

"Oh right! I almost forgot," Hayden said. He pushed his chair back, disappeared for a minute.

"So what's the big present?" Juliet asked.

I ignored her. "Six months is a lot of vacation time," Mom said.

"My problem is, I just don't believe a person should think about themselves first," Dean Neuhaus said to her. He dipped a bit of falafel into some tzatziki sauce. "There's a lot of garlic in here."

Mom stabbed her dinner with her knife. She claimed Dean was kind and responsible and had other good qualities, but you never actually witnessed them. Maybe she'd seen them once and just kept hoping they'd reappear, like a rare creature once spotted in the wild.

Hayden reappeared with the purple box. He *was* sunburned, and his nose was a happy red, the kind of red that meant fun and summer and other good things. He stood beside Juliet, holding that box, and she just looked at it without taking it.

I remembered the note I'd read when we'd returned home that day. I'd snatched it quickly from Juliet's bedside table, read it in the bathroom with the door shut and locked, returning it to its place immediately afterward. My heart beat fast as I read the words.

Juliet—
I want to wash your hair with a shampoo that smells like fruit—mango, or strawberries. I want to walk on a beach with you, dragging a big stick behind us, making a message in the sand that we try to believe an airplane will really see. I want to kiss saltwater from your lips. I want us to listen to music with our eyes closed; I want to read musty books while lying next to you—books about fascinating things like mummies and eccentric artists and old shipwrecks in the Pacific. I want to have picnics on our bed and crawl into cotton sheets that smell like summer because we left the windows open when we were gone. I want to wake in the night with you and marvel at the stars and try to find the moon through the trees. I want all the sweet things in life. But only by your side.

I thought of the letter as Juliet made a little *hnn* sound, a dismissive sort of exhale. Being impossible to please seemed the worst kind of cruelty right then. When someone gave you everything and it was still not enough, when you made them prove and prove their love again, you were the evil witch of fairy tales; you had snakes for hair and a small stone heart.

"Sweet Violet's," Juliet said, looking at the package. "I haven't seen anything from that place in way too long."

A moment passed between them. A moment that meant she was giving him information about Buddy Wilkes and about himself and about all the men who she might have let love her. He did an unexpected thing then, a good thing, because he was making it clear he wasn't a fool. He tossed the box onto the table so that it slid her direction, and then he left the room. His dinner still sat half-eaten at his place. It was quiet, and Juliet just kept eating as if she couldn't care less or maybe didn't even notice what we all noticed. You could see a whole relationship sometimes in a moment like that one. You could get all the information you needed in just a few seconds.

"That's the father of your baby, Juliet Rose," my mother said.

I thought about Jitter inside there, inside my sister. I hoped he or she was sleeping, or that the watery depths made words and experiences too muffled and foggy to really hear or feel. Juliet put her hand to her stomach, protecting the baby from who knows what. Mom's judgment, probably. Then again, she probably just had eaten too fast.

"I don't know why people bother with American chocolates," Dean Neuhaus said.

*   *   *

Dean Neuhaus drove off later in his Lexus, which had, I was sure, exactly the right tire pressure, its floors vacuumed free of any bits of dirt from the shoes of passengers. I saw Juliet in the kitchen, sneaking bites of leftover pie from a few days before, straight out of the pan with a fork.

"Remember when Mom took us to the drive-in movies that one time? She wanted to make sure we went before the theaters were all gone," Juliet said. Another forkful of pie disappeared. "God, we drove for hours, remember? Some town out in the middle of nowhere. Nothing around but RV World and Boat World and all those worlds that had nothing to do with ours, remember? That place—Chain Link Fence World."

It occurred to me that this was the Juliet that Hayden loved. The one that was funny and thoughtful, her bare feet on the wood floor, her eyes calm. When she sang, her voice was so sweet and beautiful, it could break your heart. But I didn't feel like reminiscing about old times or being open to Juliet's good qualities. I kept thinking about how happy Hayden had looked on that rock. A person could be such a happiness thief.

"God, you're a bitch sometimes," I said.

"What?" she said. She looked honestly perplexed.

"You better be careful. You lose him, and you're going to be sorry."

"You don't know what you're talking about."

"You finally found a good guy. Let alone . . ." I gestured toward her body. "You better not mess it up."

She looked at me for a moment. She set her mouth in a line. "Don't think you know anything about this," she said. "Because you don't. Not a single thing. What are you, like, seventeen?"

I shot her daggers with my eyes. I hated this trick of hers, a

Deb Caletti

trick she'd been doing forever. When she was eight, I was just a baby kindergartener. When she was in the sixth grade, I was a stupid eight-year-old. When she was in high school, everyone in my middle school looked *so young*. We were *so immature*. And the thing was, every time she did it, it worked. Every time, I felt like the little kid who had to stay at day care when she went off to big school with her backpack and her chin in the air. I didn't say anything. Just kept shooting my daggers. I was old enough to know what I knew.

She put the pie dish, fork and all, back into the freezer and the door slapped shut. It was amazing, really, how these other people, your family, held huge and great pieces of your own self, your definition, your place in the world. I could be eighty-five, maybe even have done great and powerful things in my life, our mother long gone, and I'd still be who I was in those long ago home videos of us. The one where I was the little kid at my sister's birthday party with all her friends, or the ones where Mom taped the two of us playing. There we were in our twin footie pajamas tossing dolls and plastic food and trucks from the toy box, and there was Mom's voice coming loud from her place behind the camera. *What are you guys doing?* she would ask us, and Juliet, the authoritative munchkin, would answer: *We're going to play doggy and owner*, or something like that. My voice would come next, always next, this small echo, *Play doggy*. Juliet was always in the lead, and I was her echo. Always. And she was in the lead again, right that moment, when she turned and left the room, taking all of our history with her.

My window was open, and I could hear the crickets outside, making the just-right sounds of a still May evening. You could smell the temperature change through the screen, the air turning from daytime grassy and warm to cool and wet, with that spring night smell of darkness and ripe fruit. That smell always made me feel things deeply, possibility and despair, even way back when I was a kid and didn't know those words. You just felt it anyway, something big, something about life that maybe didn't have a name yet.

The book I had given to Juliet had lain abandoned on the kitchen table after everyone had left, and so I picked it up and brought it to my room. I propped on my bed and read.

> Week three: Your soon-to-be-baby has started
> its miraculous transformation from single cell to
> baby boy or girl. This week, the fertilized egg—
> or zygote—divides several times over to become
> a tiny ball of microscopic cells smaller than the
> period at the end of this sentence.
> Week four: The blastocyst that will be your baby
> splits to form the placenta and the embryo, and
> the specialized parts of your baby's body begin
> to develop.

Jitter had been going through eons of evolution before we even knew he or she existed. It felt important to know these things about him or her. Him or her. Which, I wondered? How do you picture a person in your mind without knowing this? I decided to refer to Jitter in my mind as a he, the generic he, the he in books that meant neither he nor she, just a someone. It seemed important to decide and clarify this, even in my mind. It seemed the best way to show how welcome he was, no matter what.

Deb Caletti

I read further. *As the first trimester comes to a close, your baby's about the size of a peach.* I thought about a peach wrapped in a soft blanket. I thought about wheeling a peach around in a baby carriage. I pictured me and the peach baby in the park, park ladies leaning in to look, cooing with love and envy. I found myself reading the next few paragraphs over and over again, the way you do when you haven't been paying attention. I wasn't thinking about babies or peaches, then, I was thinking about what it might be like to have someone wash your hair, a guy someone, a man, fingers through strands, a cool rinse, your hair slicked back, the drip of water down your neck caught by a towel.

That's when I heard their voices through the wall. Muffled and heavy. The thick crackle of an argument, her and then him. A pause, then rapid fire. More silence and then her again. Buddy Wilkes's name said aloud. I listened to Juliet and Hayden and thought about my mother and Dean Neuhaus and my stalker, Reilly Ogden, and Nicole's parents and even my own parents. I wondered if maybe we were just meant to love the people who would make us most unhappy.

Juliet and Hayden fell silent. After a while, it was late enough, finally, for me to do what I needed to do. I went to my desk and took out the container of chalk; I'd first found it in the garage, still on the metal tray of the chalkboard Juliet and I had used when we played school. I crept downstairs, turned the door handle quietly. From outside, I could see Mom's bedroom window light turn off. And then Juliet and Hayden's, too.

I crossed the street, the asphalt cool and bumpy on my bare feet. I could see Goth Girl's drawing by the light of the streetlamp. Today she had finished her *Last Supper* drawing. I could see the figure in the middle where Jesus usually sat, but instead of Jesus there was a woman with brown hair and the checked coat I'd seen on Mrs. Saint George. Mr. Saint George was at the table too, I thought, next to a vampire in jeans and a T-shirt and a wild-haired witch in a tight black dress. And there was Goth Girl herself, in the figure that had her back toward the rest of them. There was Goth Girl's straight black hair, anyway, her favorite black sweatshirt.

I took my chalk and headed to the empty place just past the drawing, as I had done several times before. At first, I had tried the usual ways of being a nice person to someone who needed a nice person in their life—I had smiled at her in the halls at school and tried to make conversation when I saw her at home. But Fiona Saint George always averted her eyes, the way you do when you look straight at the sun. Her art was a message, a letter made from a single picture, and the most important thing about a message was for it to be heard. You reach out, and someone reaches back; you give, and someone gives in return—it was one of the Fair and Right principles of the universe.

So I knelt next to the painting. *This is beautiful,* I wrote, on the square of sidewalk nearest the drawing. *You are incredibly talented.* I signed my note: *A friend who believes in you.*

I brushed the chalk from my hands, stood. Across the street in my own driveway I saw something then—a tiny orange light, the glow of the end of a cigarette. My first thought was of Buddy Wilkes, that Buddy Wilkes had somehow heard my sister was back, and that he was sniffing around our driveway for her scent. Maybe he'd throw pebbles at her window while she slept beside her husband.

But when I crossed the street I saw that it was not Buddy at all, but Hayden himself.

"I didn't know you smoked," I said.

Hayden exhaled up toward the sky. He wasn't wearing a shirt, just his cargo shorts hanging at his hips. His skin glowed from the streetlight. I felt a little shy, seeing that much of him, and a strange feeling filled me, a feeling I did not want to call desire or anything close to desire. He didn't seem surprised to see me crossing the street. Or maybe his thoughts were so much somewhere else that anyone could have appeared then and he wouldn't have blinked. The president of the United States, even, and he'd have only exhaled into the night same as he just had.

"I don't really smoke. At least I haven't in a long while."

"You shouldn't," I said. He looked strange smoking. He wasn't the type. You pictured him making his own juice with carrots and ginger and raw honey, not smoking some stupid cigarette.

"Juliet likes it," he said.

"She *likes* it?"

"She likes the way it tastes."

"That's idiotic," I said. "I'm sorry, but, God."

He didn't say anything. He leaned against the side of his truck. He took another drag on the cigarette and exhaled again. It sounded like a sigh. He seemed to have the capacity for moody introspection. Juliet liked moody. I was wondering right then if maybe I liked moody too. Rational thoughts and irrational feelings were dancing badly together inside of me, out of step and offbeat, something that would have to be fixed, and fast. "You're not close," he said finally. "Some sisters are close."

"We used to be close. Closer. I did her math homework for her. She'd let me hang out with her and her friends. Complain about how unfair Mom was being. I always wished we were twins so we could do everything together. But, you know, she left. I'm still here. Do you have a sister?" I asked.

"Only child."

"Maybe we're just too different," I said. I waited for him to acknowledge this, but he said nothing. "Maybe she's . . . more like our father."

The thought had made a sudden, stunning appearance. It shocked me. This had never crossed my mind before. Our father never crossed my mind. We hadn't ever even seen his picture, so *he, his, him*—they were empty, single-dimensioned words unconnected to an actual person. *He* was that wisp of smoke now disappearing by the streetlight. I might remember what he smelled like. A cologne that smelled like oiled wood, thick as incense. At least, I had smelled incense burning once, and it had triggered a memory that couldn't quite become a memory.

Hayden just took this in. It wasn't as shocking to him as it was to me. I still felt as if I'd been slapped, and it was me who had done it. "Your mother's boyfriend is a dick," he said.

I laughed loudly. "You noticed." The corners of his mouth turned up in a smile. I wanted to open that smile up wider, to see the Hayden of the afternoon back again. But I suddenly couldn't think of anything else to say, and the smile was retreating. He was retreating. I could feel the moment of connectedness passing, my chance being lost. I wanted to play and volley and be back in that place we had been together before, that great place. I needed something, something quick—I grasped and caught something silly and lighthearted. Silly and lighthearted would do.

"So, Hayden Renfrew. What was your most embarrassing moment?"

It sounded workable until I said it. As soon as the words

Deb Caletti

slipped out I knew I had done something horribly and terribly wrong. A humiliating misstep. I felt it all in one second of pause. The night, the cigarette smoke lingering in air, the heaviness of his thoughts—my words were inappropriate and idiotic. Oh God, why had I said that? Why, why, why? And why couldn't you take back a moment sometimes? One little moment? Is that asking so much? God, I suddenly sounded thirteen. My red shorts and my white tank top felt young and shameful, my feet in my flip-flops did too. I felt so ashamed of my painted toenails in the streetlight.

"Why did I say that," I said.

He finished his cigarette, threw it to the ground, and stubbed it out with the toe of his sandal. He picked it up and tucked it into his shirt pocket. I was filled with the disgrace of my own age and immaturity. I had widened some gap between us, and there was no way to close it again. Juliet had been right. I knew nothing about this. I was seventeen and he was twenty-three, and he was a man, a man who was married and who was going to be a father.

There was the sound of a hawk overhead, the Martinellis' TV on, too loud. Hayden spoke finally.

"I was on a date with a girl once," he said. "And we had just gone to this Asian market. I had this white bag filled with hum bows. You know hum bows? Those white balls of dough stuffed with meat?"

I nodded.

"Well, I dropped the bag. We were parked on a hill, and the bag dropped, and one of the hum bows fell out, and I started chasing it. Instead of just letting it go, I ran after it, down this hill. Running and grabbing and missing. I didn't stop to think what would be better for my dignity; I just kept going after it. I chased the hum bow down the street until it finally stopped underneath the wheel of a delivery truck."

He looked at me and grinned in the darkness. But it wasn't a real grin—his eyes weren't involved. It was politeness, the kind of grin you give as a gift even if you don't feel at all like smiling. Hayden was a nice person, too.

We just stood in silence. Something occurred to me then, and I said it. "A good lot of the time, nice people are doomed."

He laughed then, right out loud. A real laugh. A loud, surprised one. "Shit, Scarlet," he said. "Shit. You." He pointed his finger at me. "Yes indeed. God, I've got to have another cigarette now."

I wanted to make him laugh again. Or say another thing that pleased him. But nothing came. "It's true, though, isn't it?"

"I think it's one of the truest things I've ever heard," he said.

We were quiet. The night settled and filled in the spaces around us. The two of us had made something better, even for a moment. "You going back in?" I asked.

"In a minute."

"Okay. See you in the morning, then."

"Good night, Scarlet."

I went back inside. I tried to close my eyes, but I kept feeling his presence there, standing just under my window, his bare skin white in the moonlight. I didn't sleep until I heard the soft click of the front door, his footsteps climbing the stairs.

Deb Caletti

Chapter Seven

*I*t was a stupid cliché, but I didn't fit in at Parrish High. High school mostly felt like a sentence I was serving because of some crime I'd committed, maybe in a past life. Sometimes being there actually hurt in a physical way, the way it hurts when you have to keep running that last bit of the mile in the PE track unit, when you're sure you can't go on anymore. Some sort of burning in your chest and heaviness in your legs.

I'd always known I was different from other people. I knew it, because I felt perpetually awkward, and I realized everyone else wasn't going around feeling like that, at least not quite so much of the time. Mr. Kennedy, our high school librarian (I was his TA for a semester), said it was because I was a *reading person*, meaning, I guess, that all the books you read made you see things differently. But Mom said I was born mature, that I was a mini-adult from the time I was four and she caught me trying to write checks in her checkbook with my crayons. I once passed the

Theosophical Society out by Honey B's Bakery, and that old lady that runs it, Cora Lee, told me I was an old soul. Then she gave me a pamphlet for their next lecture, "Understanding Ourselves in the Cosmos."

Maybe that was it, that I was a reading person, or a mini-adult, or an old soul, because I just never got the rules of high school. It all seemed silly. All the big emotion and drama and all the gushy love and spitting hate and lip gloss reapplied and reapplied and reapplied in the smudgy mirrors of the girls' bathroom. The *She's such a bitch!* And *It's just because he likes you!* and *What'd he say, tell us!* All that. Most of the time, anyway, she wasn't a bitch and he didn't like her and whatever he had to say didn't mean anything. I tried to be part of it all, but inside I knew I was only faking. To me, it felt like someone had pushed the PAUSE button of my life and I still had to wait another year until it finally might start to play again. The hope was, people like me got to finally find our place in college or in the actual world. People who understood this told you that high school wasn't the *actual world*, that it was more like a temporary alternate reality you were forced to believe in for four years. A video game you played, where you could never get to the next level no matter how hard you tried.

My mother thought my problem was all about leaping in and overcoming my *social anxiety*. She actually used those words, even though I knew from my psychology books that I didn't have social anxiety. I looked it up. The only anxiety I had was dealing with everyone else's anxiety about my being an introvert. There were always all these suggestions for how to make me less of who I was. Joining clubs—that was a big one. *Getting involved* in school events, like dances or some sport. To Mom, it was about being brave or not being brave, not about just being who you were. I'm convinced there are some people who are just born joiners of groups—fitter-inners, seamless social creatures, lovers of half-fake *happy-to-see you*'s and insincere hugs and little screams of excitement that convincingly cover what's probably boredom. And then there are others, the ones who feel every false moment to the point of bodily pain and who can't be anyone except whom they are, as much as they try.

I never understood why it was somehow superior to be a joiner. Being an introvert is judged in some extreme way, as if you're lacking some ability to cope because you don't drink beer and smoke pot in Macy Friedman's basement. In our society, introversion as an alternate lifestyle gets less respect than any other alternate lifestyle, in my opinion. You could be gay and go to homecoming with your girlfriend or boyfriend, you could go drunk, you could go and ditch your partner mid-dance, but if you didn't go at all, you were a loser. Introversion is distrusted—it makes people nervous. Maybe it seems like we've got secrets. They think the secret is that you're depressed or something, that's why you don't seek their company, when the secret is really that you're happy and relieved and almost flying at the near-miss escape of not *having* to be in their company. You're looked at like you're seriously lacking, when the only thing you feel lacking in is the ability to be an introvert in peace.

So that's why it was so strange that I actually wanted to go to school on the Monday after Juliet moved back home with Hayden. I'd never wanted that, and there I was, feeling some sense of rest just doing my regular routine: first period Art with Mr. Wykowski (who always came in smelling like weed, not too different from several guys in his class), second period European History with Mr. Chester and creepy Reilly Ogden staring at me like I was water and he was desert. Bells ringing, locker doors slamming, guys yelling, *Fuck!* and cheating on tests, what's-the-point-of-this homework, boredom—compared to being home with my now pregnant sister, it was a *haven*.

I saw Nicole in third period AP English with Ms. Cassaday, just before lunch. The minute class was over, just after the bell rang and just after Ms. Cassaday said, "Be brilliant, people," and swirled around in her batik skirt, Nicole grabbed my arm.

"Where were you yesterday? I needed you. Didn't you get my messages? Kiley was looking all over for you. She wants to break up with Ben but doesn't know how."

I didn't know anything about breaking up. I didn't know about most of the things people asked my advice about. They just seemed to need to hear something sensible that they could later ignore. "I'm not the one to ask," I said. "I can't even get Reilly Ogden to leave me alone. He gave me a note today asking me to the prom." I passed it over to her.

"'*I'd like to take this opportunity . . .*'," she read aloud. "Jesus, he's creepy. Anyway, he's a junior. *You're* a junior," Nicole said.

"*Next* year's. Look at the date."

"God." Nicole sighed. "I don't know why you just don't tell him to *go away*."

I had tried a hundred times, but getting rid of Reilly Ogden was as pointless a task as removing a stubborn permanent stain in your best jeans—a stain like grease or blood which no matter how many times you washed them, was there still. "I *have* told him," I said.

"Not in any way that says you mean it. You're afraid to hurt his feelings; I hear it in your voice. There's such a thing as *too nice*." Nicole's black curly hair was up in a ponytail, and she wore a skirt, something she hardly ever did because of her weight. Her weight was fine but she didn't think so and neither did her dad who was always on his bike or running somewhere. He wore those spandex shorts that were as tight as Saran Wrap over a bowl of leftovers, which meant that Nicole was destined to hide her own body in every way she could.

"Hey, you look great today," I said.

"Really?" I knew from my psychology books that Nicole lacked self-esteem. She was talented and a great writer, especially, but she didn't believe in herself. It was sad, and I felt sorry for her. We'd been friends since elementary school, best friends, and her dad still thought my name was Sharon.

"You ought to wear skirts more often," I said.

We walked toward the lunchroom, which was full and noisy and smelled like it always did no matter what was on the menu—some combination of gravy and cut apples, Pine-Sol, and the rubber from tennis shoes. It was enchilada day, I guessed, because Leo Snyder shouted to some other guy on the soccer team, "*Pico de gallo* is just Mexican for *salsa!*" and then Renny Williams (who hadn't legitimately passed a class since elementary school even though his mom was vice-president of the PTA) shouted, "Hey, I still got half a burrito in my car from last night!" and then Leo Snyder said, "Duuum-ass" in a deep, dumb voice and Renny said, "Suck my *Pico*," and everyone at his table hooted those laughs meant to make everyone look.

"Hopefully Kiley's there already. You've gotta answer your phone, Missy," Nicole said to me and flicked my arm with her finger. "I don't like when you leave me. Don't leave me ever again, okay? Dad bought himself a new car and Mom went nuts. He says he can't help her pay her bills anymore and he goes out and buys a new car. You're the only one who understands."

"I was busy," I said. "Showing Juliet's new husband around."

"I can't believe your sister's having a baby. Wait, there's Kiley." Kiley was already at our table, waving us over with both arms. "See? She really needs someone to listen."

The way I'd coped with my term in high school was to find meaningful work, kind of like a prisoner who gets a job in the prison library. I was the Designated Listener, DL, the one who stayed emotionally sober while everyone else was falling apart, letting their feelings out in a way that was sloppy and off balance and dangerous. It wasn't just my on-the-fringe friends who sought me out either. Casey Chow cornered me in the girls' bathroom once when her period was late, even though she never spoke to me when anyone was looking. Olivia Gold confessed to me that she hated her perfect life when we used to ride the bus in middle school. I guess I had the kind of face that looked like an open invitation.

I had read in some of the psychology books about Maslow's Hierarchy of Needs—that we had these life requirements that ranged from the lowest and most basic ones of food and safety all the way up to the highest level of need, something called self-actualization. Self-actualization was the uppermost point, the nothing-else-to-need-now need, and it included things like morality and problem solving and helping others. I liked to picture myself at the top of the pyramid chart I saw on those pages, imagining, truly or not, that I'd risen through the fat horizontal chunks of *Safety* and *Belonging* and *Love* and *Self-esteem* and had arrived at the smallest tip of *Self-actualization*.

It was a fancy rationalization, probably, for saying that being needed sometimes made me feel good. It had a high purpose, anyway. So I listened and advised Kiley to break up with Ben because it wasn't good to get so serious so young and reminded Nicole that her parents' problems were out of her control, and then we all tried to tell our friend Jasmine that she should just talk to her parents about quitting orchestra if she hated lugging her cello around so much. This, as Custodian Bill walked around the tables, sweeping around us with his big broom as if we were guests in his house and he was anxious for us to finally leave.

"I can't believe I almost forgot," Nicole told us. "I talked to Shy today. Actually *talked*." She swirled the tip of her spoon around the bottom of her container of nonfat yogurt.

"He spoke?" Jasmine said. "I can't fucking believe it." Jasmine was a tiny girl with shiny black hair, so small and delicate that she was forever given the kids' menu at restaurants and asked if she were lost in stores. Jasmine swore a lot, but it was always goofy and unconvincing. I was pretty sure she would start drinking and having sex, too, as soon as she got the chance. Not that she wanted to do those things, but only because it might convince people finally that she didn't need crayons and a picture of a smiling hamburger to color whenever she ate. Jasmine's parents were so overprotective, they were practically running an in-home prison system and a fine one at that. But they didn't have to worry, not really. Badness needed the right landscape, a landscape Jasmine would never have. Jasmine with a beer in her hand seemed as silly as a baby with a driver's license.

"I said, 'Can you pass those papers down?' and Shy said, 'Sure.'" Nicole grinned at us.

"You always knew he was an intellectual," I said.

"And he's obviously got a sense of humor, too, huh?"

"The comic timing . . . ," I said.

"We really connected," Nicole said. "The conversation just flowed."

"You're obviously soul mates," I said. I didn't tell Nicole about seeing Shy in my neighborhood. I don't know why, or maybe I did know why. It was one of those times I believed in the subconscious, that it existed, at least, like the books said it did. I just wasn't so sure it was always doing those things without us knowing. Probably, you and your subconscious only pretended to keep secrets from each other. I pictured the subconscious as this thing the general population had to get us off the hook for the stupid things we did, the same as Catholics had confession.

Another image came up then, a wrong one. Hayden, with his man wrists and capable shoulders. How he held Zeus's collar in a way that told Zeus he meant what he said. I found a strange comfort in that firm hand. It was something Juliet had better appreciate if she knew what was good for her.

"Don't look now, but Reilly Ogden is heading our way," Nicole said.

It was true. Reilly, in his stiff new jeans and Bazooka Joe T-shirt, which was trying its hardest to display a playfulness that Reilly Ogden probably had never felt in his life. He tucked that shirt into his pants with one hand as if he were some old guy who meant business.

We crumpled our lunch bags, got up in a hurry.

"See you around, bitches," Jasmine said.

Jasmine's brother, Derek, always gave us a ride home from school even though Jasmine had track. In the parking lot I headed over to his Camaro, with its low back and its two wide white stripes along the hood. I was the first one there and so I waited, careful not to lean against the paint. Derek would have gotten pissed off at that. Derek never said much, but you could tell when he was mad. He was always quiet, but he got more quiet when he was angry. Quiet wasn't one thing. It had levels.

I watched Mr. Wykowski get into his beater car and wondered what his private life was like other than what we knew, which was that he was a pot-head. This occupied me for about two seconds until I saw Shy cross the parking lot, his backpack over one shoulder, his jeans low and sloopy, and his hair a little over his eyes. He looked over at me and I smiled at him. He waved his hand without raising his arm, just a little lift of his fingers at his side, and then I could see his face change color, from a nice easy tan to a sudden red the shade of a pomegranate.

You sure got that guy all shook up, I heard Hayden's voice say in my head. But I didn't have time to think about it, because I saw something else then. Something I knew was important, only I didn't know why. It was Buddy Wilkes's El Camino, pulling into the school parking lot. It was an old car, with a cream-colored convertible top that was down in the sun. I didn't know what Buddy Wilkes was doing in the high school parking lot. He'd graduated three years before and had no business being there—his car gave off some sense of wrongness, of boundaries broken, same as when Wiley Rogers's older brother came around the school selling drugs, hanging around just off campus by the cemetery across the street.

And then I saw why Buddy Wilkes was there. He pulled right up to the curb by the school's front doors, where it was painted No Parking red, where only the buses were allowed. The radio was loud enough for me to hear, though he did lean forward and turn it down, his long arm reaching to flick off the sound. Not out of politeness, I realized, but to be heard better. He cupped one hand around his mouth and shouted, "Alicia!"

Alicia Worthen, of course. It made sense why Buddy was there. Alicia was a senior and beautiful. Not just ordinary beautiful, not just cheerleader or popular beautiful, but really beautiful. The kind of beautiful that seemed like it was too much even for Alicia Worthen. She tried to get rid of it, the same as you give away something you have two of—she tied up her chestnut hair and went without makeup on her olive skin. But it was there no matter what she did. Alicia Worthen's beauty was the determined sort.

I wondered for a moment what kind of pull Buddy Wilkes had over beautiful girls. He went through them fast, like they were paper towels to be used and thrown away. He'd had three girlfriends in one week, I'd heard once. Juliet had been with him the longest, but if she thought he was faithful, she was an idiot.

"Would you hurry it up?" he shouted again, and maybe that was my answer about beautiful girls. Maybe he found that dark place that even they have, that hollow and impossible to understand need to not be good enough.

Nicole arrived then, grabbed my arm. "Jesus, girl, what's that look on your face?" she said, but before I could answer, Derek arrived too, talking all about how Kevin Frink got caught in the boys' locker room with a pipe bomb and how he might get expelled. I'd never heard Derek speak quite so many words. Bombs got him pretty excited, I guess. We got into the car, and I watched Alicia get into Buddy's El Camino as we left the parking lot and turned the corner.

"I just don't get the need to blow things up," Nicole said.

"It's a reordering of your personal universe," Derek said,

causing Nicole to look at me and shrug and for me to shrug back. "A bomb will change things forever."

Looking back, I would remember his words. You'd have never guessed that Derek, with his *C*-minus average and motor-oil hands, was some sort of prophet.

Chapter Eight

A s soon as I got out of Derek's car, I saw something unusual on the sidewalk across the street where Goth Girl's drawing had been. When I'd left messages before, they'd just get washed away with the drawing itself, by the rain or someone's garden hose, leaving the cement clean and empty as if she'd always been silent. But even from across the street I noticed something different now. The drawing was gone, but my words were still there. A new color had been added. I crossed the street to look.

I knelt down. My heart rose. All around my own message were the tiny, tiny words *thank you thank you thank you* written in a circle.

I couldn't believe it. I couldn't believe this sudden progress, this new place where Fiona Saint George had now put the two of us. I felt so happy, the kind of happy that makes you want to sing, or kiss, or eat cake. I had reached out and she had reached back and it was fantastic. I looked around to share the great moment with someone, anyone; I would have smiled and waved at Ally Pete-Robbins, even, or scooped up Ginger, but no one was outside. There was only the *whick-whick-whick* of the Mr. Pete-Robbins's sprinkler system shooting jets of water in an efficient circle.

I heard a screen door slam, and I was ready with my smile and friendly words for whoever it might be, ready for generosity to bring generosity and more generosity. That's how good I felt about what had happened. But the whole train of joy and good will stopped with sudden screeching brakes.

It was Clive Weaver. But, oh God, *wait*. This was not what I was hoping for—not at all. This was some sort of emergency. It was Clive Weaver, and Clive Weaver was naked, completely naked, and heading out toward his mailbox. Gone were his usual blue shorts and white knee socks, shirt tucked in tight. Instead, there was only his round white stomach and dangly, embarrassed penis. Blue veiny legs, and a wide, flat floppy butt. I shielded my own eyes and gasped. Oh God, what was I supposed to do? I peeked to make sure he wasn't going to dodge out into the street. I could hear that nasty ice-cream man, Joe, with his cheerful truck and tinkly music and glaring eyes, somewhere on the next block. It would be a death or bad accident Clive Weaver didn't deserve. Death by Creamsicle. Death to the tune of "The Entertainer."

Through the space between my fingers, I could see that Clive Weaver wore his old man slippers, too, and worse yet, his former mailman helmet, which all gave him the unfortunate look of an old nude guy in search of a mail safari. I felt a little panic. Should I do something? What should I do? The tiny dangly penis was understandably distracting. His slippers scuffed along the sidewalk until he reached the mailboxes. His wide white ass sagged in the direction of the street. He opened his box, empty, and he shut it again.

"Fools," he said loudly.

I was too embarrassed to move. His exposed flesh had stunned me into inaction. Instead, I peeked from a distance and made sure he got back into his house. I hoped he was okay. I wondered if I should tell Mom or call his daughters, something. Then again, he hadn't continued out to the freeway or anything. He'd just gone to get his mail and had forgotten his clothes. Maybe this happened after a person worked forty-five years for the postal service.

Mom must have left Quill Stationers early, because her car was in the driveway. Hayden's truck was gone, though. I had no idea what combination of people I might find there, in my formerly pre-dictable house. Inside, though, it was as quiet as it usually was when I got home. No sign of my mother or Zeus. I heard the scrape of a lawn chair against the cement patio, though, through the propped-open kitchen door. Juliet was outside, lying out in the sun in her bikini. She reached one arm down to a squirt bottle of water, sprayed herself down and up as if she were a dry houseplant.

"Hey!" I shouted. "I'm home!"

"Out here," Juliet shouted back without sitting up.

I dropped my backpack, grabbed a Fresca from the fridge. The whole bottom shelf of our refrigerator had been packed with diet sodas since Dean had come along to blow my mother's self-confidence to smithereens. I made my feet happy and took off my sandals, headed out to the back. I noticed that Juliet had a Fresca too popped open beside her.

"Oh God, don't look. I'm so fat," she said. She looked fine to me: she had only the small mound of stomach us regular people always had. She made no move to cover herself up. That was another difference between us. Juliet was never shy about her body. I loved my body and all that, I just loved it more covered up.

"Clive Weaver was just outside naked," I said.

"Who?"

"Clive *Weaver?* Come on, it's not like you haven't lived across the street from him practically your whole life."

"Maybe he was hot," she said, and squirted her calves with the bottle.

"Where's Mom?" I asked. I wanted to ask, *Where's Hayden?* but I didn't.

"Next door. Wacky Mrs. Martinelli couldn't sign on to the Internet and she came over all frantic."

I sat on the lawn near Juliet. Picked up a tennis ball that must have been Zeus's and threw it against our fence where it bounced and landed in Mom's oregano bush. One of the neighbors behind us was getting their house worked on. I heard the *chink-chink-chink* of a ladder rising, the bass hump of music, lyrics drifting. *Some people call me the gangster of love, yeah. Some people walking round calling me Mau-rice. . . .* "I like Mrs. Martinelli. I like her a lot, actually."

Juliet turned her head on the lawn chair and looked at me, annoyed. It was the same look she'd been giving me throughout our whole childhood, the kind I'd gotten in the backseat of the car when she felt I had taken too much space for myself or when my elbow accidentally touched hers. "What, are you going to fight me about whether Mrs. Martinelli is a kook now too? What is your problem? You've argued with every word I've said since I got home. You never even said congratulations. Not really."

I waited. I guess it was true. "Congratulations, Juliet," I said. I let my sarcasm show. I wondered how often people meant it when they said that word; *congratulations* was probably one of the biggest mixed-feelings word in the English language.

She rolled her eyes in exasperation. It was weird to look at her body sprawled out like that. She didn't seem to realize that she was different now, at least to me. I looked at that small mound. I remembered the pictures from the book; the tiny curled baby sea creature who now waited and grew inside of her while she swigged her Fresca, then set it on the glossy pages of the magazine she was reading. But it wasn't just the tiny creature that made her different. Decisions could make you different too. A person could decide something that made them seem totally unknown and unknowable, even if you'd been with them nearly every day of your life.

"You shouldn't drink that diet stuff. It's bad for the baby," I said.

"Thank you, doctor," she said.

We sat there for a while. You could feel the fight there sitting between us. I hated conflict, but conflict with my sister was allowed. Conflict was part of our personal, forever playground. She would fight with me in a moment, but I never forgot that she'd fight for me too. "You know, I just don't get the whole pregnancy thing," I said. I picked at the polish on my toenails. I hoped Jitter couldn't hear this. It was nothing personal. This was something between me and Juliet.

"What's there to get? We had sex; there was an accident; we're having a baby."

"Jesus, Juliet."

"Oh come, on, Scarlet. Don't be such a prude."

"I'm not being a prude. You're just so flip about it. *Accident.*"

"Those things happen."

"Not when you're being *careful.*"

"I thought I *was.* Believe me, Hayden in bed can make you forget just about anything. It's one of his finest qualities."

"*Jesus!*" I wished I'd never said a word. God. "Never *mind.*"

"You brought it up."

"You were on the *pill,*" I said.

"What are you implying? Are you accusing me of something? For God's sake."

"There are other *options* here."

"Neither one of us wanted that, all right? Satisfied? It's not like I trapped the guy, if that's what you're saying."

"I'm *saying* it's a little hard to understand. I'm *saying* you hugely disappointed Mom."

"Oh, you're kidding, right? What, I'm going to live my whole life for Mom?" She blew air out her nose, a huff that said what an idiot I was. She sounded like she was in middle school. "I've got to make my own decisions. Am I not allowed to *grow up?*"

Grow up. The words sounded childish. You don't fight for your right to grow up if you already have. "You've wrecked everything you said you wanted." I said.

I remembered when she got the job at the Grosvenor Hotel, how we'd popped open a bottle of cider, clinked our glasses; how Mom had grasped Juliet's hands and told her the world was hers, how she needed to follow her dreams, even if we all knew how much Mom wanted her to go to college. I remembered, too, how Juliet had packed up and left her room nearly empty, tiny holes in the walls where her posters had hung. We'd tacked up all of the postcards she'd sent us to cover those holes—postcards of the Grosvenor Hotel at night which were in every desk drawer in every room there, next to the free pens and stationery that no one used.

"I didn't wreck; I reordered," she said.

I stopped picking my polish and looked at her then. *Reordered*—the word Derek had just used not twenty minutes before, half hour tops, about why people blew things up. I listened to signs like that—a song heard twice when you turned the radio station, a line in a book read at just the right moment. Little clues given by the universe. The word was suddenly important. It seemed like maybe it was a sign that I should do some reordering of my own. They'd argued about Buddy Wilkes the night before. Buddy Wilkes was her unfinished business. Business I could finish up right then and there.

"I saw Buddy Wilkes at school today," I said.

Juliet sat up then. "You saw Buddy? What was he doing at school?"

"Picking up Alicia Worthen. They looked pretty serious. Really serious."

"Alicia *Worthen*? She hasn't even *graduated*."

"You're so lucky you didn't stay with him. He just sat in his car and shouted at her." I was making up some of it as I went along. I guess reordering wasn't always a precisely planned thing. "Hayden would never act like that."

"What'd he say?"

"He didn't exactly yell *at* her, more *for* her. Just, 'Alicia, get over here.' Something like that. Like she was his *dog* or something. No, Hayden wouldn't even treat Zeus like that. You wouldn't believe it. He's such an ass."

"Alicia *Worthen*. God." Juliet didn't look well. I felt the alarming sense of things all at once going wrong—that slipping feeling, the movement in an unintended direction. The way the ground starts to roll under the flat surface of your shoes just before you fall. Maybe the reordering had been a bad idea. Maybe I had opened a door when I'd tried to shut one. Maybe the truthful part of me knew I wanted to hurt her and had.

The smugness I had seen Juliet wear every day since she had arrived seemed to melt, as if she had gone from having everything to having nothing.

"I shouldn't have drunk that Fresca," she said. She got up and went inside and in a few moments I heard her retching, the toilet flush, the faucet running.

I sat there on the grass, ran my hands over the blades. I felt a little sick myself. I smelled a whiff of Varathane or some other soupy, gleaming chemical coming from over the back fence. I heard a small burst of man-talk, a shout. *Whaddya say?* More faraway man-talk. Music. *I'm a joker, I'm a smoker, I'm a midnight toker. . . .*

And then another sound, closer. Right there, from our own bathroom.

Juliet, crying.

Chapter Nine

This is what I call reciprocity," Mom said, holding a pie dish on one palm.

"Lemon meringue?"

Mom nodded. It was Mrs. Martinelli's specialty. "I perform the computer miracle called turn the machine off and back on and look what I get. Want some?"

"No thanks." I gestured to the white bread I'd taken out of the cupboard for a snack, the jar of peanut butter.

"Tell me why it's nice to have superior computer knowledge over someone, anyone." Mom loved Mrs. Martinelli too. Sometimes Mrs. Martinelli would have lemonade with Mom at our umbrella table outside or coffee with her while sitting on the living room couch. They would pat each other's hands and tell stories. Mom always said that she respected the sequined sweatshirts. Sequins required a certain confidence, especially when worn while gardening.

"I guess you got her connected again."

"Maybe I shouldn't have. Did you know they're writing back and forth with some scammer? She said you knew all about it." Mom didn't wait for an answer. "Where's Juliet?" she asked.

"She's not feeling well." I stuck my tongue out, mimed a throw-up face.

"Oh," Mom said. "Poor thing. That's too bad."

"Why aren't you at work?" I asked.

"I thought maybe I'd take the day off. Make sure Juliet was settled in."

The words fell before I could catch them. "You didn't even stay home with me when I had the flu and a hundred degree fever."

"Scarlet," she said as if it were the end of what she had to say even though it was the start. "I asked you over and over if you wanted me to stay. You said you were fine. You insisted. I took you at your word."

I was going to tell her about Clive Weaver naked in the street, but I didn't feel like it anymore. Some worm of jealousy and resentment was working around in my heart. I put my knife into the new jar of peanut butter. No matter what seemed to be going wrong in my life, there was something satisfying about that act. It was a mini-sense of triumph, a culinary groundbreaking ceremony, with me holding the special shovel.

Mom left the kitchen. I could see her through the door, standing in front of the stereo. She pulled her hair back in a ponytail and then let it go as she pretended to contemplate what to put on. She looked young like that. It was always strange when you saw your parent as a person, not a mother or father. I guessed that happened more when you had a single parent.

They couldn't hide in that thing called marriage. Mom stared down at Neil Diamond's face on the cover of *Neil Diamond's Greatest Hits*, the one where his eyes are brooding but kind, and then on came the deep thrum of the guitar, and his voice. *Melinda was mine, 'til the time that I found her . . . holding Jim. Loving him . . .*

"Mom, God," I called from the other room.

"What?"

"I'm so sick of that I could scream."

She put her hands on her hips. "I'm not exactly forcing you to stand there and listen, am I?"

"Play 'Sweet Caroline.'" Juliet had reappeared. She looked pale, even after her day in the sun. She'd tied a sarong around her hips, sleeked her hair back in a long blond braid. "Remember how we all used to sing that loudly in the car? *Sweet Car-o-line, bum, bum, bum . . .*" She sang with that voice that could make you think about beautiful things—water droplets and tulips pushing up through frost. "Summer time," Juliet said. "Scarlet with her teeth perpetually blue from Otter Pops."

"I loved that," Mom said. "Everywhere we went, we played this. You, me, Scarlet, and Scarlet's *monkey.*"

"Jibbs," Juliet said.

"God, he was so dirty, and you'd never let him out of your clutches, Scar," Mom said. "I had to sew his head back on twice."

"Remember when she used to get the words mixed up to 'Jimmy Cracked Corn'?"

"'Jimmy crapped corn, and I don't care,'" they sang. How could I forget? I'd only heard the story a million times.

Juliet and Mom laughed, but I didn't feel like playing. I took a bite of my sandwich. Something was irritating me. And irritating me even more when Mom put her hands on the sides of Juliet's cheeks and looked into her eyes. "You okay, baby?"

Juliet groaned.

"I know."

The doorbell rang then. "If it's Mrs. Martinelli again, I've reached my end of computer knowledge," Mom said.

Juliet went to the door, opened it. "Silly, you don't have to ring the doorbell," she said. I heard the happy *tick-tick-tick* of Zeus's toenails arriving on the wood floor, and Hayden's voice in the hall.

"We are now officially employed!" he said. He appeared in the kitchen. His sunburn from a few days before was turning brown. His hair was sweet-rumpled, and Zeus pushed past him and came toward the counter, his nose up in the air, sniffing for something that *might be/maybe/is it?* peanut butter.

"You got a job?" Mom asked.

"I'm calling myself a dock manager," he said. "But I'm really just hired to fix stuff there at the marina, work on Will Quail's boat. I was afraid to commit to anything more permanent since we haven't decided"—he knew to be careful, paused to choose the right words—"things."

For a moment, Juliet said nothing and Hayden said nothing which meant they were saying a lot. The moment passed. You could feel a decision being made, hers, an instant mental pro-and-con list. She looped her arms around his waist then, and you could also feel something melt, fast as butter in a hot pan. Hayden put his hand around her bare back and sniffed her hair. He was someone who fell easily into forgiveness.

"Old man Quail used to teach Driver's Ed," she said.

"He's deaf as a stone," Hayden said.

"He's always been deaf as a stone," Mom said. "Too many rock concerts during the Age of Aquarius."

Juliet released Hayden, turned to place herself against him, standing with her back against his chest. "He used to go, 'Turn that radio off!' when it wasn't even on." She grabbed Hayden's arms, wrapped them tightly in front of her. She hadn't been this affectionate with him since they'd gotten here. The whole aloof business was gone. *Thank Alicia Worthen for that*, I thought. It was the law of diminishing options.

I felt the wave rise—the wave of vague *pissed-off*—a pissed-off without a name. An edge of anger that might really have been disgust. All of this easy forgiveness wherever you turned. I shoved my feet into my sandals. I suddenly just wanted to get out of there, away from all of them.

"Tacos for dinner?" Mom said. "Can you eat that, you think?" She peered worriedly at Juliet.

Juliet nodded. "Oh yeah. Let us help." She lifted up one of Hayden's arms, pretended to bite it.

"I hold the record for cheese grating," he said.

I choked back the bite of my sandwich. "I'm actually heading out," I said. I heard the edge in my own voice, the letting-them-know but not-letting them-know anger. It pushed up against me inside, made my face flush.

"Oh?" Mom said.

"Dinner plans with friends."

She didn't even ask her usual twenty follow-up questions. Who would be there, what time I'd be back, if a parent would be present. She'd either given up on my doing anything different from babysitting or hanging out with Nicole and Jasmine, or she was too preoccupied to really care. "The car needs gas," she said. "Take my card and get some."

Anger and irritation were fighting for first place inside of me, and I made some attempt at a rare dramatic gesture. I swiped her keys off the counter and stormed toward the doorway, realizing too late that *shit, shit, shit,* one foot was suddenly bare and landing on the linoleum floor. My shoe, that traitor, had abandoned me, and it now sat alone over by the counter. I had to do the one-shoe limp back to retrieve it. It would be so much better if humiliation was private.

I heard a little *hnn* sound from Juliet, a laugh trying not to be a laugh. Forget that shit. I got out of there. I left my half-eaten sandwich, left my backpack full of homework. Left cloudy motivations and strange workings of the heart. Left small humiliations and big disappointments.

Neil Diamond was still crooning. *Good times never seemed so good . . .* If I never heard that goddamned Neil Diamond again it would be too soon.

The tick of Mom's gas gauge was as far into the red as it would go, so dangerously low that it was Dean-Neuhaus-would-never-do-this low. My psychology books would call this passive-aggressive behavior, subtly striking back at someone who seems more powerful, only my mother was getting it wrong, because she was the only one who was sure to be punished. I pulled into Abare's, which we all still called Eugene's, since that's what the gas station had been for a hundred years before the old guy died. It was sold after he was gone and a mini-mart was put in, and the only thing that stayed the same was that they still hired guys from our high school to pump gas for elderly ladies like Cora Lee from the Theosophical Society and Mrs. Dubbs, who worked in the deli at

Johnny's Market. Buddy worked at Eugene's, too, but I didn't see either him or his car. I pulled into the lane marked SELF-SERVE, chugged gas into Mom's tank as the wavy lines of fuel fumes made a psychedelic escape.

"Hey," a voice called. I assumed not to me. Maybe someone was shouting to the chunky motorcyclist in his chunky leather jacket.

"You."

I looked up. It was Jason Dale, a guy who had graduated a few years ago, one of Buddy's friends. He obviously didn't know my name, but I knew things about him. He'd been a hard-core partier. He'd gone out with Renny Williams's sister, Wendy, and some people said she'd gotten an abortion. Juliet thought he was an idiot. She thought all Buddy's friends were idiots.

"Aren't you Juliet Ellis's sister?"

"Yeah," I said. If I had business cards, that's pretty much what they'd read.

"Is it true she's back in town? Someone said they saw her."

I played a mental chess match, with Hayden on my team. I calculated how long that news would take to reach Buddy. I hung up the gas pump. "Nope. Someone saw wrong."

"Shopping downtown?" He still sounded hopeful.

"She's in Mexico," I said.

"Oh cool." He rubbed his angled cheeks with his palms as if feeling for a nonexistent beard.

"Yeah." I was ready to expand on my story. I had her singing for some cruise line, docked in Aruba and heading out to sea where she would be unreachable for months, but the details didn't prove necessary. Jason Dale walked back to the minimart without a good-bye; his jeans droopy in the back like Clive

Weaver's bare skin. The motorcyclist gunned his engine and arced out of the lot.

I got back in Mom's Honda Accord. I moved the seat and changed the radio station because I knew she didn't like that. I turned the radio up loud enough to feel it thrum inside my body. I needed music that loud sometimes, loud enough to feel like a heartbeat.

I didn't really know where I was going. Not to Nicole's or Jasmine's. If I had a father, I thought, this would be the time I would go to wherever he was. It was not the kind of thought I usually allowed myself. It was stupid. But this time I gave myself a pass for one visiting-my-perfect-father fantasy. I tried it on for about two seconds until it felt like I was wearing a silly and pointless hat in public. Awkward, embarrassing, never mind.

Instead I drove over to Point Perpetua Park. I had another fantasy on the way—me putting Jitter into a baby seat and driving far away where I could make sure he was never around unhappy parents. I would buy him soft clothes and read him books and teach him to aim high. It was still early evening, and the light was just dimming to twilight and turning thoughtful. I walked down the forested path and out to the beach. An older lady with poofy white hair walked with her small poofy, white-haired dog, and Bea Martinsen, who told fortunes at the Sunday market, sat at one of the benches eating a take-out hamburger from one of Pirate's Plunder's bags. When I reached the beach, I saw a couple who looked like they were having an argument and the guy who always played the bagpipes around town, who now sat on the sand and watched the waves. I picked my way over to the rock where Hayden and I had sat. A small collection of shells was up there—someone had been there since we had and had forgotten their treasures.

The water was choppy, and the waves were traveling at a rambunctious angle. A tanker inched by in the distance. The wide sea and rocks and beach should have set things right for me, that's how it had always worked before, but I still felt some ugly feeling in my chest, something metallic and twisted, some kind of wreckage. I tried to untwist and understand. It didn't feel good. It felt a little close to hate. Maybe I was hating Juliet, and it felt wrong to hate Juliet. Maybe what I hated was that Juliet could do no wrong even when she did one of the biggest wrongs.

The arguing couple made up, took hands, and then kissed deeply by the shore, the water wetting their shoes. The old lady appeared with her dog and they walked a bit, and then she picked him up just before he headed toward a glittery pool of broken glass. Maybe I had also always felt sure of something I wasn't so sure of now. That if I followed some rules of being nice and good, everything would work out okay. That at least this meant I was giving fate its best shot to follow through the way it should. Good people would get good things; wrong acts were punished. You'd get back what you gave, because that was only fair. Maybe being good to other people was often really only about hope—your hope that if you acted the right way, the pieces of the universe would fall into their true and just place. If you were being honest, that was a good part of why you did it, right? It was a way to protect yourself. Sort of a shield against wrongness, only maybe wrongness just didn't care about rules or hope or other people's good intentions.

I sat there for a long time, until everyone had left and there were only two guys smoking cigarettes on the beach. The shadows were getting long and night was falling, and so I finally left. I went down to the marina and picked up a hamburger and fries and a shake at Pirate's Plunder, because I tended to catch other people's food choices, same as a yawn. I ate it in Mom's car with the windows rolled down so the lingering french fry smell didn't give away what I'd actually done with my night.

The TV was on in the living room but the lights were off when I got home. I didn't want to catch Juliet and Hayden making out, so I crept upstairs. There was a crack of light under my mom's door. I made my way over the creaks in the hall, shut my door by turning the handle oh-so-quietly.

There was a tap then.

"Scarlet?"

"Yeah."

Mom poked her head in. "You okay?" One hand was on the doorjamb, the other at her side. Plain, ringless hands. She never wore rings. I had asked her why, once. She had said she liked her hands to belong to herself.

"Yeah."

"You don't seem okay. Can I come in?" I nodded. She sat on the edge of my bed. She looked up at my wall of photos— Mrs. Martinelli in her frog sweatshirt, the back of Nicole and her mom looking into their refrigerator, Buster standing around with Ginger, as if they were catching up on dog gossip, a little girl staring with wide eyes into Randall and Stein Booksellers as if it were a toy store.

"I like that one," she said.

"This?"

A shot of Goth Girl's *Mona Lisa*. The Saint Georges' lawn took up the top half of the frame; the painting filled the bottom.

"Next to it." It was the back of Mr. Martinelli's neck. The straight line of his crew cut set against a blue sky. "You've got a really good eye, you know."

"Thanks."

She tucked her brown hair behind her ears, and then tucked it again, as if she were about to deliver some bad news. She opened her mouth to say something, shut it for a revision, tried over. "I know this is hard. This stranger, coming and moving into our house . . . His dog. All this with Juliet. This situation thrust on us. I know that even I don't understand how this happened."

I looked down at my comforter. Traced the threads with my finger. Boy, was she getting it wrong.

"It's new for me, too," she went on. "We don't even know anything about him. And then, a *baby* . . ." She sighed. "God. She's so young. I think about how young I was. . . ."

I tried to imagine this, a younger version of my mom, pregnant with Juliet. Some stranger with white-blond hair who spoke and ate and made decisions and maybe loved Mom and maybe didn't. Twice in one day was more than I'd thought about him in years.

"I don't understand how she could do something so stupid," I said.

Mom thought. "Well, sometimes . . . you think it's going to decide something. Marriage. A baby."

I didn't know where she was going with that. Mom could be fond of misty and beside-the-point musings. The kind you got when you'd been listening to music and were therefore in some mood to be profound. I didn't care about any of that. *Profound* was just a way to keep your distance from prickly life truths. I didn't want soft, misty talk. I hated conflict, *hated it*, especially with Mom, but I chanced the truth. "You don't seem that upset," I said quietly.

"What?"

"Not really. You're not that mad at her."

Mom shook her head. She looked at me like she couldn't quite understand where I was coming from. Her face changed, lost its softness. Her voice was irritated. "I'm just trying to do the best I can here."

I kept tracing the threads with my fingertip. I could go farther, but it might mean a real argument, a guilty and unsettled night's sleep, and the dreaded waking up with the knowledge that things were wrong between us. I kept quiet. We just sat there silently. I listened to Mr. Martinelli drag his rubber garbage cans down the cement driveway to the curb.

"All right, Scarlet. If this is the way you want it . . . ," Mom said. She waited, but I gave her nothing back. She got up and left me alone again.

I tried to get into bed and go to sleep, but sleep was stubborn and taunting, staying just out of reach. I wondered if I should make a list of things we needed for the baby. I listened to crickets and folded up my pillow and tried it that way and then unfolded it again. The sheet had gotten all scrunched at the bottom of the mattress and I was sorting out my confused bed when I heard a noise out on the street. Footsteps. A voice? I peeked out my window.

Oh God, it was Clive Weaver outside again, naked as the day he was born. He was out by the mailboxes. He muttered something. And then he said, "Roscoe Oil, those bastards!" so loudly that he caused a far-off dog to bark and Ally Pete-Robbins's porch light to go on.

"Mr. Weaver!" I whispered as loudly as I could.

He looked around as if God were talking to him. I could only imagine how surprised he'd be when God turned out to be a seventeen-year-old girl.

"Up here!" I whispered. "It's me, Scarlet."

"I thought maybe the mail was late," he said.

"It's not late," I said. "It came this afternoon."

"They'd never have let us get away with that shit," he said.

"I think you'd better go inside and go to bed," I said. His nakedness was not as shocking the second time around.

"What?" he shouted.

"Go inside and go to bed."

"So long," he said.

Mr. Weaver shuffled back in the direction of his front door, his slippers scuffing along on the sidewalk, his flabby white ass making a sad retreat. I climbed back into bed. Someone was going to have to do something about him. Probably that someone was going to be me. Ever since way back in kindergarten, when Mr. Keneely needed "someone" to walk with Renee Horton to the office when she was about to throw up and nobody, *nobody* offered to help, I'd been the someone who would finally raise their hand. Whether someone ever got to be anyone—that was what I wasn't so sure of anymore.

Chapter Ten

*I*n the morning, there were cars out in front of Clive Weaver's house. Two cars. Serious-looking cars. I hoped he hadn't died or anything. It didn't seem like a death-type morning. The guys working on the house behind us were getting an early start; I heard the cheery *chink, chink, chink* of the ladder rising, the clatter of lumber being dropped. A crow heckled his nasty *caw, caw* from a tree, as another, more positive-thinking bird group twittered cheerfully from farther off. A milk truck from Daly Farms was stopped in front of Ally Pete-Robbins's house, the driver hopping into the wide-open truck door and starting the engine back up with optimistic vigor. Blue sky, a tree shimmering in a slight breeze. All in all, not a day someone's life was over.

I walked past Juliet's closed door. It seemed heavy with sleep and secrets and entwined bodies and sheets in disarray. I tried not to think about what my sister had said, about Hayden in bed.

I pretended not to see the door the way you pretend not to see things not entirely hidden that should be entirely hidden, life's little moments of too much information—Wiley Rogers's older brother selling drugs across the street from our high school, for one example; Hailey Benecci's anorexia, for another.

It was not exactly like I hadn't been faced with Juliet's sex life before. There were countless times she'd come home with her hair smashed up and tangled and her makeup long gone, and sometimes I'd actually catch her and Buddy on the couch in our living room. There would be a panicked flurry of jumping up and adjusting clothes and Buddy looking around on the floor with one hand for his shirt that had fallen, wearing underwear so tight he could have been on the swim team. But this was different, even though Juliet was married now. Hayden wasn't Buddy or Adam Christ or Harrison Somebody. He was more real. He had strong-looking shoulders, and life goals, and a dog he scruffed under the neck and crooned at. He wasn't some idea of a man, he actually *was* a man. It made that closed bedroom door—

"Morning," Hayden said from the kitchen.

"Oh!" I said. I felt some weird relief at the sight of him standing there in his jeans and his favorite soft green T-shirt, his cheeks stubbly and unshaven, his hair a bird's nest tangle of curls. Assumptions were sometimes tricky territory.

"I'm afraid this coffeepot may have stopped working." He was holding an empty cup, *World's Best Mom* written on it, with a picture of a trophy cup. Mother's Day from a thousand years ago.

"Mom unplugs it every night," I said.

He shook his head to indicate he couldn't believe his own stupidity, looked behind the coffeepot, and lifted the cord up as evidence that I was right. "I see," he said. And then: "Every night?"

Deb Caletti

"She's convinced it will burst into flames."

"Mothers," he said.

"Mothers," I agreed. "Do you have one? I mean, where is yours? *Are* yours. Your parents?" It was true what Mom had said—we didn't know anything about him. He could have been raised by wolves for all we knew. I got a cereal bowl, poured breakfast. Mom had already gone to work, and if I wasn't waiting at the curb in fifteen minutes, Derek would drive on without me.

"I don't see my father much anymore. Not a great guy. Actually, a bad man. You know." I did. "Mom is in Portland. She's a sculptor. Really good. She's getting pretty successful now, I'm proud to say."

"How does she feel about . . ." I waved my arm in a circle.

It was quiet except for that stupid crow. He was cawing along and then got frenzied as crows do sometimes, the caws turning into that *garble-garble* strangled-turkey sound. Zeus leaped to his feet and trotted out to the kitchen window as if to protect us from imminent danger. In his mind, as long as he kept his eye on things, we'd be safe.

"That crow," Hayden said. "Turkey murder."

"I was just thinking the *exact* same thing," I said.

I thought for a moment he would skip the answer to my question, but he finally spoke after the coffeepot began to burble. "Mom's um . . . disappointed. I'm the only child, and this isn't how she saw things going. Or how I did, honestly. She offered to help so we could stay in Portland, but Juliet . . ." He shrugged a well-you-know-how-this-story-ends shrug.

"But I guess you and Juliet have that in common," I said.

"We both have disappointed mothers?" Hayden leaned with his back against the counter as he waited for the coffee. Zeus turned his attention back to him, looked up at Hayden as if he was the center of everything great—steaks and dog biscuits and shady spots and car rides.

"Fathers. You know."

"Asshole fathers?"

"Absent ones."

"Mine was around; he just wasn't a nice guy."

"Maybe we had it better, then. We didn't know *what* kind of guy he was."

"You knew he was a coward," Hayden said.

My chest filled with an unfamiliar feeling. Something large. It was the great rising flood you feel when the kid you know is cheating from you gets caught, or when the creep driver who's been riding your tail gets pulled over. I didn't answer him right away, though. It wasn't something I liked to think about. But the place he'd just brought me to was a great place, where he was standing up to the bully just by speaking the truth.

"A coward?" I said.

"Absolutely, Scarlet."

He held my eyes, driving his point home. I looked down. All the greatness was too much suddenly; the awareness of how much his words meant embarrassed me.

"Anyway," I said. "You and Juliet. A match made in childhood."

The coffeepot filled cheerfully. Hayden tilted his head and narrowed his eyes at me. "There you go again," he said. "Jesus. Nothing much passes you by, does it, Scarlet Ellis? You are a life-watcher. You take it in, all of it."

I willed myself not to blush. "I gotta run," I said. I rinsed my bowl, jammed it into the dishwasher.

"Look both ways and don't talk to strangers," he said.

"Okay, Dad," I said.

I waited outside for Derek. The day was sunny and you could smell flowers blooming. I swear I could smell the orange red of Ally Peet-Robbins's bed of primroses. I had that big, big feeling that sat right next to *giddy*. Where you feel like you could build a building or stop warring nations or create a masterpiece, and you want to start right then. I life-watched; I took it all in, it was true. That was me. That's who I was. That's who I was exactly.

Usually you could hear Derek Nakasani's car before you could see it. The Camaro made the sound a large animal might make in the back of its throat when provoked. I once made the mistake of making Derek wait because I was late, or should I say making Derek not wait. So I tried to be early and stood in front of our house with my backpack at my feet. The cars still sat in Clive Weaver's driveway, quiet with importance.

My eye caught on something on the sidewalk in front of Goth Girl's house. Something pink. A new design started already? I crossed the street to get a better look.

A new design, yes, but it was nothing like anything she'd ever drawn before. It was simple. The sparest message. No hints of famous paintings, no family members in punishing poses. No vampires with fangs and blood. Just a red Volkswagen. A tuxedo. A dress, one that a princess might wear—pink, with a full skirt. Underneath it were the words *Prom dress*. A pair of shoes, and the words under that: *Prom shoes*.

Every bad thought I'd had the night before about helping people, about being a good person—they vanished, just like that. *This* was why you helped people. This was why you did the right thing. Because you could make a difference when no one else could. Because you were actually *needed*. You watched life, you took it all in, and then you did something about it. Goth Girl was talking to me. Goth Girl was telling me her deepest secret.

Goth Girl wanted to go to the prom.

"Are you ignoring me? Because I have the feeling you're ignoring me." When I shut my locker door and turned around, I found Reilly Ogden standing there.

"Jesus, Reilly, you scared me." Reilly had a way of appearing out of nowhere. That day, he wore a black dress shirt open to his chest, a traveling salesman stuck in the seventies, ready to pick up foxy chicks in a hotel bar. His hair had something slippery on it; it was stuck up in some punk-cool, circa 1980. His tennis shoes were high-tech millennium cool. Who knew what year the actual Reilly Ogden was inside.

I had seen Reilly's house once, the night I made the mistake of going to the dance with him. It was one of those flat fifties houses with small windows and that white stuff that looks like Grape-Nuts sprayed onto the low ceiling. There was a BMW out front, his parents' car. Inside, the living room smelled like someone had just cooked bacon. It had a sort of creepy basement. I don't know about anyone else, but I'm really only about sixty-eight percent okay with basements.

"Scarlet, what's wrong? Things haven't been the same between us."

"Look, Reilly," I said. "I'm just not ready to get involved with anyone, okay? Don't take it personal." Which you only said, of course, when something was *very* personal.

"We're already *involved*. You came to my *house* . . . ," he whined.

I shoved past him, remembering the cold sweat on his palm that night at the dance when he had tried to hold my hand. I headed for Ms. Cassaday's AP English. I sat in that hard plastic seat and tried to concentrate on *Tess of the d'Urbervilles*. My mind couldn't be still, and that rarely happened in Ms. Cassaday's class. She was bold and important and never spoke about her personal life, even though we all knew she lived with Elaine Blackstone, who worked at the oyster beds. You wondered what their house looked like inside, and if, every morning, sitting on the edge of their bed, Elaine put her work boots on—the green rubber ones you saw her wearing at Johnny's Market, her jeans tucked down inside.

But that day I couldn't be hooked in by Ms. Cassaday's words. I was unfocused and gaze-y, staring out the classroom window which looked out over the baseball field, with its dry yellow grass and padded white bases set on dusty ground. I wondered if Hayden had played baseball in high school. I pictured him with a mitt on his hand, a dog running around his legs. I wondered who he was as a boy. If he rode his bike or collected bugs or grew a sunflower in a Styrofoam cup in the first grade. A person can seem like a whole country you've never been to.

The deep desire to see someone again, to know more: Was it fate shifting its pieces, or just what my psychology books would say—that instant connection is your past at work, the reminder of something, or the hope of something else? My mind kept bumping into him. God, I was acting like someone with a *crush*. I'd better *not* have a crush on him. First, he was Juliet's husband, and that was not something you conveniently forgot. Besides that, I hated the word *crush*, a pink candy word, a frosting word, something for giggly girls who wrote their name with his surrounded by a heart. I wasn't the kind of person who had crushes. I didn't believe in stupid insta-connections with people you didn't even know. It needed to matter, it needed to come to something, be *real*, or it wasn't worth all the wasted feelings. Everyone else, even Juliet, fell in love with Mr. Gregory Hawthorne (who let us call him Gregory), our middle school algebra teacher. But I'd only noticed how he paused by his reflection in the classroom window, and how his breath smelled of coffee when he stood too close.

And what was curiosity or gladness or intrigue, anyway? Just regular human being feelings. People could have all kinds of feelings, and that didn't necessarily mean anything. It didn't mean that anything would *happen*.

I hurried through lunch. There was someone I had to talk to. Goth Girl had reached out to me, and hers was a problem I could do something about. She had drawn a red Volkswagen, and there were only two red Volkswagens in our school lot. Henderson Law, super-jock, perpetual Homecoming King—I knew it couldn't be him. But the other Volkswagen belonged to Kevin Frink. Bomb Boy. Kevin Frink, with his heavy jacket and averted eyes and pocket full of matches. It made perfect sense, the kind of perfect sense that's actually the strangest and most bizarre perfect sense possible.

I knew Kevin usually hung out around the football field bleachers at lunch. The last time I saw him there he had a couple of firecrackers and a small package of matches from some seaside motel in Oregon. I walked through the stadium gate and down the bleachers, but didn't see him until I looked out onto the field

Deb Caletti

itself. He sat on the AstroTurf with his back against a goalpost. I wondered if I should ask him about Clive Weaver, but I could imagine Kevin's voice. *Just because my mother drives a hearse doesn't mean I know when everyone* dies. When I got down there, he looked up from a roughed-up copy of *The Anarchist Cookbook*.

"You said you weren't going to want something for not ratting on me and now you want something," he said.

"How'd you know?" I asked.

"People always end up wanting something," he said. He shoved his hair up out of his eyes with his palm. He had dark long hair that fell over a big forehead. Kevin Frink was a big guy. He had been known as the Kid with the Big Head since elementary school. This had changed to Bomb Boy when he lit his first cherry bomb in the gym during the PE basketball unit in the seventh grade.

"Can I sit down?"

"Whatever. I don't own the place." Kevin Frink breathed heavily when he spoke. It was the exertion of weighty things—his bulky body, his burdened life.

"Do you know Fiona Saint George?"

"Vampire. Who doesn't?"

This didn't seem to be a good start. "She's a great artist," I said.

"What does that have to do with anything?" Kevin Frink grabbed at a clump of AstroTurf as if it were grass and pretended to throw it a few inches away.

"I think she really likes you."

Kevin snorted.

"No really. Maybe a lot. Maybe enough to go to the prom with you."

"You're out of your mind."

"No. I know it's true."

"Is this some kind of joke?" I knew Kevin Frink was thinking about the time those kids put a dead deer in the hearse his mother drove for Simmons and Sons Funeral Home. Or maybe about that year that Steven Gardener and his friends spent every lunch trying to step on the back heels of his shoes. "Not me," he said.

"I wouldn't lie to you," I said.

"I can't dance."

I thought about this. "Maybe you don't have to dance. Just go."

"I hate shit like that. What's in it for me?"

"She really likes you," I said. He wouldn't look at me. Just down at the big leg of his big jeans.

"Fucking freak, she'll stick her fangs in me," he said, but I could tell he was wavering.

"Just ask her. I'll pay for dinner. The Lighthouse." It was one of those places on the water. Nice, but not so fancy that they still didn't have the captain's wheel from a ship hanging on the wall and menu items called Surf and Turf and Wally's Oyster Special.

"I'll give it my personal consideration," he said.

"Thanks, Kevin. You won't regret it." I touched his arm. He wore a puffy ski coat, even in the heat. His arm was in there somewhere. I stood. This was great. Great! My heart sang with Everything Working Beautifully hope. Something good could happen, not just for Fiona Saint George, but for Kevin Frink, too. "I'll see you tomorrow," I said.

"Go get another *A* or something," he said.

Buddy Wilkes's El Camino was there at the curb again when school got out. I passed by it. You could feel the heat and energy of Buddy's presence even as he sat in the driver's seat.

"Hey," he said. He was looking right at me.

"Me?" I said.

"Give this to your sister for me," he said. He had a folded-up piece of paper in his palm and he held it out.

I wanted to hit his hand, make the note go flying. I wanted to say something brave, something I'd never say, *Fuck you*, maybe, something bold and definite. But I was so surprised at his eyes looking right at me and his voice aiming right my way that I barely remembered to lie.

"She's not around," I said.

"Just give it to her," he said.

I took the note. It felt hot from his own palm, hot enough that its heat transferred to my own hand. I stood dumbly holding the note as Alicia Worthen walked out the school doors. I still held that note as Buddy Wilkes started his car back up and drove off, held it as Alicia just stood there at the curb calling, "Buddy, Buddy! Wait!" as the back of his El Camino left the school lot and drove out of sight.

Alicia Worthen started to cry. Right there, with her backpack on one shoulder, her clarinet case in her hand. I unfolded the note. His writing looked nothing like Hayden's. It had the childish, blocky innocence of a fourth grader's report on earthquakes or volcanoes or the pony express. But not his words, though. Innocent is not what you'd have called them. *Saturday. Five o'clock. You know where. I know you want to.*

After school, the cars were gone in front of Clive Weaver's house. No one was out in the neighborhood except Ally Pete-Robbins, who was a planting a tidy row of marigolds up her walkway, and her twin boys, Jeffrey and Jacob, playing kickball in the street. Jeffrey kicked the red ball and it rolled under the Martinellis' RV, the Pleasure Way. Jacob ran over and looked underneath, his butt up in the air and his shirt rising to show his smooth eight-year-old back.

"You dummy, Jeffrey!" Jacob shouted to the underside of the Pleasure Way.

"Jacob!" Ally Pete-Robbins called with a trowel in her hand. Her hair was up in a bandanna, and she had on those high-waisted shorts that are in the clothing Constitution for some women over thirty. "What did Mommy tell you about name-calling?"

"Don't name-call," said a serious Jeffrey from first base, which was a red jacket thrown on the ground. Jeffrey looked like his father.

"Dummy, dummy, dummy," Jacob said. He fished out the ball with one arm and stood up. "Don't dummy do that dummy again."

"Jacob!" Ally Pete-Robbins yelled again. She brushed the dirt off her hands like she meant business. "What would Jesus say?"

"He'd say he wished he could play kickball," Jacob said to Jeffrey. This cracked them both up. "Jesus loves kickball," he said again to maybe see if the joke was as great the second time.

It was. Jeffrey held his stomach. "I'm gonna pee."

Ally Pete-Robbins decided to ignore them. Not Reinforcing Bad Behavior was right up there in the top ten in the parenting rule book, just after Presenting a United Front and Being Consistent. Jeffrey and Jacob were basically monsters.

"Mrs. Pete-Robbins?" I asked. "Have you heard anything about Clive Weaver today? I saw these cars. . . ."

"Oh!" she said, and stood. She held a marigold released from its pot in her hand. The loose dirt fell between the fingers of her gardening gloves, the roots of the plant as exposed and white as her own arms in that plaid sleeveless shirt. SPF 45, I was sure. Jeffrey and Jacob were as white as she was too. A ray of sun likely never touched their skin except on the days Mr. Pete-Robbins was in charge. "Yes, he's fine. I did call his daughters last night. Unfortunately, Mr. Weaver was walking around disoriented."

Ha—she saw him naked too. I guess I wouldn't have to be the someone to call for help after all. Ally Pete-Robbins had beaten me to it.

"Is he okay?"

"They brought him to the doctor. He had tests all morning. Perfectly fine. A case of Restless Leg Syndrome, but otherwise in perfect health. My aunt had it too, and my uncle had to sleep on the couch or he'd be up all night! Of course, Mr. Weaver only has his dog."

"Corky," I said.

"Thank the Lord, the doctors said Mr. Weaver might just be depressed."

"Really?" Depression didn't seem like something to thank the Lord for.

"Retirement," Ally Pete-Robbins said, as if this explained things.

"Ah," I said.

"A loss of purpose. Nothing to get up in the morning for. Nothing to look forward to."

"Okay, thanks."

Ally Pete-Robbins smiled at me. It was a smile that said how glad she was that we both cared like we did. How glad she was that we were together on this. The smile worried me. I really couldn't stand Ally Pete-Robbins.

"Slow and straight or fast and bouncy?" Jacob asked.

"Slow," Jeffrey said, as Jacob pitched a ball as wild as a kayak on the waters of the Strait of Juan de Fuca during a storm.

I heard barking in the backyard. Hayden was there, in his shorts and no shirt, chasing Zeus around Mom's flowerpots on the patio. Hayden lunged, and Zeus skirted him sideways. Then he clapped his hands and called Zeus's name firmly. Our old big metal tub sat in the center of the lawn, filled with sudsy water.

"You get fired already?" I called.

"Short day. Juliet's upstairs sleeping." He was out of breath. His back was shiny with sweat. "Damn dog. I hate that dog."

This made me smile. He loved Zeus in the most permanent way. "Bath?"

"He smells like a wet rug. I'm worried your mom might want him kicked out or dry-cleaned."

"Want me to try?"

"Might as well," Hayden said. He rested with his hands on his knees, catching his breath.

I clapped my hands. "Zeus! Come here!" I tried to sound as excited as possible. Zeus just sat there on the far corner of the lawn, his tongue hanging out. He wasn't having any of it. He looked like he was having the best day of his life.

Hayden lunged again and Zeus took off and made two furious laps around the yard, his ears tight against his head from his racehorse speed. He hoped to break the sound barrier, to be the fastest dog on earth. I headed him off over by the hibachi, where he was cornered. He was no match for the two of us. Hayden leaned down and picked him up, all of his big dog self gathered up in Hayden's arms, Hayden's muscles straining at the effort, Zeus's skinny legs hanging down.

"Teamwork," Hayden puffed, as he set Zeus into the tub. After all that running around, Zeus didn't protest or try to jump out. He was flexible about this sudden change of plan. He actually just sat there with his best manners as Hayden poured water over his head with a measuring cup.

"You forgot how much you loved this. You love this, remember?" Zeus sat quietly. His hair was all wet and flat. Hayden poured more water slowly over his back.

"So what was all that running around about, huh? You made me carry you. It was humiliating for both of us."

Silence.

"He loves it," I said.

"Big fool," Hayden said. "Can you give me a hand? If you don't mind getting wet?"

"Sure."

"That soap—" Hayden gestured with his chin to a plastic bottle near his bare feet. I grabbed it. "Just squirt it right on him."

I did. I kneeled beside Hayden. I put my hands in the warm water, soaped them along Zeus's back. His solid self felt so good. I rubbed my fingers in the hair on his butterscotch-and-vanilla chest, where my fingers bumped into Hayden's under the water. My arm against his. I felt a shutter click of stop-action—an awareness of his slippery fingers, his wet arm. There was silence except the sound of the water against skin and the soft sound of the construction guys' radio across the back fence. Okay, God. I stopped thinking about Zeus and backyards and pregnant sisters. I stopped thinking about anything and everything but the sudden and overpowering sense of skin on my skin. Wet, soapy skin on wet, soapy skin.

I breathed. I tried to breathe.

"It's amazing what another pair of hands can do," Hayden said.

I would have spoken, had my heart not been in my throat.

Chapter Eleven

uliet had woken from her nap. I heard the shower on in the hall. I passed by her room. Their room. The covers were tossed back. I could see a sheet of paper on the floor, where it had obviously been slipped under the door and left where it was found. I would not read it. It was not my business. I went to my own room, shut the door with my back against it.

I argued with myself a full ten minutes before I did what the truthful part of me knew I was going to do all along. I don't even know why I bothered with this moral charade, except maybe to show myself that I did have a little decency before I went ahead and did the bad thing I was planning to do anyway. My mind somehow awarded me conscience points for the meaningless inner protest. I had restrained myself for a few minutes, so I couldn't be all bad, right? When all that messy business of ethics and principles was sorted out, I went back to Juliet's room. The shower was still on, but I still had to act fast.

I left the paper right where it was. I leaned down to read it without touching it.

Dear Juliet—

You only met my mother once, and I know how you felt about her, but I hope this will change over time. She is someone I love and respect, and her experiences have given her a wisdom I trust. She taught me a lot about life, stumbling through it, running to it, climbing around and over its crevices and peaks. She saw some bad times with my father, Trent. Bad. Yet even stuck in that place, she believed that a limited life was your own doing. She believed your life was in your own hands.

She always kept a list on our refrigerator. I remember it there from the time I was very young. It went through two moves, countless years, and it became faded and splotched and worn as some recipe handed down from generations. Finally, I took it down. I've kept it in my wallet since. It's a worthwhile thing to keep near.

She called it The Five Rules of Maybe. *Maybe* was her favorite catchphrase for hope or anything close to it— dreams and possibilities and wants and wishes. . . . This is the list:

The Five Rules of Maybe

1. Respect the power of hope and possibilities. Begin with belief. Hold on to it.

2. If you know where you want to go, you're already halfway there. Know what you desire but, more importantly, why you desire it. Then go.

3. Hopes and dreams and heart's desires require a clear path—get out of your own way.

4. Place hope carefully in your own hands and in the hands of others.

5. Persist, if necessary.

It's deceptively simple, I've come to realize. But I saw how this list got my mother out of bad places and into good ones, to the work she loves, a life she treasures. I accept that a limited life is my own choice, and I'm holding tight to my belief in us. My hopes for you and me and our child are numerous and galloping—I am going to be the best man I can for you, Juliet, that's what I desire, and I desire that because you deserve that. That's who I want to be. Let's dream and believe and make all the best for ourselves.

The possibilities are there in your eyes, Juliet, swimming in those pools of blue. Let's get out of our own way. What did you say to me? Waiting is for cowards. Let's go get the life that's ours.

You could almost hold a wide sea in your hand, an endless, beautiful valley, a whole city where anything could happen. The biggest sky, stretched on forever. Was it true, really, that you could get what you want? That you could desire it and seek it and make it your own? I thought about those hands under that water, the slippery skin, some shiver of need, and right then it seemed like a want was doomed to be either a small flame too impossible to fan or else a secret fire blazing out of control. Never just a daily thing, yours, both wild and confined, burning bright in your very own fireplace. Juliet could have whatever she wanted though. It was right there for her. A life was there, a pair of outstretched arms, *two* pairs, something wonderful, and she was going to ruin it.

> Welcome to the second trimester! Your baby is
> now about the size of a clenched fist. . . .

Right then, I told myself I wanted only one thing. I convinced myself, or thought I did. I wanted only what was best for Juliet and Jitter and Hayden. Coming to the rescue of other people was something I knew, and something I was good at, and so was wanting the best for other people. I *could* have those things. I took the note from Buddy out of my pocket. I ripped it up and ripped it up until it was only a hundred tiny flakes of paper. I put them into my garbage can, thought better of it, and wrapped them in an old lunch bag full of sandwich crusts and orange peels and then threw that away again. I shoved some old Biology handouts on top. I buried those words so far down that they would never hurt anyone.

That night, I claimed to have too much homework to even have time for dinner. I ate in my room instead of acting like the stupid younger sister with a crush. I did not look for long minutes at the photo of Hayden with his eyes closed that I had taken out at Point Perpetua, now taped up on my wall with all the others. The one where his whole face seemed to be taking in the sea and the rocks and the sky, taking in the pure pleasure of the day. I made it equal in my mind with the photo of Mr. Martinelli's crew cut. Sometimes willpower is really more like won't-power.

I let Zeus come and stay in my room. He'd eaten two rolls of LifeSavers out of Juliet's purse, and his breath still smelled a little minty fresh. I did my Math and Biology and English homework, and after that, I started a new assignment. I planned the steps, imagined the end result. It made me pleased to think about. I decided to call it the Make Hope and Possibilities Happen for Clive Weaver project.

I went downstairs, to the back porch, looked around in the recycling bin for old mail. The screen door opened. Hayden stood there with an empty beer bottle in his hand.

"I was just going to toss this in," he said. Zeus peeked around his legs. He still looked fluffy from his bath.

"Don't mind me," I said.

"You okay?"

"Yep."

"Did you lose something?"

I stopped and looked up at him. His face was stubbly with the day's beard. The porch light gave him a soft glow. "I'm just doing something for a friend. A depressed friend."

"Oh," he said. I thought this would send him on his way, but instead of going back in, he opened the screen door and came outside. He sat just outside the door in the old wicker chair that Mom had had forever, the one that needed repainting, the collector of jackets and tossed-off things, where we'd sit to take off our muddy shoes before coming in.

"That's too bad, about your friend."

"I don't know. Somewhere along the line, life seems to give you something to be depressed about. Seems like it's just a predictable season in the human condition." He didn't answer. I was still looking through the old mail, but I glanced up at him. He was spinning that bottle on its end in his palm, thinking.

"I suppose you don't stand much of a chance if you think that happiness is the absence of unhappiness," he said. "Good luck ever being happy, then."

"Yeah, the odds just aren't in favor it, of things being perfect your whole life long. I don't know. I think it's a basically acceptable fact. Like Halloween candy. You're always going to at least get some disgusting Good & Plenty."

"Oh God," he groaned at the thought. "Or those Root Beer Barrels. That single Root Beer Barrel in cellophane. I can't believe they still make those."

"They don't. People have had them in their cupboards for thirty years."

"That explains it," he said.

I stopped hunting through the bin and watched him. He tilted the bottle back to get some last drop, and I looked at his long neck, arched. "Maybe we'd all be happier if we expected to be sometimes miserable," I said. I guess I was trying to tell him something about Juliet.

"But not always miserable. Not when miserable becomes a way of life." He tossed the bottle into the bin for glass, and it clanged against the bottom. I didn't want him to go in that direction. Not at all. His words opened a door of possibilities I hadn't considered—his not sticking around. Not putting up with her crap. Juliet going too far with that barbed wire that was Buddy Wilkes. But Hayden *had* to. He had to stick it out.

He couldn't run and disappear forever. Jitter needed him.

I didn't know what to say. I went back to the conversation we were having before, tried to steer him there too. I hoped he'd stay on that path, not go off onto other, dangerous ones. "My friend's depression—it isn't about unrealistic expectations, anyway. He's seen a lot of life already. He knows it isn't always perfect." Clive Weaver's wife, Mary, had died a dozen years ago. A wife he had loved and who had loved him back; at least, he still had her high school graduation picture on the fireplace, her with horn-rimmed glasses and swooped-up hair and a string of pearls. He'd told me once, too, the story of how he had helped invade the peninsula during the Korean War. He left out the most important details. A former soldier was under no misconceptions about what life held.

"Well, it's a fine thing that you're helping him," Hayden said.

"I don't know. Maybe it just makes me feel better."

We both stood there on the porch. Zeus was peeking at us from the other side of the screen. It was all quiet there between us.

"Remember, Scarlet. A good lot of the time, nice people are doomed."

I smiled, and so did he, and then he went inside, letting the screen door slam shut behind him. I looked at the moon for a while. It seemed both so far away and close enough to touch. Finally, I went inside too.

I laid out the mail I had found. Credit card applications, a magazine subscription solicitation, ads for mainland appliance stores, and a seed catalog. I stuck some white labels over Mom's name, wrote in Clive Weaver's instead. I filled out a postcard of the Eiffel Tower that I'd snitched from Mom's craft box from her scrapbook club. *Dear Mr. Weaver,* I wrote. *Paris is enchanting. Wish you were here.* On a whim, I took a pizza advertisement, cut the paper to make a square, folded it corner to corner and back the other direction into a triangle. A thousand paper cranes makes a wish come true, right? Wasn't that what they said? Maybe a few less than that could make your wish come pretty close. I made a good day's worth of progress toward the goal, stashed away the whole project in an old shoe box.

I woke that night from a dream. It was a smell that woke me, not a sound. A smell drifting in my window. The smell of a cigarette. I sat up, got out of bed, and crept to the window. I could hear the night screech of the island hawks, who circled endlessly above us looking for rabbits to swoop down upon. I expected to see Hayden's muscled back, his skin white in the moonlight, his jeans around his hips, the orange tip of cigarette. If it had been him I might have gone out there again, because I was still sleepy and sleep could soften things, could make you forget your promises. But what I saw instead was a pair of triangular red lights. The red lights of the back of Buddy Wilkes's El Camino, heading down our street.

Chapter Twelve

I trusted you," Kevin Frink said.

"What's the matter?" He stood by my locker. His big face was red. His arms were folded across the front of his puffy coat.

"I thought you were my friend."

"God, I am. What? Tell me! I'm so sorry." I didn't know what I was apologizing for. It was a cover-your-bases apology. A please-don't-bomb-my-locker apology.

"She said no."

He looked crushed. He hit the side of his head with his palm as if his ear had water in it. Or maybe as if he were trying to displace the memory of prom rejection.

"You're kidding," I said.

"You set me up."

"No," I said. I put my hand on his arm, but he yanked away. "I swear, I know she wanted you to ask her."

Two red Volkswagens. Henderson Law? *Goth Girl?* Was she out of her mind? In terms of hope and possibilities, this seemed ridiculously out of reach. She had to know that.

"She's a vampire," Kevin said. And he was Bomb Boy. They would have made a great couple.

"I know," I said. "You're right. I am so sorry. I don't know what happened." Henderson Law happened. How could this be? This was terrible. I felt awful.

"I didn't want to go to that stupid fucking dance, anyway."

"It's all my fault," I said.

"You can say that again."

I would have—I would have said it again and again if it would make him feel any better. But Kevin Frink had already turned and slumped away, his huge head morose over his huge body.

"I've got a plan," Reilly Ogden said next to me as I walked into the cafeteria. Nicole had gotten to our table early, and I gestured to her, indicating the salad bar. I'd skipped making my lunch that morning, purposefully avoiding the kitchen. I'd heard Hayden down there, sipping coffee and reading the paper and telling Zeus that he didn't know what the world was coming to.

"Reilly," I warned. He wore tight black jeans and a T-shirt that said *Hang Ten!* over a surfer cresting a wave. His eyes looked as big and wide and gawking as Mrs. Martinelli's behind her glasses.

"Just listen. All I'm asking is that you commit to me until the end of the summer. Three months. And if you're not satisfied, it's over."

I couldn't help myself. I laughed.

"You don't lose a thing that way. It's like a money-back guarantee."

"Reilly, no. I've told you a thousand times. You're a great guy, but no."

Evan O'Donnell and Jake Tafferty came along then, cut right between me and Reilly in the lunch line. Their girlfriends, Melissa DeWhit and Casey Chow, joined them, sending Reilly farther and farther back. I felt a little bad for him, but not bad enough, and it was other people's cruelty anyway, not mine. I put my money into the lunch lady's bread dough hand and moved ahead with my tray.

I reached for a pair of salad tongs just as Shy reached for the other. I looked up at him and he blushed red-fierce. And then he grabbed the tomato spoon just after me, and then the garbanzo one, and every other spoon just after I did. I looked at him again and he grinned a little, shrugged. He was playing with me, I realized. I smiled. Our eyes had a conversation.

"See ya," he said.

When I got to the table, Nicole hit my arm with the back of her hand. "Did Shy just talk to you? I swear I saw his lips move."

"He said, 'See ya.'" Jasmine scooted over to make room for me.

"Are you kidding me? He talked to you? On his own? I'm so jealous."

"We really got to know each other," I said.

"I told you he was an intellectual," Kiley said. She'd gotten over the breakup with Ben and was doing her Biology homework due after lunch.

"God, he's cute," Nicole said. She watched Jesse leave; we both did. I didn't want to call him that name anymore, Shy—he had his own name. He had a Coke under his arm, his salad in his hand. He had a book, too. Some kind of Roman history, I thought, by the look of the cover. I didn't know where he went to eat. Maybe the track. Maybe the lawn that looked over the north waters of the strait.

"What he said about politics and the economy was mind-blowing," I said.

"Classical fucking music, too," Jasmine said. Her life was that cello.

"He's probably a science genius," Kiley said. She was the science genius herself. She could do that homework with her eyes closed. She was pretty and smart but still managed to be mostly unnoticed by anyone but us and Ben, who was cute and smart and basically unnoticed, too.

"Definitely well rounded," Nicole said. No one mentioned the Roman history book. The actual details of him didn't matter. "Did I tell you I saw him running all the way out by the ferry terminal with the cross country team? Mom and I were picking up my aunt Suzie. Dad's sister? Mom figures it'll piss off Dad to have her stay with us instead of him. Anyway, I got this picture when we were driving past." She took out her phone, pressed the buttons with her thumb. She passed various ghostly images her camera had accidentally taken of the inside of her purse until she came to an image that she handed over for me to see. A blur of white and a blur of blue. "That's his tank top. The car was moving."

"Nice. It really captures his true personality," I said.

Nicole put the phone back in her purse. "I can't believe he talked to you." She seemed almost mad. It made me a little mad back. Shame on him for not following the script of her imagination.

"We're getting married next month," I said.

"Ooh, bitch fight," Jasmine said in her little tiny voice.

Mrs. Martinelli's flowered stretch pants were pulled tight over her big rear end as she bent over her sprinkler, adjusting it on a new place on the lawn. She looked up when she saw me slam Derek's door shut.

"Scarlet! Wait right there."

Oh no. I stood at the edge of her grass, surveyed things. There were no new messages from Goth Girl, and there was no sign of Clive Weaver. The twins sat on the sidewalk with their tennis-shoed feet in the gutter, eating Popsicles and watching Mrs. Martinelli's sprinkler water disappear into the drain. Their mouths were purple.

"Let's stick stuff down there," Jeffrey said, looking down into the darkness of the grate.

"Let's stick dog poop down there," Jacob said, and they both cracked up.

Mrs. Martinelli reappeared. She had her reading glasses hanging on her neck, and she held another sheet of paper out to me.

I read:

> I hope this mail meets you in a perfect condition.
> If you do not remember me, you might have
> received an e-mail from me in the past regarding a
> multi-million-dollar Business Proposal which we
> never concluded. I am using this opportunity to
> inform you that we are awaiting your future reply,
> as the fate of my cocoa plantation depends on it. My
> sources say that your efforts, Sincerity, Courage,
> and Trustworthiness are widely known. . . .

"Morin Jude!" Mrs. Martinelli exclaimed. "She is persisting, Scarlet. Mr. Martinelli and I appreciate persistence." She popped her glasses on her nose and admired the note.

"Mrs. Martinelli." I sighed.

"Oh, I know what you're going to say. But you can't tell me Morin Jude sent this letter to just anyone. She chose us."

"Thousands of people," I said. "Mass, mass mailing. Morin Jude lives in Cleveland, or something, I promise you. Morin Jude's real name is Buck Johnson. He shoplifts beef jerky at mini-marts in his spare time."

"Mr. Martinelli won that citizenship award at Rotary," she said. I shook my head—I didn't understand. "Sincerity, courage, trustworthiness? We protested the Vietnam War, you know." She took her glasses off and stared at me hard. Her eyes were the light violet color of the lavender bush in her yard. The skin of her neck drooped in folds.

"I know how tempting it is," I said. I didn't know at all, actually. "You're going to have to trust me. You give any money to these people, and it's *sayonara*."

"We wouldn't give *money*."

"Okay."

"We're not idiots."

"Good."

She clutched my wrist. Her arm had a thin gold watch on it. She was surprisingly strong. "We've been around the block," she said. I think the block may have been the only thing they'd been around.

Jeffrey's Popsicle slid from his stick then. He wailed his protest. He held up the empty purple stick for Jacob to see.

"Feed it to the sewer," Jacob said, and they both cackled.

I heard the vacuum on, but there were no back and forth sounds of actual vacuuming—only the steady roar of the machine standing still. That's why she didn't hear me come in, either. She didn't hear me come up the stairs or pass by Juliet's room. There were vacuum tracks in the hall, but they stopped where Mom stood, right over the threshold of Juliet's doorway. Her face was soft and serious. Her mouth was open slightly as if she'd been taken by surprise. She held the note, *The Five Rules of Maybe*, in one hand. She looked down at it and down at it, as that vacuum roared beside her. She looked down as if it were telling her things she'd needed to know for a very long time.

I understood her in a way I never had before as I watched her. I felt so close to her. I saw a narrow fiber of our connection, me and her, us—not her and Juliet. Was that even a real or likely thing? It seemed so. Maybe it was deep in our bones, submerged far in the rivers of our bloodstreams, but the two of us seemed joined then by something Juliet would never feel—the hunger for things too far away to touch, the need to believe in private and impossible longings.

Chapter Thirteen

There was no sign of Juliet or Hayden as it grew closer to dinnertime. Mom was in the kitchen, ripping lettuce into a bowl.

"I wish he'd stop staring," Mom said. Zeus sat very straight next to her. So straight he was sure she'd notice his fine behavior and drop him a nibble of something. His triangle ears looked like they were trying very hard to be as upright as possible too. "It's like he knows things about you."

"Zeus!" I clapped my hands, but he just kept sitting like a little soldier and staring at Mom. He could really focus for someone who also had these wild ADD moments.

"Never mind," Mom said. "I suppose I'm getting used to him. He's not the worst company in the world. By the way, Dean's coming for dinner."

I noticed how close the words *worst company in the world* and *Dean* came to each other. The psychology books would have something to say about that. Zeus tried a different tactic. He lay down, set his chin on his paws. It was the cutest thing in the world, and I'm sure he knew it. We looked at each other, and he blinked one eye. Sometimes, I swear he winked on purpose. "It's like he's a person but not a person," I said.

"Dean?" Mom said. She kept ripping lettuce.

"*Zeus.*" I laughed. Maybe in her most secret, honest places she hated Dean as much as we did. You couldn't help but see what he was really like, could you? I'd always thought telling the truth to other people was hard, but maybe that was a snap compared to telling the truth to yourself. Sometimes we just refused to know what we knew.

"Where's Juliet?" I asked.

"Doctor's appointment."

"For sure?" I asked.

She stopped with the lettuce. Wiped her hands on a towel. "For sure."

"Did Hayden go with her?" Juliet couldn't see Buddy Wilkes if Hayden were there.

"Yes, Hayden was with her. Is there some reason you're so concerned?" Mom opened the fridge, took out a cellophane bag of mushrooms. Then she looked at me, narrowed her eyes into a question. There were little wrinkles at their corners that I'd never seen before. Those wrinkles, and the few brand-new gray hairs at her temples—they made me want to be a better daughter from here on out.

"I'm worried about—" I stopped before I said it. *Buddy Wilkes.* I had no real proof, not yet. I played the scene in my mind. Mom would defend Juliet; I knew that. That's how it had been forever. Perhaps when things were too close, you just couldn't see them.

Same as when you held a piece of paper right up to your nose.

"The *baby?* You can say the word, Scarlet. It's okay. We might as well get used to it. They're seeing Dr. Crosby. Marla. Juliet didn't want to go to old Doc Young, and I don't blame her, even if he's delivered every baby on this island for the last forty years." Old Doc Young had hair coming out of his ears in surprised tufts and a little ancient car as old as he was with fluff coming out of the seats. Some people look like their dogs; old Doc Young looked like his car.

"Juliet shouldn't be eating so much sugar," I said. "I saw her scarf half a box of chocolate doughnuts. It's not good. It puts her at risk for gestational diabetes."

"You're worried about *Juliet.* Oh I know, honey, me too. The idea of her going through *labor* . . . Our Juliet? Come here." She opened her arms to me. She hugged me with the mushrooms over my shoulder, and I hugged her back and took the sympathy she was offering even if it was misdirected. "Juliet's going to be fine. She and Hayden probably stopped at the park or something. It's good for them to spend some time together."

The hug and those wrinkles made me feel especially open toward her and I chanced the truth again. "She doesn't seem to love him enough," I said into Mom's shoulder. *He could leave,* I wanted to say; that's what I most needed to tell her, what we most needed to talk to each other about, but right then Zeus started to bark madly. He took off, his toenails skittering and sliding across the floor. He knew the sound of Hayden's truck—he could hear it blocks away. He stood by the front door, barking and wagging and waiting, his rump turning circles of joy.

"They're here now," Mom said. She didn't hear me. She let me go and went to the door.

Juliet was already inside, and she tossed her purse on the couch. "God, that was too real."

Hayden came up behind her. He was grinning widely. He scruffed Zeus under the chin, then grabbed a handful of Juliet's peasant blouse and pulled her backward to him. I felt a sharp pinch of want, which I quickly shoved into the recycle bin of my mind. "We heard a heartbeat."

Mom held her hands to her mouth. "Oh my God." Her eyes were shiny as if she might cry.

"Remember when I was in that play, *The Bat?* Middle school?" Juliet said. Mom nodded. Mom had moved her hands from her mouth to her own heart. "They had this big piece of metal they used as a thunder machine. It sounded like that."

"*Shoo, shoo, shoo*," Hayden demonstrated. His eyes were bright.

"Beautiful," Mom whispered. "Really. This is a beautiful thing."

Juliet pushed away from Hayden a little. "Kind of creepy, if you think about it. A heart inside my own body."

"Jeez, Juliet," I said. I hoped and hoped again that Jitter with his real beating heart couldn't hear anything in there. He needed to know he was one hundred percent loved and wanted.

"Beautiful creepy," Hayden said. "Fantastic creepy. Maybe not even creepy at all creepy."

"I'm hot," Juliet said. She lifted her hair up from her neck. "I'm going to change."

Juliet walked upstairs as we all stood below. It was perfect, really. Juliet above us, Juliet away, us gawking and wanting more. It seemed wrong that she was taking Jitter with her. He should have been there with us instead, with me and Hayden and Mom.

Hayden looked at us. His eyes pleaded.

"Pregnant women are very emotional," Mom said.

"It's the couples who are ordering wedding invitations and who argue over everything that get me," Mom said. Her cheeks were rosy with wine, and her voice was lively at dinner. We sat around the table, Zeus right by my chair, looking up at me. I really liked his furry chin. It was so small and serious.

"This one groom got outraged over an embossed rose. Outraged!" Mom went on. "A really ugly peach rose. He stormed out. 'Just because your parents are paying for everything, I don't get to exist.'"

"And they lived happily ever after," Juliet said.

"He was not angry about the rose," Dean Neuhaus said. He was under the impression that we would not be able to figure this out ourselves, not without his help. It was lucky we could function in the world without him.

"The in-laws'll be at that guy's house every night for Sunday dinner," Hayden said.

"I know!" Mom said. "Right?" She looped pasta on her fork but the whole enterprise slipped off and she had to try again. Her bra strap was showing and she hadn't noticed. She was enjoying herself.

"He better run for his life," I said, though only part of me was paying attention. I kept thinking about tomorrow. Saturday. Saturday and Juliet and Buddy Wilkes's note. I'd gotten rid of it, but that didn't necessarily mean anything. He wouldn't have heard back from her, and maybe he would try again, then. There had to be something I could do.

"In two years, your business will be closing its doors," Dean Neuhaus said. "Even wedding invitations will be electronic."

"I don't believe it," Mom said. "You can't tell me that. There's something special about real paper, real ink. A message written by hand? It has an importance, *permanence*."

Dean scoffed. "Shredder? Recycling . . ." He was counting his points on his fingers.

"What if a message is not destroyed but is saved forever in a small cedar box?" Hayden said. He really was a romantic. Who was a romantic anymore? Even his hands were romantic hands. Long, strong fingers. The kind that might carve something out of wood for his beloved, that cedar box, something everlasting.

"A letter is a gift," Mom said. "It's tactile. Intimate."

"An e-mail's about as passionate as a Post-it note," Hayden said.

"A handwritten letter—one heart to one heart," Mom said. They were both nodding. Juliet looked amused.

"Or to two hundred fifty, depending on who's on the guest list," Dean Neuhaus broke a breadstick in half. God, it must have gotten tiring being him.

"A letter means something could happen," I said.

Hayden looked at me. "*Yes*. Yes."

Mom nodded. "A letter is about possibilities." But then she blushed. *Possibilities*. The blush already in her cheeks now spread down her neck and into the collar of her shirt. A guilt blush from reading the contents of that note. Maybe we both should have been blushing.

"Two years, stationery stores . . . gone." Dean Neuhaus made a slash in the air with his manicured hand.

"Nonsense," Mom said. Dean Neuhaus raised his eyebrows. He was that kind of man—you were stepping out of place if you disagreed with him. "A letter is an art form," Mom said. "Art forms tend to last. People build *museums* for art forms."

"Your scrapbooks are an art form," Juliet said. "God, I used to love watching you cut and glue and arrange. Show Hayden."

"You did? You liked that? They're silly maybe," she said.

"Show him," Juliet said. It was funny how sentimental she was about our past life suddenly. She had never seemed to care before. Before, all she wanted to do was to leave us. Now she seemed capable of getting gushy about our old microwave.

"If you want," Mom said, but she sounded pleased. She shoved her chair back and went upstairs. I could hear the weight of her footsteps above us, the creak in the floor where her room was.

"I almost forgot. I have a present for you guys," I said to Juliet. It was best to avoid Hayden's eyes. They were dangerous flood-waters you might be swept into. "A belated wedding gift. Dinner, tomorrow night? Saturday night date? The Lighthouse. Romantic evening, whatever."

"That's really nice, Scarlet," Hayden said. "You don't have to do that."

"I want to," I said to Juliet. "Tomorrow? I'll babysit, ha."

"It's got to be tomorrow?" Juliet said.

"We'll take it, if you don't want it," Dean Neuhaus said. He chuckled to himself like he had just made a great big fat joke. *We'll*, meaning Mom and him. Sometimes the word *we* could feel poisonous.

"I didn't say I didn't want it," Juliet said. She couldn't stand him either.

"You have a secret trust fund, girl? That's a big gift," Hayden said.

"A secret second job."

"Pet Palace?"

"Did my belt buckle give me away?"

He laughed. I'd forgotten about not looking at him. And, God, I did like looking at him. "Nice to involve us in private jokes, people," Juliet said.

"I'm not sure elopement requires a gift," Dean Neuhaus said.

"Well, then, that decides it for sure. If elopement doesn't require a gift. Tomorrow," Hayden said.

"Good," I said. Good. Settled. I set my napkin down on the table, a napkin period at the end of a dinnertime sentence.

"This is one of the first ones I did," Mom said, as she walked back in. She looked around at us and paused; she caught the moment of something in the air, decided to dismiss it just as quickly. She hated conflict as much as I did, maybe more. She placed the book in front of Hayden, leaned over him as he opened the pages.

"Prague," she said. "Well. You can see."

"Wow," he said.

"Nineteen twenties Paris. Etcetera, etcetera . . ." She started flipping pages.

"Wait," he said. "Slow down."

It could have been embarrassing, this show. I remembered the time she'd spent on these, her head bent down over pages, the glue stick in her hand. Concentration that seemed to mean a mission I couldn't really understand and maybe wasn't meant to. It wasn't a mission that had anything to do with me. I hadn't really looked at them in a long time; maybe I hadn't really looked at them ever. It was just Mom doing an inexplicable Mom thing—listening to "Be" for the millionth time, exercising on a beach towel in front of the TV, buying a new scarf or hat, something we knew she'd never wear (and, of course, didn't ever wear), and then later shoving it into the closet with the rejected cowboy boots and animal print leggings and lime suede skirt.

But looking at the scrapbooks again, I saw something else, something I'd never appreciated before. The pages were collages of postcards and cut-out letters and bits of things—small shells and sand glued down in swirls. A key, a stamp, a picture of a clock face or train schedule. They seemed old, made of memories, places and experiences of a long life lived. The life of an interesting person with stories and secrets. But not the person who stood above Hayden, chopsticks holding up her hair, two deep lines now on her forehead that I hadn't noticed before, wearing an old tank top I remembered since elementary school. That person wanted things she had never gotten. I could see that now.

"I always thought they were beautiful," Juliet said.

"Really?" Mom said.

"Paris," Hayden read. He turned the page. "Morocco."

"I never knew you went to Morocco," Dean Neuhaus pouted. The idea seemed to bother him.

"Oh, I never did. Only time I've been out of the country was Canada," she said.

"You never went to any of these places?" Dean Neuhaus couldn't imagine the point. He squinted in the direction of the book, but you knew he couldn't even see it from where he sat.

"It's about *art*," Hayden said. "It requires *imagination*."

"Not that I wouldn't love to go," she said. "I would have loved to go."

"Of course you would," Hayden said. "Of course. You were raising kids. You couldn't, is all."

I was watching Mom's face, so I saw what happened when she heard those words. *Of course. Of course*, given to you when you maybe weren't used to *of course*. I don't know if I ever realized before how important those words were—those words that meant you were completely understandable. Words that meant you were reasonable and sound and valid. It was funny how often we didn't feel any of those things on our own. Not that we were a trembling mess and incapable—just that a lot of the time we weren't so sure all by ourselves.

Mom looked almost stricken. The idea of actual understanding came as a shock to her. My throat closed then; I thought I could cry. Her own self, her person, the woman she was and wasn't and wanted to be, the person who had and never had—she stood in front of us, her own story right there on her face. I hadn't done a very good job of trying to understand her myself, and Juliet wasn't, even now—she was just shooting her narrow eyes at Dean Neuhaus to let him know what a creep we thought he was.

I swallowed. The moment passed. Still, I felt this arrow of sorrow. Most of our parents wanted the best for us, I knew, but we also wanted the best for them. Mom showed Hayden the rest of the albums. She put on some music, and after dinner, Dean Neuhaus had his hands on Mom's waist when we did the dishes. She left those hands there and didn't stop him either when he patted her butt as she passed by to use the bathroom.

When he said good night at our door though, I noticed, she only offered him her cheek. And when that happened, I silently cheered for her.

Chapter Fourteen

You're a toilet," Jacob said.

"*You're* a toilet," Jeffrey said.

"You're a toilet *face*," Jacob said, and they both laughed so hard they held their stomachs. They sat on the sidewalk behind their mother's Acura, hiding. Jeffrey seemed to be holding something in his hands. Fishing line, I realized. And it was tied to an old purse lying in the middle of the street. God, I hoped it wasn't Clive Weaver who jetted out there to grab it only to have it yanked away. He was already fragile as it was; he didn't need one more thing snatched from him.

"I don't understand why you require me for this outing," Juliet said as we got into Mom's car on Saturday morning. "Mom can take you."

"God, Juliet. You're kidding, right? I'm going to trust Mom with fashion advice? You. You're the one I need. Juliet, this is *huge*."

"Fine," Juliet said. But it wasn't fine. Juliet looked stressed. She kept running her fingers through her hair and her mouth was in a tight line. "Who did you say you were going with? And where did you get money for a dress? Mom only paid half of mine, and this isn't even your prom."

I had to think fast. What name did I give? Justin? Johnathan? "Jared. Finnley. You don't know him, I told you. He's new this year. And I'm using my own money."

"I can't believe you're going with a senior."

"God, you make it sound like you're surprised anyone might actually like me." Okay, I might be surprised anyone except Reilly Ogden might like me, but it wasn't okay for her to feel that way.

"I didn't mean it like that. Just, you're getting so old. Growing up. Look at those brats," she said.

"Let's run it over," I said. But Juliet didn't seem to hear me. She drove right past the purse. She was already looking at the clock in Mom's car, and we hadn't even gotten out of the neighborhood yet. Saturday was now officially and completely booked. Screw you, Buddy Wilkes.

"This is going to take all day," Juliet said. She rubbed her temples.

It was impossible to understand why it was so hard to get people to do what was best for them.

"I don't see why you won't let me come in there with you," Juliet said.

"No way. Uh-uh. I'm the only one who gets to see me naked."

"Not even Jared?" She poked me in the arm. I had no idea what she was talking about until I remembered. Jared! Right!

"Ha," I said. I had an armful of dresses. This would take a while. I made her take me onto the ferry and into Kingston where there was a mall. Now we were in this store called Vibe! and it was the kind of place I hated. High school girls with clothes so tiny they rivaled Clive Weaver's latest favorite outfit for fabric square footage and salespeople who asked if you needed help as if your presence there was seriously imposing on their personal time. The music in there was so loud and pulsing, you could feel it like a pop-song earthquake. Shiny, overconfident clothes you could never imagine yourself wearing hung along the walls. I felt some sort of clothes-store consumer shame creeping up my insides. It was all the insincerity of high school with the added humiliation of mirrors.

"Scarlet, please. I've seen your body before. Since I was three, for God's sake. I'm your *sister*."

Precisely. "Uh-uh."

"I'm tired. I'm *pregnant*, remember? I need to sit. I'll shut my eyes."

"Fine."

We closed ourselves in the little dressing room with the slatted wood door. Juliet sat down on the triangular corner seat. I hung the fat bunch of dresses on the hook, slipped off my shoes. I could see the sock clad feet of the person next to me under one side of the wall.

"So tell me about this Jared," Juliet said. She leaned against the tight corner of the dressing room, eyes shut. She looked sort of sweet then. I remembered how much I loved her. She didn't look capable of ripping Hayden's heart to shreds.

"Jared," I said. I stepped into the first dress, wiggled the zipper up behind me. The bust of the dress gaped out and I pushed my palms against the material to flatten it out. "Jared is . . . No boobs," I said.

She popped open her eyes. "Yeah, no. That won't work. What do they think? If you had a chest that big you'd fall over every time you stood up."

I plumped out the material to its fullest full to make her laugh. "Triple Venti Double-Tall implants," I said.

"Move on," she said. Eyes shut again. "Jared."

"Really nice, you know. Wants to be a . . ." I wriggled free from that dress, put on the next one. It was black, with white decorative piping. I was a human Hostess Cupcake. "A chef."

"A chef?" She popped her eyes open.

"A pastry chef."

"Oh." She seemed to ponder this as she pondered the dress, realized they both left something to be desired.

"No comment even necessary," I said.

"You should try something sexier. You could pull it off. You don't have to be virtuous *every* minute."

"Right, what, low-cut black lace? I'm sorry, I'm not *you*."

"Look at you. You turned gorgeous. I go away for a year and, well, *look* at you. Jesus."

I did—gave a good long look in the dressing room mirror. I looked back at me, unimpressed. I looked through the hangers, deciding what to try next.

"Tell me about Hayden," I said.

"What's to tell?"

"You make it sound like he's so simple. Like it's all right there to see."

"It is. He's sweet. A good person. Etcetera, etcetera. You can see it. Anyone can see it."

"Does he like the mountains? Did he ever go to camp? What is he afraid of?"

"I don't know, Scarlet." She was getting pissed at me.

"I'm just saying, there's a lot to a person."

The little room shuddered as the door next to me closed. A mom with two small children by the sound of it. There was a lot of shuffling and bumping, and then, "Sit here with Sarah, okay, Benjamin? Make sure she doesn't fall."

I unzipped a satiny brown dress and tried to lift it over my hips but it wouldn't go. Plan B, try again. I raised my arms and scootched it down. There was a small voice: "I like what's in your purse, Mommy."

And then: "Benjamin! Don't play with that. Put that back!" And then, a thump and a wail.

"Brown satin," I said.

Juliet looked. "I really like that. That's great on you."

It was hard to see anything since the mirror was so close up, but from what I could tell, I looked like me, only shinier. The kid was still wailing next to us and Juliet squinched up her face as if the sound pained her. I did the same. "Can't you do what I ask you for one minute?" the woman next door said. The second kid started to yell-whine. "Mom! Give it baaaaack! I want it baaaaack!"

"We'll put this one in the maybe pile," I said.

"What did you say? I couldn't hear you," Juliet said too loudly. I hated when she did things like that. Juliet wasn't one to just be nice and go along.

"Juliet!" I whispered.

"Well, for God's sake," she snapped back.

"Fine, here. Take it. Just don't take everything out," the woman said. The sock-clad feet in the dressing room on my other side put their shoes on and got the heck out of there. Smart.

Getting out of the dress was harder even than getting it on. I was sure it had shrunk a size somewhere between lifting it up over my stomach and up to my shoulders, where it appeared to be jammed. "Ow," I said.

"Are you okay?"

I managed to get one arm free, hoisted the dress over my head so that it was basically stuck on my face. "God! How do they expect you to get these things off?"

Juliet laughed. Damn it, she was peeking. "Don't look!" I said. The dress was hanging on my head like a turban, with one of my arms in the air out the neck hole, when the wailing stopped next door and a face peered under the door.

"Hi la-dy," the little kid said.

"*God!*" I said.

"Hi-ii," the kid said again.

"Go back on your side, honey," Juliet's voice was a hostile, too-loud message to the mother next door.

"Sarah! Come here! Quit that! The lady needs privacy!"

"Can I have gum?" Benjamin said.

I finally managed to free the dress, and I stood there, clutching the brown satin to my mostly naked self as the little girl retreated and appeared again, and as I watched Juliet's face change in a moment from pissed to horrified. She put her fingertips up to her face, as if their touch kept the thoughts in her head.

"Juliet?"

She looked ill. I got scared. What did I know about any of this, this pregnancy? Was this some medical emergency? I tried to remember about anything I might have read in *What to Expect When You're Expecting*. What if something happened to her right here? What if there was some sort of pregnancy disaster right here in Vibe!?

"Oh—" It was more a sound than a word. Pain. I didn't know what to do. I just stood there clutching that strangulating dress and looking down at her.

"Tell me," I said. "What? Are you hurting? Is something going wrong?"

"I just . . ."

"What?"

"I didn't think about this," she said.

"Juliet, what?" Okay. This was okay. It was an emotional crisis not a physical one.

"*This.*"

She pointed down to the floor, where a pair of little kid legs now stuck into our dressing room. One of the small pink tennis shoes had the laces undone. The bottom of the other shoe was scribbled on with some sort of ink pen. There was a pink-and-purple swirly Band-Aid on one plump knee, hanging on by only a single sticky end.

"That kid?"

Juliet gave a small nod. A tear rolled down her nose. I felt something big then. Something too large to have a name. The weight of mistakes and the lifting heart of compassion. Human beings colliding with the most complicated parts of themselves and the weird bravery of that. I held my sister against that brown satin dress. Held her head as the tears darkened the fabric. I felt all the choices that come out wrong in spite of our small hidden hopes. But I felt something else then too, something for the small someone inside Juliet whom I couldn't seem to make entirely real. A someone who was growing and becoming in spite of our confusion, a someone whom I felt right then that I maybe just might love.

I listened to Hayden's truck back out of the driveway. He and Juliet were going out to the Lighthouse, with its candles on every table and tri-fold menus. Hayden had rubbed his hands together happily at the thought of a baked potato wrapped in foil, and Juliet smelled like perfume. Buddy Wilkes's allure—his slim hips and lank hair, the six-pack too often dangling from his long fingers, the poison of his coyote thinness and dark need—it had been kept away from my sister's new life. He was just an outsider. For that day anyway.

Candlelight and dinner, facing each other across a table—this was a setting for love, or else it was supposed to be. Hayden's hand was on the small of Juliet's back when they left, and she leaned into him as they went out the front door and down the walk. I would lean into that hand, I would. It would be easy. I would rest against that chest and it would be the rightest feeling in the world because he was a man who understood kindness. You could rest where there were good intentions. If you really cared for someone, though, really cared, you wanted what they wanted for themselves, right? You wanted that for them more than anything else, even if it made your heart clutch up. Even if you wished the hand was there on the small of your own back.

When they left, I read the new note on the bedside table.

Dearest Juliet—
Beautiful places: The tip of the Baja peninsula, Lover's Beach, a slim stretch of white sand below an arch of rock. The Northern California coastline, wild rock shorelines, tumultuous waves, trees bent and twisted by insistent wind. The Cinque Terre—rugged, ragged

Italian hill towns spilling out toward the sea, oranges
and reds and old stone and clotheslines of white sheets
set against blue azure waters. Ile Saint-Louis, cobbled
streets and winding alleys and immense old doors and
secret courtyard gardens.

None, though, is as beautiful as the land of your
body—the curve of hip, breasts, ass, mouth. Skin white
and smooth as eggshells. Softness, woman, a country to
disappear in forever.

I put on some music and sat at my desk. Zeus lay underneath, and I kept him close by petting him with my foot. Hayden
asked me to keep my eye on him so he didn't have a revenge pee
on the carpet. He didn't always take well to being left behind.

I folded paper cranes out of roof-washing advertisements and
credit card applications and real estate flyers. I sifted through
Mom's postcards and chose one from Madrid with a bullfighter on
the front. *The weather is superb here,* I wrote. *We saw the Vazquez
collection at the Prado and thought of you. . . .* I took another sheet of
stationery, yellow with a wildflower border, and wrote, *Mail carriers
are AWESOME!* on its empty center. I folded it three times and
tucked it into the yellow wildflower-bordered envelope.

Being needed was a handy trick. It could fill you up so full you
never even noticed all the places that were empty.

I heard them come home, and for a long time, the house was
silent. *Hayden in bed could make you forget just about anything. . . .*

But then I heard the door handle turn, slowly, with effortful
quiet, and then I heard the creak of stairs, the shushing of Zeus,
who thought he was waking for a night adventure.

My heart was beating fast, and I was weirdly excited, the way you are on your birthday morning, or when you're taking something new you've bought out of a shopping bag, or when you are about to see someone you really like. Really like. I didn't stop to think, or maybe that was just another lie. Maybe I decided not to stop and think. I tossed on my shorts and my sweatshirt. I made the same quiet path down the stairs.

"What are you doing here?" I whispered.

"Scarlet."

"Can't sleep?"

"Nah. You? What are you doing up?"

"I'm the worst sleeper in the world," I lied. "Happens all the time. Sometimes I just need to get up and out. Sometimes I go for a walk. I walk and look at all the quiet houses."

"Yeah? Same here. I like to drive, though. Once I crossed the state line. The night I met Juliet."

"I thought you would have slept like a baby after your night out tonight. Romance, dinner, tra-la-la."

"We had a great dinner, thank you, Scarlet. It really was great. Your sister just puts a lot on my mind. She can't help herself."

I left that alone. The joy I had felt when I heard him head outside started to slip a little, and I didn't want it to slip. It felt so good. I had a sudden idea.

"Let's go for a drive now," I said.

"I don't think so, Scarlet. I don't think that's such a great idea."

"Come on, why not? A spin around Deception Loop. It'll help us both."

"No car keys," he said. And then he seemed to reconsider. He felt up inside the bumper of his truck, near the tire. He held up a small metal box. "Car keys."

I smiled.

"I have a feeling your mother would not like this," he said.

"We're not doing anything wrong. It'll be our secret."

I liked this idea, us having a secret. No one would need to know, just like no one needed to know any private feelings I might have. They would be a secret between me and myself, kept from doing anyone harm by staying locked away. They would be mine and mine alone. A person, a girl, could have all kinds of thoughts and none of them mattered, none of them could betray or embarrass or complicate as long as she kept hold of them, made them her own business and no one else's, kept them tucked in a box of metal, same as those car keys, which Hayden now slipped out and dangled on one finger.

"Windows down . . . ," he warned. "Night air blowing in."

"No other way," I said.

We got in and he started the engine. It sounded so loud there on that late, dark street. I closed the door so softly that I had to open it again at the stop sign to shut it hard.

"You've got to warn me when you're going to do that," Hayden said. "I was just about to push the gas pedal. Maybe you'd better buckle in. I'd hate to lose you."

The sound of that pleased me. "I'm buckled. See?"

"All right, then."

"Music?"

"Just night music."

"Better," I agreed.

The windows were down and he drove just a little too fast on the long road around the island. As he drove, you felt all of life there, stretched out and sleepy in the black night—the still cars and dark houses, the glow of porch lights and the tiny red beams of sailboats bobbing in the waters of the sound. Gardens resting, hawks not, rabbits huddling together for safety. People dreaming, toes touching other toes under quilts, fretful tossing, all of what might be waiting when morning came. The slow, permanent rhythms of the tides, of trees doing midnight growing, of humans forever tangling and untangling their own stories. I breathed it all in through the open windows, felt its grandness, and beside me, felt Hayden's presence there too, him with his one elbow out the open window, his T-shirt sleeve flapping in the cool air.

I watched his profile. The *tick-tock tick-tock* of the turn signal sounded both tired and important at that late hour. It reminded me of arrivals and departures, the sound of coming home when you were a child and it was past your bedtime, and you'd been asleep in the backseat of the car.

The tires crunched gravel, and he pulled over at the small curve where there was a scenic view labeled with a sign. We sat there for a while, listening to crickets through the open windows. The night smelled like blackberry leaves and the ocean's nearness, something sweet and deep and full. His presence seemed so large there beside me. I felt it in every part of me. It was bigger than the sound stretched before us, a sea of creamy blue-black tinged with silver moonlit waves.

"Hear that hawk?" he said.

"Yeah."

My voice seemed to surprise him. He looked over at me. He seemed startled. Maybe he'd forgotten who was in the car with him.

"We'd better get back," he said.

He reversed out of the lot, set us on the road again. We didn't amble and stray this time, just made a straight shot there. We were nearing home when he spoke. "She's scared about getting close. She says she's scared; that's why."

"She's scared about getting close," I said. Right. She had seemed really scared of getting close when she was wrapped up with Buddy Wilkes on our living room couch. Getting pregnant on purpose sure seemed like being scared of getting close. Uh-huh.

"You know, after . . ."

He didn't finish. I wanted to say, *after what?* What big crisis had she had that we didn't know about? But I felt irritated at the direction things were going in. We were almost home. The ride was almost over, and maybe I'd never have another like it again. I picked up his pack of cigarettes on the seat. I shook one out.

"You could teach me to smoke," I said.

"You don't want to smoke, Scarlet."

"I do. You could teach me." I put one between my lips. It tasted brown and sweet, sweeter than the gray, ashy smell it made when lit. I let it hang there. "How's this? Like in the movies." I pretended to smoke, blew out the imaginary air. I was feeling a little reckless. The wind and the night and the late hour and watching Hayden's profile, it all made me feel like I could toss things away, everything, all. Like I would want that, and it would be good.

"Give me that," he said. He snatched it from my lips, and I could feel his hand brush against my mouth. His fingers, brushing against my skin.

"My smoking days are over already? And I wanted it so much."

"You don't want that, Scarlet."

"I don't?"

"It's not who you are."

We pulled up to our driveway then. He cut the engine, and there in front of our still house, the night seemed quieter than quiet.

"We don't know that."

"We *do* know that. And it's a good thing. It's a great thing," he said. "Come on, let's get some sleep."

We went inside again. There was the shushing of Zeus, the creaking steps, the turning door handles, in reverse. He stopped at their door. I wanted something bad. I could feel the rumble of that want filling every bit of me. If you had asked me right then what I wanted, though, I might not even have been able to say exactly what it was.

"Good night," he whispered finally.

"Good night," I whispered back.

Chapter Fifteen

ey, Miss A plus." I closed my locker and turned around.

"Kevin," I said. I had a moment of fear-panic, looked at his hands. I saw with relief that they did not hold some round cartoon bomb with a sparkling, lit fuse, nor a Wile E. Coyote crate labeled *Dynamite!* Actually, he was smiling. I had to think a minute. I wasn't sure I'd ever seen Kevin Frink smile. He smirked, yes, but that only involved one corner of the mouth, not both.

"I don't want you making anything of this," he said.

"Okay."

"She called me. Fiona Saint George."

"She did?"

"She told me she may as well go to the prom with me since no one else was ever going to ask her."

I looked at his big face and wondered if her words had bothered him, but I guessed not. He seemed pleased. He even had a new T-shirt on. I could see the thin plastic *T* still attached to his sleeve, the one that had once held the price tag. I pointed it out to him and he lifted his sleeve to his mouth and ripped it off with his teeth.

"I said, 'Maybe you ought to wait for Dracula. He'd take you to the prom. And she said, 'Fuck you' and I said, 'Fuck you back' and then she said I'd better get her a corsage and I told her I wasn't stupid and she asked me to come over today after school."

"Wow, Kevin!" I wanted to hug him, but Kevin Frink wasn't one you actually hugged. Even if you touched him, he seemed to flinch, pulling tight back inside his coat. His coat—wait. He wasn't wearing his coat.

"Where's your coat?" I asked.

"It's hot," he said. "What do I know about corsages? What do you do? Do I have to call that place? STD?"

"FTD? Nah. Even the grocery store has corsages."

"What do I get?"

I thought of the pink dress drawn on the sidewalk drawn in chalk. "Pink roses. For her wrist."

"All right. I got that. Pink roses."

"You're going to do great!" I beamed. I felt so happy, my insides beamed too. It was beautiful, this plan. Everyone could get just what they needed. I felt like a proud parent.

"Fucking prom," Kevin Frink said, but when he went back down the hall, his usual big head slump had turned into something like a big head bob.

And then, the salad bar again. Jesse's knuckles accidentally grazed mine as we both reached for the sunflower seeds.

"I don't understand the kidney beans," he said.

I knew what he meant. "Every day they put them out here and no one touches them," I said.

"It's like the cafeteria ladies keep hoping."

"Hopeless kidney bean hope," I said.

"Pathetic," he said. "To give your hope to a kidney bean." He smiled. Raised his eyes to meet mine.

"If you take him away from me, I'll be devastated," Nicole said, back at the table.

I had a feeling she meant it. I wouldn't do that to her, though. Nicole had enough problems already. I had a responsibility to her. My heart seemed too full with other things anyway. Other people. *Person*, even.

"We're honeymooning in Cancun," I said.

She socked my arm, put her head for a second on my shoulder. "I know you'd never hurt me," she said.

I leaned against the streetlight by Derek's car, feeling the sun-warmed metal against my back. I even closed my eyes for one perfect and satisfied moment, but that's only how long the perfect moment lasted. *Perfect* is a frail thing, though, maybe one of the most frail. I heard laughter coming from the cemetery across the street then. I knew that laughter. That laughter had been part of my personal sound track from the day I was born.

I looked over. I saw a flash of yellow. Disappointment and panic immediately rushed in to take the place of what had felt so right. A flash of yellow and that laughter and a memory: three years ago, walking home from middle school past that very same cemetery. Juliet and Buddy Wilkes were there, their bodies leaning against a tall granite obelisk, both of his hands up her shirt, his thin hip bones pressed hard against hers.

I started walking that way. Fast. I was compelled, the same as you might be if there had been a sudden accident. And that's what this was, I knew. A sudden catastrophic collision, an imminent one anyway.

I saw the yellow again. Juliet, in that yellow dress, all summer invitation. Of course it was her. There was Buddy Wilkes, too, in the cemetery. He wore ripped jeans and a tank top. She was laughing. He was laughing. He gestured to himself in some sort of joke. And then he grabbed her. Pulled her close. She steadied herself with one hand against a tombstone, some poor dead somebody who was probably a nice person who didn't deserve this on their place of eternal rest.

Juliet had one hand against Buddy's ribbed shirt which was worn oh so tight against his chest. He reached one hand down between them, rested it right where our baby was. Rested it there like he had every right to.

I was practically running. I *was* running. "Hey!" I called. "*Hey!*" I was too far away for them to hear. I watched him lean in to her as if to kiss her, and she gave him a little shove away. A yes-no game, as if a halfhearted protest was some excuse.

Just as I made it across the street, they disappeared, winding their way around gravestones and elm trees and the leafy shadows that swallowed them up and made me think that maybe I hadn't seen what I knew I'd seen.

I was out of breath. I clutched the chain link of the cemetery fence and called. "Juliet!"

But there was no answer. Goddamnit! How could she do this? I heard an engine start up, probably the engine of Buddy's El Camino. And then a moment later, Derek's car pulled up beside me, and Nicole stuck her head out the window.

"What are you doing over here, you crazy girl? Get in."

I unfurled my fingers from the fence. Opened the door to Derek's car.

He leaned across the seat. "There's no such thing as ghosts," he said to me.

When I got back home, Kevin Frink's red Volkswagen was parked by the curb next to the Saint George house. I could hear the *tick tick tick* of its engine cooling off. Kevin Frink didn't waste any time. Mom-and-Dad-We-Went-to-Yale, I'd like you to meet Bomb Boy.

I headed inside our house, but before I got to the door, I heard the smoker's cough rumble of a motorcycle. A Harley, actually, with a thick, large man with long dark hair riding it, black leather jacket with the orange Harley emblem on his back, metal-studded saddlebags. He looked familiar to me; I knew I'd seen him somewhere before, but I didn't have time to think about that. Jeffrey and Jacob sat on their lawn, holding that string which was connected to the purse in the middle of the street.

The man stopped just short of the bag, cut his engine, put both feet to the ground, and swung one meaty leg over his bike. Okay, Jeffrey and Jacob were brats and would no doubt be unleashed into society to be lousy husbands and fathers who would have affairs as they got their sports cars detailed, stealing office supplies from work and complaining the house wasn't clean enough, but I didn't want to see them get killed. Their eyes were huge as they sat on the lawn. They even gripped hands in some oh-man-we're-in-for-it-now solidarity.

A few birds cheeped in bird innocence, but that was the only sound as the man sauntered toward that purse like some tough sheriff in a Western, though then again, maybe it was just the

Deb Caletti

leather chaps, well, *chapping*, that made him walk that way.

"Wait!" I called. I didn't know what to follow this up with. But I knew those kids were in for it. You get in over your head, sometimes. It's stupid, but you're thinking Clive Weaver and that purse, not some prison felon escapee on a motorcycle and that purse. You have this stupid idea. But you're not thinking something's going to destroy you.

The man didn't hear me. He took off his black shiny helmet and shook his hair free. He had one of those mustache beards, the kind that go all the way down your mouth and around your chin, the name of which escaped me then. This would be the time for Jeffrey and Jacob to pull on the string, right as the man reached down to pick up the purse with his hunk of a hairy arm. I knew they wouldn't do it, though. I didn't think they would do something that bad, because we all have self-preservation at least, right? They were probably about to wet their pants in fear.

But then, it *did* happen. I was wrong about the boys' not doing something that bad, because right then the purse leaped as if by magic from the motorcyclist's hand. It jerked for a second, rose up off the ground, and then it landed with a splat on the asphalt. The motorcyclist looked up. He scanned the horizon. Stupid, idiot kids! I was wrong about their future of stealing of office supplies, too; they were destined for worse offenses—white collar crime, tax fraud. Lewd acts in public theaters. I wanted to stop what was going to happen next, but no sound came out. One foot stepped forward, but that was it. The motorcyclist lifted his large arm and pointed to the boys.

"You!" he roared. Why, why, why weren't they running? Why didn't they take off to hide inside their house, hide underneath their twin beds with race car sheets? The man's body was huge. His voice came out as big as God's. "That is . . . Awesome! That's fucking *awe*some! Right *on!*"

Jeffrey and Jacob looked too stunned to respond. The motorcyclist was nodding vigorously, as if he'd just had one of the greatest moments of his life. He was happy. He was thrilled. He got back on his bike. Flashed a pair of thumbs up. "Right *on.*"

I watched the orange Harley emblem on his wide back disappear down the street. I was stunned too. Now Jeffrey and Jacob bounced on their knees and shrieked and clutched each other. I'd almost saved them. I'd almost intervened and yet, this was a fabulous, glorious moment for them. For all of them. Something good had been heading their way, not something bad.

God! How were you supposed to do the right thing for people when you couldn't even predict what the right thing was? Did you have to be able to predict the *future* to make things come out the way they should?

"Don't tell Mom," Jeffrey said.

"Don't tell the cops," Jacob said, and this cracked them both up.

"Let's do it again!" Jeffrey shouted, as Jacob ran out into the street and set the purse straight again.

The minute I saw Juliet, she was going to hear it from me. If she wanted to mess up her own life, fine. But there was Hayden to think about. There was Jitter. I didn't know who exactly Jitter was going to be, but I was starting to want the best for him. I felt the rising heat of my words, waiting for the chance to erupt and spill. I didn't care how young she thought I was. She'd better knock this off, and fast.

Deb Caletti

I heard Juliet's and Hayden's voices in the basement later that afternoon. Maybe I would ask to speak to her alone; I'd say something like *Can I have a word with you privately*, the way people did on television. I walked down the stairs, to the cool paneled room. No one ever spent much time down there, except our old Barbies and their pink Corvettes, packed away in boxes marked TOYS in fat black marker. It was the room that collected the past, the same as that one kitchen drawer collects the rubber bands and loose screws and take-out menus until you can't even open it anymore. I didn't even realize how much stuff was down there until now.

"Knock knock," I said.

"Come on in," Hayden said.

I felt shaky with held-back anger. The sliding glass doors to the backyard were open, and Zeus trotted in and out with the glee of sudden free access to grass. Juliet sat on one box and had opened another; she had some of our old stuff laid out—my old Ernie Halloween costume; her Princess Jasmine one; Lambie, a stuffed lamb she used to keep in the corner of her room. She wore the Princess Jasmine headpiece on her white-gold hair.

"Hey!" Hayden said to me. Zeus trotted back in, sniffed a hello into my palm, and then trotted back out again. He couldn't believe his good fortune at being able to come and go as he pleased. I had felt that same way when I first got my driver's license. "We're trying to get our new digs ready," Hayden said. "Studio apartment."

"You're moving down here?" I asked. I tried to keep my voice steady. I avoided looking at Juliet.

"We're leaving the nest," he said.

"Mom just wants more distance between her and a crying baby," Juliet said.

"I doubt that," I said. In fact, it was a stupid and selfish thing to say. "The way she's been acting, she'd be happy if you let the baby move into her room. You, too." I tried to keep back my fury, but my voice came out sounding snotty, even to me.

Hayden looked up, but kept quiet. He directed his focus back to the boxes. "These will fit into the garage," he said.

"'Member this, Scars?" Juliet held up an old rabbit we had that was actually a puppet. She put her hand up his backside and made his head look around. It felt wrong of her to dig inside all of those old boxes. What do you do with the past when it's *past*? You box it up, label it, move it out of sight. Opening it all back up again—it was going the wrong direction. Walking backward when you were trying hard to go forward. What good could come of it?

"Better hide that from Zeus. He'll rip it up and take out the fluff so all that's left is stuffed-animal road kill," Hayden said. "He loves fuzz."

"Oh, this used to be our favorite." Juliet held up our old over-sized Richard Scarry book, *Busy, Busy Town.* She opened it to the drawing of the inside of a house, where little kittens were waking up in one room, and a father cat was putting on a tie in another, looking into his dresser mirror. Outside, a pig mailman delivered letters and a pig milkman in a white hat drove a milk truck. If someone made the *real* Richard Scarry book, I thought, you'd look inside the split-open house and see fighting sisters and single moms. Outside there'd be depressed mailmen wandering around naked on the lawn, and the ice-cream truck would be driven by a glowering psychopath.

"Ohhh," Juliet said. "The little cats." The book was open on her knees. She turned the page of the book to study the construction scene of small pigs in hard hats. The reason people said, *Can I have a word with you privately* only on television was that it just didn't work in real life. It would tell Hayden all the things he shouldn't know. Instead, I dripped sarcasm, gave her a full lecture with my tone alone. "What did *you* do today, Juliet?"

"Haircut, can't you tell?" she said. She still didn't look up, only flipped the ends of her hair with one hand. "What is it about hairdressers? You tell them 'not too short' and some part of their hairdresser brain hears this as 'whack the shit out of it.' If you never say, 'not too short,' everything is *fine*. You say it, and it's a guarantee you'll come out ready for the military."

"I think you're supposed to say *stylist* now," Hayden said.

"And it's hardly short," I said.

"What's wrong with *you*," she said.

I looked straight into her eyes. Buddy Wilkes is what's wrong, I told her. If she couldn't read that message, she was more of an idiot than I thought.

"Wow, I feel a sudden chill," she said. She reached over and closed the sliding glass door with her palm. A second later there was a *bam!* as Zeus smacked right into the glass. I could see him there on the other side, looking momentarily stunned.

"Aw, Zeus!" Hayden said. He opened the door and let Zeus back in. "Poor kid. Come here, you okay? That was funny but not funny."

"Oh, I'm sorry Zeus," Juliet said. But she was looking at me. Figuring me out. Like maybe she got my message loud and clear, after all.

"Big dumb kid. That was sort of humiliating," Hayden said. He was patting Zeus and looking him over but you could tell

Zeus had already moved on from the sudden shock of something gone awry. Hayden opened the door again, and out Zeus trotted once more. Running into a wall of glass at full speed couldn't begin to touch his general sense of optimism.

"Honey, I'm sorry about Jared and the prom. You must be so disappointed," Mom said after dinner. She rubbed my back in a sympathetic circle. We sat on the couch together, watching but not watching some Hollywood entertainment show that neither one of us cared about. We weren't the type of people who connected to other worlds involving floor-length gowns, but it helped us pretend not to hear the raised voices coming from downstairs.

"Well, Nicole told me he was the type, but I didn't believe her." I was "getting over the breakup" with Jared, the senior who was leaving soon to become a pastry chef.

"Oh, I know. I know," Mom said.

"I'm just glad I didn't buy that dress, is all."

"Things have a way of working out for the best," she said. We flinched right then.

We both heard Juliet: "*You act like everything is my fault!*"

And Hayden: "*I'm doing everything I know how to do!*"

"I saw Juliet today," I told Mom. I think I needed her help. It felt like things were growing too big for me to handle on my own. "At the cemetery." She looked puzzled. "With Buddy Wilkes."

"No," she said. She shook her head. I thought she was shaking her head in disbelief, at the tragedy Juliet was playing out. Some small form of outrage. But then I realized it was something worse. She held both hands up as if she wanted to hear no more. The *no* was for me. "This isn't our business, Scarlet."

"You're kidding me," I said.

"She's a grown woman."

I knew it had nothing to do with being a grown woman. This was how it always went. When Juliet was caught skipping school in the seventh grade, Mom only gave her a lecture about making life choices. In the ninth grade, she took Mom's car and drove onto the ferry and over to the other side and back, and Mom just had a talk with her that left them both crying. Eleventh grade, she was hanging out with Buddy and Jason Dale and whoever, drinking. Caught by Officer Beaker, and there were only more whispered, urgent talks, them with their heads tightly together like they had private issues I would never grasp. Juliet could even yell and slam doors, and the next day Mom would be making her lunch as usual. Juliet could do no wrong, ever.

"This time she's hurting other people," I said. I would risk the conflict this time, even welcomed it. But Mom's voice was firm and calm.

"Scarlet, you need to let this be her business. I mean it. She's got to work things out herself."

"He doesn't deserve this," I said.

"I'm sure it was nothing."

Right then I knew we were all liars, Mom and me and Juliet. I just lied to other people. Mom lied to herself. Juliet, it seemed, did both.

His voice woke me that night.

"I don't know, I don't, boy," he said. I thought I was dreaming it. Through my open window, below me, rising from the night, I heard the truck door open and close, and then the rustle of cellophane. The *flick, flick, flick* of a lighter. He was having trouble getting it to work. "Fuck," he breathed. And then *flick, flick, flick* again.

I didn't care that I was only wearing my long T-shirt, the one Nicole had brought back for me from Las Vegas, the time her mom took her on a pissed-off spending-spree trip to run up her dad's credit cards. I didn't stop to check how I looked, only swiped on a quick fingertip of toothpaste as I went past the bathroom and headed downstairs. I knew where Mom kept the matches gathered from various restaurants over the years or from somewhere—I didn't exactly even know where they came from, because I doubted she'd ever been to those places. I grabbed a red box labeled *The Flame*. No restaurant by that name around here. Some objects—pens, matches, coins—liked to travel.

The air was wet and thick and it smelled like it had rained, even though it hadn't yet—that wet earth smell, wet streets, wet evergreen boughs, wet, simmering campfires.

I threw the book of matches and he caught them against his chest. "Here. In spite of the fact that it's not who you are either."

He was shirtless again—the night was warm. My whole body noticed this, the valley of his chest, the curve of his muscled arms. The noticing surprised me—it was a bold feeling, and I was not exactly known for being bold. *Want*, even, and I was not known for wanting.

"I woke you," he said. "You shouldn't have gotten up. And you've got school tomorrow."

"Hmm," I said. "I didn't look at the clock, but if it's past midnight, it's officially Saturday."

"Jesus," he said. He shook his head as if it needed clearing. He struggled with the matchbox, lit his cigarette. He inhaled deeply.

Zeus lay down at his feet, as if it were okay to rest now that some-one else was on duty. "Another week gone by," he said.

"Time flies when you're having fun," I said.

"Ah. You heard."

"She's not the easiest person in the world."

He blew smoke up to the sky. "This isn't the easiest way to begin a relationship."

I thought about what to say. I looked down at my feet on the cool cement, curled my toes under so I couldn't see the polish and then out again so that I could. I wanted to be careful. The moment was careful. The night held its breath.

"Maybe you shouldn't love her so much," I said quietly.

He looked at me, straight on. Hs eyes were direct, his gaze shooting straight inside me. My stomach dropped. It was like he was staring right in, seeing the way I worked; seeing, maybe, all the things I wanted to hide and couldn't say and might never say.

"But that wouldn't be the truth," he said.

"If you knew her . . . I don't mean to say you don't *know* her, but if you knew-knew her . . . She likes the cool, distant thing, right? You hold back, she chases, you get; she pulls back again, you pull back, she chases. . . ." I was talking fast. He needed to know these things if Juliet was ever going to love him like he wanted. "It's dangled, I think. Out of reach. Somehow she wants it more then."

"If I did that . . ." He thought. "I'd be acting more out of fear than love, wouldn't I? Fear would make me a liar. I shouldn't have to be a liar to make someone love me. I shouldn't be so afraid of losing someone that I'll do anything to make them stay."

He was looking right into my eyes, and all at once my throat closed up. All at once, I felt the hot press of tears. They came out of nowhere, and I swallowed hard. I didn't feel ashamed about what I'd said. I didn't feel like I'd been stupid to give him such unwanted advice. No, instead, I saw his compassion, and the way he understood things about himself and about me, too. He'd seen it in me, or just felt it himself, the way you try to do certain things and be certain things and give and give more and change and fix and hold back and not hold back all in order to keep people close. A million little lies to get that one thing.

I felt a clear truth, and that truth hit some deep part of me, the deepest, most secretive part. The part of who I most am and why I am that way. You can hold a secret, hold it so far in that it drives nearly every thought and every move you make, your very heartbeat, almost. And then someone can come along and name it, gently name it, call it forward in kindness, and when that happens, all you can do is stand there in the night doing everything you can not to cry.

"I know, Scarlet Ellis," Hayden whispered. "I know exactly."

Chapter Sixteen

aybe Mom was right, maybe Juliet just needed
to work out things on her own, because for the
next few weeks before the end of the school year,
Buddy Wilkes seemed mostly gone. There was no yellow dress
in the cemetery after school, no laughter filtering through leafy
trees. Maybe Juliet had just needed to see him to get him out of
her system the way you need to eat a little chocolate to get over
your craving.

Jitter was growing—Juliet's form was becoming blocky,
and, according to my book, at over five months, Jitter had eyes
and eyelashes. I would find Juliet with her hand at her back
from her growing weight, and she said she could feel flutters
like a butterfly let loose inside. I had heard her once on the
phone, muffled voice through her bedroom wall, angry words
that were not directed at Hayden, who had come through our
front door not a moment later, whistling. Juliet had greeted him

with a long kiss, and he had put one hand in the back pocket of her shorts. She seemed so happy with him sometimes, the real and true kind, not the Buddy Wilkes anxious and uneasy kind. The butterfly candleholder by her bed had gone missing, too. There one day. Then, not.

I saw Buddy Wilkes during that time, not at school in his El Camino, not driving down our street but, oddly, at the library. The library was one of the most beautiful buildings on Parrish Island, and I liked that about it, it seemed fitting. The library should be the best building. It was a tall white structure with a long set of steps and a pair of elaborate columns; inside, the floor was shiny and wide, and the stairwell curved toward a domed ceiling painted like the sky. It was a place for book reverence, reverence for ideas and words and thoughts, not a place for boys with narrow hips and thin, sallow cheeks—manipulative boys whose only special talents were unhooking bra straps with one hand and talking middle-age grocery clerks into selling them beer.

But there he was. Sitting at one of the dark, solid tables, right there where I wanted to be, in fiction. Creeps didn't belong near fiction. I could smell already-smoked cigarettes coming off his jacket. He might as well have been a rank-smelling animal in an art museum. He had a book open in front of him, but he wasn't reading. It was a big book, with glossy pictures of Victorian furniture—red velvet sofas and heavy chiseled chairs, nothing he'd be interested in. I looked around for the real reason he must be there. One of his friends was in the stacks, maybe, Jason Dale or Kale Kramer, preparing to pull some kind of practical joke on the respectful people there; or maybe some girl, some Alicia Worthen, trying to graduate in a hurry before it was too late. I'd know her when I saw her—she'd be wearing a tiny tank top and the shortest shorts possible, clothes somehow not fitting for the religious place that was the library.

But I didn't see anyone who might be with Buddy Wilkes. No Jason Dale or Wendy Williams. Only Elizabeth Everly with her cart, shelving books. Sweet and quiet Elizabeth Everly, who'd graduated with my sister, with her whispered voice and teacup-fragile wrists—not exactly Buddy Wilkes's type. Most likely we'd be reading in the morning about some crime that had been committed at the Parrish Library, and I'd know who did it.

I walked by Buddy's table, but he didn't look at me. I don't know why I did it, but I knocked my hip into the chair across from him so he'd notice me. Maybe it was some useless attempt at warning on my part; I needed him to know that I was aware of things, and that he couldn't always do as he pleased simply because he wanted to. The wood chair bumped hard against the table and Buddy Wilkes looked up. He saw me and I stared back at him, but it was as if he didn't even recognize me. He did not hand me some note for Juliet, or speak to me, or even give me a look that said we knew each other. I'd seen him countless times—in my driveway, my kitchen, hopping around half-naked trying to get his pants back on in a hurry, but his gaze right then was as blank as if we'd never met. It made me wonder if he only saw you when he wanted something. Some people are like that. You don't exist, unless you are of use.

I didn't tell Juliet about seeing Buddy Wilkes at the Parrish Island Library. I had learned my lesson about opening closed doors that snakes and thieves stood behind. Anyway, Hayden seemed to be managing Juliet on his own, and full-time managing of Juliet was part of life with her; I knew that. Hayden seemed to have taken two pieces of my advice, and it appeared to be working. He was giving her both compliments and presents—flowers and soft words and little books of poetry and elegant slices of desserts from Alice's Bakery. She opened them with delight as her stomach grew, the smallest mound forming into a more distinct rounded hillside. I had to go downstairs to find the letters now, into their basement "apartment." The letters were usually left on the nightstand, which was made out of the old crate that used to hold Mom's college textbooks, and before that, according to the label, Valencia Oranges. I would hold the letters and try to breathe and let my secret be its own, full self for a while. I'd let my feelings out into the room, the way you might let out an animal who'd been traveling too long in a cage so that he could be free and remember how good that was.

Juliet—
Some decisions are a struggle, a thrashing effort of
back and forth, the tormented wakefulness and night
sweats and tangled sheets of a bad night's sleep. But
other decisions—there's a purity. There is a simplicity
and rightness about the decision. It's the simplicity
and rightness of air, of snow, of apples. Marrying you,
Juliet, was that kind of decision for me. I made it with
the straightforward ease of taking a drink of water,
closing one's eyes to rest.

I wondered about Hayden's words. *Straightforward ease.* He didn't seem to be feeling very easy. He seemed to be working hard, and what I was learning, beginning to learn, since he had come was that there were relationships that were hard work and relationships that weren't. Most often, you worked

Deb Caletti

hard like that when you were really worried you weren't going to get what you needed back. Maybe he thought that working hard was honorable somehow, an honorable thing, but I saw something different. I saw him making himself small for her. Making himself less than and lower than and below. He said he didn't want to be a liar to make someone love him, but he was being a liar by doing those things, by trying so hard to get her to love him. Working hard with someone else—it was a sign of serious trouble ahead, bumps and heartache and things going unexpected directions; doom, even.

It was coming. We should have known that.

"Oh my God," I said out loud when I saw my locker.

"It is *dripping*," Nicole said. "This reminds me of people who write in blood in those awful horror movies."

We stared at the metal door, with *I love you 4-ever* written in shaving cream, now sliding toward the floor. It looked less like blood and more like the time I made a milkshake in the blender with the lid loose. "This is so humiliating," I said.

"I'll get some paper towels," Nicole said and hurried off. I think she just didn't want to stand there any longer than she had to.

"You're the one for me," Reilly Ogden said.

"God, Reilly!" I hated how he appeared out of nowhere. His eyes were big and his breath smelled like a mix of onions and spearmint gum. He wore a *U2 World Tour* T-shirt tucked into his jeans that were cinched with a cloth belt.

"Reilly . . . ," I said. I tried to make the word say everything I needed to.

"You're mad," he said. "I can't believe you're mad."

"It's a little embarrassing," I said. The words oozed and seeped. Nicole had been right.

"Why would you be mad after what happened the other day?"

"What? *What* happened?"

Nicole showed up with the paper towels. She gave Reilly a look of disgust and began to wipe up the mess.

"I gave you some notebook paper in AP English and you took it."

"I said I was out, and you offered!"

"You could have said no. That means something. You can't tell me it doesn't."

"Reilly," I tried again.

Nicole clapped her hands like he was a bad dog on her lawn. "Get. Out. Now," she said firmly.

He turned and left, just like he *was* that bad dog. Just like that. He slunk off. His jeans were too high on his hips.

"Just like that," Nicole said, reading my mind. She handed me some paper towels. "Watch and learn."

"So I know he comes out of the gym after second period," Nicole said. We all knew who "he" was. "I wait there, over by the garbage cans? Every day. I pretend I'm throwing stuff away, and when I see him coming I turn and smile, and he smiles back."

"You never told us," I said.

"I know. It was just this thing I did. On my own. I didn't want to tell you guys. But for the last three days, he hasn't been there. We know he's been at school. I think he's taking a different way on purpose." She looked a little sick. "Do you think it's because he likes me? Maybe it's just because he likes me, and he's too afraid to show it?" Her eyes pleaded. It was one of the really bad things about rejection, the pleading that came with it. Maybe we should all have a personal law against pleading. We should forbid ourselves from doing it. That smallest person inside who was the one doing the pleading—they deserved our protection. They should be guarded to the best of our ability and only let out under certain careful conditions.

"Maybe he's been hurt. Do you think that could be it?" she asked.

"Probably," I said.

"Definitely," Jasmine said. "Stupid bitch, whoever she was."

"Roses?" I asked. Mom snatched the little tiny card in its little tiny envelope out of my hand.

"Don't look," she said.

"Who are they from?"

Mom looked puzzled for a moment, then made a funny little gasp. "Oh my God, I can't believe it. I almost forgot his name! I was drawing a total blank. *Dean.*"

The psychology books would really have something to say about *that*. "I thought Dean didn't believe in wasting money on flowers," I said. "I even heard him say so once, after you bought tulips." I felt a small prickle of dread. I hoped flowers weren't enough to veer Mom from the iciness she'd been showing Dean lately. Flowers may have worked for Juliet, but I thought, *hoped*, Mom was different.

"People change their minds," Mom said. The vase of flowers still sat in the cardboard delivery box. She flicked this box with her fingernail. It was the trying-to-decide gesture people used with grocery store melons.

"But *why* did he change his mind?" I asked.

"There doesn't always have to be a why."

Maybe there didn't always have to be a why, but there almost always *was* a why. If I had learned one thing from all my psychology books, it was that.

"Huh," I said. And, then, just like that, I got it. "He's afraid he's losing you," I said. Those were the kinds of things you did when you were afraid of losing someone.

"Don't be ridiculous," she said.

But she kept those flowers in that box, and that told me everything I needed to know.

Kevin Frink's Volkswagen was parked on our street every day after school. The chalk drawings had disappeared. Kevin Frink would drive Fiona Saint George home, and they would sit inside the small curved space of his car. I could see his big head and her small dark one, and she was talking, the girl who didn't talk. Sometimes they would get out; Fiona Saint George would sit on the rounded hood of Kevin Frink's car with her ankles crossed in a way that was flirtatious, and Kevin Frink's bare arms would be exposed to the sun. Once I saw him disappear into her house; he followed behind her, their fingertips touching. The Saint Georges were not home, and I imagined the empty house. Orderly rooms. Buster, the sausage-fat bulldog, too lazy to follow them up the stairs. And I stopped my imagining there. They were due their privacy, even in my mind, and I later saw Kevin Frink leave the house with his head down as he zipped up his jacket and headed to his car. He was smiling. The curtains of Fiona Saint George's room were open just enough for her to watch him drive away.

The romance between Kevin Frink and Fiona Saint George was

going better than I could have ever expected. I was actually happy about it. I didn't stop to think about the things that might happen when you lit the personal fuse of a Bomb Boy, when you led two breakable people into the dangerous territory that was love.

If everyone right then was working hard for love, if Hayden was and Nicole and Reilly Ogden and Dean Neuhaus and Kevin Frink, well, I guess I was too. Or working hard not to love. Because that's what my feelings for Hayden were, love. Wrong or stupid or forever hidden—still, love. I would watch the way his thoughts showed themselves across his face like a movie screen, notice how the sun made his hair turn from brown to gold. He took care of things—fetched cold drinks and watered forgotten plants and noticed when Zeus's feelings were hurt. *Crush* was flimsy and unfair and inaccurate. I knew why I loved him.

The feelings were good and awful at the same time, pressing against my insides, begging to be let out. I knew when you had that particular combination, the sweet and the terrible, the terrible always won out eventually. So I would write postcards and letters for the Clive Weaver project and try not to become distracted by that photograph on my wall—Hayden with his eyes closed and his face full of that moment when we sat on the rocks. I folded paper cranes for Clive Weaver and began to fold them for myself. I stood on my bed and hung them from my ceiling with strings and small bits of tape.

Sitting on the rock at Point Perpetua, I had felt an ease with Hayden that I was unfamiliar with. But I had been wrong then. I was still on a rope bridge, all right, one with fraying knots and old jute. He was my sister's husband, and even if she didn't love him, he wasn't mine. I could stand on that bridge with all my wants and desires, but beneath me, there were the raging waters and the hard fall of heartbreak.

One thing I knew, *straightforward ease* did not cause you to awaken night after night, did not cause you to turn the knob of the front door and walk out to the only place that was really yours, your own truck, so that you could lean against it and feel the comfort of it. Straightforward ease did not cause others to go out after you because they worried, because some part of them wanted to save you, because they knew you deserved better.

Sometimes we would talk.

"We are the worst pair of insomniacs," he said once.

I nodded, though I'd never had trouble sleeping before, not until he came and I would lie awake and listen for the sound of him, or sometimes, go outside myself first in hopes he might appear. "It's the curse of the busy head," I said. "They could make a horror movie with that title."

"Too bad busy heads aren't given mandatory work hours. Nine to five, no overtime," he said.

"Otherwise, fired." I slashed the air.

"We've got to be more strict with our heads."

"Absolutely." I shivered, even though the night was warm. "A mind is a tyrant." Mine was, anyway. Sometimes, I got so sick of being in my own head, it would have been nice to be anywhere else for a while. I wished for a mind that was peaceful and orderly, like a well-run office. Mine was more like a hospital emergency room.

The smell of Hayden's cigarette rose up and wandered off. It was one bad habit he had, a habit Juliet wrongly appreciated. I imagined her curling up to him when he came back to bed,

Deb Caletti

her head on his chest, the smell she liked on his breath.

"So, what brings you in to see the doctor today," I said.

"Hmn. I'm afraid I have a chronic desire to save people." He put his hand through his curls and they fell back to where they'd been before. He wore cargo shorts low on his hips, the loose, soft-looking sea-green T-shirt he loved. That wedding ring, catching the streetlight.

"I know about that," I said. "I've got it too. Maybe it's catching."

"Not catching enough," he said. He thought about this. We both did. "The need to rescue . . ." His words drifted off.

"I know all about it," I said. *It's you I want to rescue* I wanted to say but didn't. It was funny. He saw Juliet in need of saving, when he was the one who needed it most of all. Sometimes, I guess, we couldn't see past our own intentions.

"I was even a lifeguard in high school." He shrugged. It was apologetic. God, he looked good in the streetlight on those summer nights.

"You were?" I tried to picture this. Maybe for a moment I saw myself pretending to drown. "Did you wear that white stuff on your nose?"

"Nah. Urban lifeguard myth. Mostly I had to tell little kids to walk, not run."

The sky was beautiful, and we were both looking at it. Deep, dark, intense white speckles spread out like the grandest present ever. "That's it, probably," he said upward, to the night. "See there? Those people we want to save? They're the intense flashes of fire across our otherwise empty black sky." He nodded, as if agreeing with his own self. He sounded like one of his notes then. I could almost see the words written in his firm, small handwriting. Was he right about this? I just thought being a rescuer was who I was, and that helping others was the right thing to do. I didn't like this idea, that there were people who were sky and people who were stars. I think I wanted to someday be a flash of light across a plane of darkness.

"I don't know. Maybe we're just nice people," I said. "Not boring ones."

He leaned down, stubbed out his cigarette on the driveway, showing the long curve of his back. He held the cigarette butt between his fingers, looked around for somewhere to toss it, then tucked it into his T-shirt pocket instead. Hayden never seemed to mind my presence there at night. Actually, he seemed glad when I appeared. I wondered if that's what us rescuers really wanted—that same feeling of protection offered back to us, just once. Maybe I wanted to give Hayden something because of how badly I wanted him to give me something. In my most private thoughts, too, I sometimes felt like Reilly had—I offered something and Hayden took it, and that had to mean something, didn't it? I repeated rule four of *The Five Rules of Maybe* over and over. You had to place hope carefully in your hands.

"Think about it," Hayden said. "At the center of the most empty, hollow places there's a vortex of activity and motion . . . Astronomy 101."

"Are you calling us empty?"

"I'm just saying that maybe we ought to be making our own vortex, you know? Instead of using everyone else's? I've been thinking about this. I don't even know how to put words to it. But we *could* stop getting sucked into every available black hole. We could want things."

"We *do* want things."

"For *ourselves*."

What I wanted was to circle my fingers around his wrists, to feel his arms around me, to rest my head on his chest, to breathe the smell of night in his hair. That's what I wanted for myself. He was looking at me, urging me to hear this thought of his, and I did hear then. *Want* was a shut door, and I opened it just a small bit, just enough to get through, the way you push a door just a bit with your toe when your arms are too full of other things. It's what the rules said anyway, right? Before you got to rule four about holding hope carefully, you had one and two and three, about belief and pursuit of it, about clear determination. *Know what you desire. . . . Then go.*

At that moment, Clive Weaver came outside. He had rediscovered his robe, thankfully. He shuffled down his walkway and looked down the street as if it were two o'clock when the mail came. He was out there more and more often with us, the people who thought too much during the time when other people rested.

"Evening," Clive Weaver said.

Hayden gave Clive a two-fingered salute in response.

"I believe I've lost Corky," Clive Weaver said. Corky, Clive Weaver's little black-and-white dog, was actually sitting upright on their porch step then, smiling. He never usually got to stay up this late.

"Behind you," Hayden said.

"Ah," Clive Weaver said, as if this were the answer to a great mystery. He looked at Corky for a while. "It's over faster than you think," he said finally.

You could hear crickets off in the blackness somewhere and the sound of a distant airplane. As we watched Clive Weaver wander back across his grass in his tired robe on that June night, I suddenly wasn't so sure about what Hayden had said, about wanting things for yourself. Hayden didn't look so sure either, anymore. Clive Weaver wanted things badly.

"As you were saying . . . ," I whispered.

"Shit, man." Hayden sighed.

I looked up at our sky, stars *twinkling, twinkling, twinkling* their forever-ness. "If this were the movies, this would be the time a shooting star would streak across the sky," I said. "To make us think something great was heading our way after all."

Hayden looked up too. The sky just kept looking the same as it had before, and both of us caught the moment of hilarity at the same time. We both laughed, oh God, we laughed so hard, trying to be quiet, holding our stomachs. There was no shooting star, of course, not a one, and Hayden was bent over laughing and saying, "Fuck. Fuck," and I was gasping for air. Then he mimed looking up again, and so did I, and of course there was still no dramatic cinematic moment, only regular life, and it was hysterical all over again.

I was bent over and my arms were crossed against my stomach, and I wasn't even looking at him because I was laughing so hard and trying to be quiet at the same time. And that's when I felt each of his hands behind me on my shoulders, giving them a shake, the way a father might shake the shoulders of a kid he was joking with. But then he turned me around and I turned to him and we hugged there. We hugged for a moment and then he released me and he was still grinning.

I had felt his back under the flat of my hands, his soft shirt, my cheek ever so briefly against him, there where his heart was. He had held me, and I had held him, too. God, it felt

"I'm not disappointed," I said. "I move on quickly. I'm not one of those people who really cares about stuff like that." Actually, I was happy. Really happy. I had that excited feeling, the one you used to get when you were a kid and it was Halloween night. I'd even offered to mow the front lawn so I wouldn't miss a thing. I couldn't wait to see Goth Girl and Bomb Boy all dressed up and heading out to dinner. I'd seen Kevin Frink at school and offered him the money I'd promised for dinner. He'd refused it. He wanted to take Fiona to the Harbor Tower instead, the nicest restaurant on the island. He had a hickey on his neck, just above the collar of his T-shirt.

"Well, you can hang out with us if you're feeling depressed," Juliet said.

We all sat on Mom's checkered tablecloth laid out on the grass and ate dinner on paper plates. I wolfed down my hamburger and the potato salad that Mom made and hurried out of there. I changed into my old ragged shorts that used to belong to Juliet and this T-shirt I'd had for a billion years, hauled the push mower out from the garage. I hooked up the grass catcher and looked for a second garden glove just to pass the time.

When I heard Kevin Frink's Volkswagen come down the street, I realized how anxious I was. Both my stomach and heart were doing the tango surges of nerves. Kevin parked and got out in his big black tux, his hair smoothed back on his large head. Shiny shoes. He must have lost weight in the last few weeks—his usual large, bulky overhang seemed contained or at least well hidden. I bet he even smelled like cologne. He carried a small gold corsage box in one hand.

"Kevin!" I shouted.

I put both thumbs in the air, shook them in victory. Kevin

did a very non-Kevin thing. He spun a full circle on the bottoms of those shoes, showing me the whole look. I wanted to applaud. I wanted to take pictures and show them to all the relatives.

"Fantastic!" I said instead. "You look great!"

He grinned. "I'm not dancing, so you know," he said, and then he walked up to Fiona's door. He rang the bell, and Mrs. Saint George answered. She wasn't smiling. She shook his hand and let him in and the door closed.

I cut six or seven stripes of lawn, stopping the *flick-flick-flick* of blades often. Our yard was small, and I needed to do slow-motion mowing or the task wouldn't last. Finally, the Saint George door opened, and there was the sound of conversation. Kevin said something that made Mr. Saint George laugh a hearty obligation laugh. Fiona's mother chirped a few words in response.

And then there was Fiona herself. I actually gasped. She wasn't wearing the fluffy pink number she'd drawn in chalk, but a sleek apricot dress that clung tightly to a body she'd never before shown underneath her usual sweatshirts and jeans. Her raven black hair was swooped up, and her bangs were sprayed across to show her deep eyes rimmed with her dark eyeliner. She was a little uncertain in her shoes, holding a bit of Kevin Frink's tux sleeve to steady herself. But she looked beautiful. Goth Girl looked *beautiful*.

I went back to my lawn mowing as they drove away. I finished in two seconds. When I was done, I sat down on the short, scratchy grass and looped my arms around my legs. I felt so satisfied. The night was sweet summer light. When Jeffrey and Jacob came out to play, when Jacob laid down on the sidewalk with his legs straight together and his arms flung out, and said, "Look, I'm Jesus on the sidewalk," I actually smiled.

For a good while after Kevin Frink and Fiona Saint George drove off together in that car, I was sucked right into the whole idea that said the Prom was the end of that story, same as the Wedding was the end of the story. But there was something big and long and important called After the Prom and After the Wedding which was basically all the time that came beyond dancing in uncomfortable shoes. Of course, sometimes *after* isn't long and important. Sometimes it's brief and shattering. *After* is fate's own personal cinematic moment, the one when you're sure the movie is over and the bad guy is dead and gone forever but when he pops back up instead, reaching for the knife on the floor beside him.

School got out, and summer eased all the way in, and I worked most days helping at Quill Stationers. On my days off, I continued to make progress on the Clive Weaver project, to read psychology books about how to fall out of love. I listened to Jeffrey and Jacob ride their bikes over wooden ramps, fight and make up, ride their bikes again. I watched Juliet grow round, watched her hand move to her stomach when she'd feel the fluttery butterfly movements of the baby that we could finally feel too, if we held still long enough.

The construction workers over the back fence kept working on the house behind us. The songs from their radio—*You can't always get what you wa-aant . . .*—were our summer sound track, along with the noise of lumber dropping and hammers against nails and the *keshank* of a shovel into gravel. There was the perpetual smell of newly sawed wood. Joe, the miserable ice-cream man, made increasingly insistent loops around our streets now that school was out. Juliet and Hayden went to see Dr. Crosby, and we got our first real picture of Jitter, a black-and-white sono-gram image—a tiny curled-up body with small fists, an image that looked more like an incoming weather system than a baby.

And then things were different.

I heard Mr. and Mrs. Martinelli's garage door lift on its squeaky hinges as I sat outside on the lawn waiting for Juliet. Soon, Mr. Martinelli was bringing out card tables, unfolding their thin metal legs.

"Lemonade stand?" I joked, but he didn't hear me. He was focused. Mrs. Martinelli called out something to him from the garage, and then they began hauling out armloads of stuff to the now upright tables—crystal dishes and old suits, blocky clock radios and record albums, a TV that looked heavy enough to anchor a ship.

They both disappeared inside the house, and then there they were again, struggling to get a large wood bed frame out the door. Mr. Martinelli was sweating.

"Slow down, sugar," Mrs. Martinelli said. She could bite when she wanted to—I'd heard her snip and nag at him over the years, in ways that made you feel bad for him. But her words were patient this time. Cheerful, even.

"Do you need some help?" I called. I could just see them both having a heart attack right there. I tried to remember how many times you were supposed to compress the chest and how many times you were supposed to blow into the mouth. "Just a sec." I jogged over.

Mr. Martinelli puffed air out of his cheeks. "It's not that heavy, sweet pea," he said to Mrs. Martinelli. But he looked relieved to set it down.

"You always were my muscle man," she said to him.

I lifted Mrs. Martinelli's end easily. "What is it?" I asked.

"Our old water bed," Mr. Martinelli said. "Set it by the curb. This oughta draw the folks in."

"What are you guys doing?"

"A little housecleaning," Mrs. Martinelli said.

"A little housecleaning," Mr. Martinelli repeated.

They looked guilty. I couldn't figure out why, unless they'd just held up a Saint Vincent de Paul truck. I poked around a Tupperware container of old-guy tools and a dish of necklaces. A stained-glass lamp, a fondue pot, macramé plant hangers, saucepans . . .

"Hey, you guys had this in there." I held it up. I think it was a picture of their grandkids. One of those creepy, stiff images of two kids sitting at an angle against a blue photographer's backdrop. The little boy wore a plaid tie and a navy blue vest; the little girl had a matching plaid dress. "Probably don't want to get rid of this, right?"

"Someone might want the frame," Mrs. Martinelli said.

"Two bucks," Mr. Martinelli offered.

"No thanks," I said. We had our own relatives.

"Cute kids, though," Mrs. Martinelli said. She hunched over a table with a fat marker in her plump hand.

I set the picture down. I was poking through a dish of groovy old-lady earrings when I heard the slow squeal of bike brakes behind me.

"Hey."

I turned. "Oh!" Straddling his bike, right there, was Jesse Waters, Shy, on my own street on my own Saturday morning. Nicole was going to be pissed. He shook his dark hair out of his eyes.

"I was just riding around," he said. "Okay, that's probably pretty obvious, since, you know, I'm on a bike. . . ."

I did a mental inventory of how stupid I might possibly look. Since Juliet and I were about to take the ferry into the city, I had reasonable clothes on. Makeup, check; teeth brushed, okay; all was pretty well. "Do you live around here?"

"Not too far," he said. "I saw the signs." He pointed. I looked in the direction of his finger. Whoa—I don't know how I'd missed them. Signs were on the telephone poles and streetlights, going down the street and heading around the corner. GARAGE SALE! EVERYTHING MUST GO! Red paint on pieces of thin cardboard.

"Those look like cereal boxes," I said.

"Yep," he said. "One fell off a telephone pole two streets over. Frosted Mini-Wheats."

"Mr. Martinelli's favorite," Mrs. Martinelli said. She was listening in.

"What?" Mr. Martinelli shouted from the garage.

"FROSTED MINI-WHEATS!" she shouted back to him.

"I thought maybe you were the garage sale," Jesse said. He got off his bike, laid it down.

"Nope. Not us. We're sale-less." I gestured over to our driveway, which was empty except for Hayden's truck and the Neilsons' cat lurking around its tires.

But I'd caught what he'd just said. He knew where I lived. I knew what that meant. I was only pretending not to know what that meant to buy myself a little time to figure out how I felt about what that meant. And how *did* I feel? Well, I wasn't so sure, but I picked up one of Mr. Martinelli's cuff links anyway. It was very large and silver and had a fat chunk of turquoise in its center.

"This would be nice for you," I said.

"If there was only a tie clip to match." He grinned.

"Two dollars," Mr. Martinelli said. He emerged from the garage carrying a box labeled CHRISTMAS DECORATIONS.

"Oh, let him have it, sugar. He's Scarlet's friend."

"Whatever you say, sweet pea."

"That's the man I married."

I rolled my eyes in Jesse's direction. I'd never seen them so lovey dovey before. Usually, they were either ignoring each other or doing the functional back and forths that I guessed were what was left after a long life together. I wondered what happened. Maybe you just woke up one day from fifty years of TV watching and gutter cleaning and table clearing and realized that you had to have a garage sale and that you were in love. Maybe there was hope for Juliet and Hayden. Someday when they both had white, poofy dandelion hair, Juliet would look at Hayden and realize the depths of her true feelings.

"Those will look very handsome," Mrs. Martinelli said to Jesse. "We got those on our trip to Arizona." She searched around for the pen cap.

"Under your chair," I said. I smiled, shrugged, and handed Jesse the single cuff link. Who knew where the other one was.

"Thank you very much," Jesse said to Mrs. Martinelli.

"Look through the record albums. I think we have Bay City Rollers."

Jesse bent his head to attach the cuff link to the pocket of his denim jacket, next to the silver snap.

"That will look very handsome," I whispered. He grinned.

He looked up and we had an awkward moment, where you're both in that vacant space where there are a thousand things to say and nothing to say.

"I should go."

"I'm heading out to—" Our door opened then, and Zeus came charging out, and Hayden yelled, "Catch him!" and I lunged, but Jesse caught his collar with one quick hand.

"God! Sorry guys. Prison break," Hayden said. One thing about Zeus, he completely broke training when the front door opened. You had to walk out sideways, or he'd shove through and run for it. He was fearless about going after what he wanted. Who cared about streets and cars and the chance of death when there was all that open, endless space full of high speed possibilities?

"Zeus . . . ," I explained to Jesse, who seemed surprised to be suddenly grasping a dog, let alone one crazy with near-escape joy.

"My fault!" Juliet said from the doorway. Hayden retrieved Zeus, and they exchanged hands on that collar. I saw them standing together, and I had an unfair moment, a comparison moment, when I saw Hayden's sure strength, his firm grip, and Jesse's uncertain one, Hayden's known pieces and Jesse's unknown ones, the way Hayden filled the space in my mind like few people ever had, maybe no one.

"Thanks for the catch," Hayden said, and smiled at Jesse.

"I'd better be going," Jesse said. He got on his bike. I felt guilty, like maybe he could read my thoughts. But maybe not, because he just smiled and said, "See ya," and shoved off on his bike, that cuff link still shiny on his jacket.

"Who was that?" Hayden said, and knocked me with his elbow.

"Someone from school," I said.

"I don't know, Scarlet Ellis. I got to wonder what's going on here. It looks like a *someone* from school."

"No, not at all."

Deb Caletti

It sounded harsh and definite. I didn't want him saying that. I wished he hadn't seen us. It was wrong to think like I was thinking; stupid, I knew that, but there it was. The nighttime talks meant something to me. I was loyal, even if Juliet wasn't.

Mrs. Martinelli held up a large ancient drill and waved it my way. "Your young man didn't want any of these nice tools?" she said.

I wouldn't have agreed to go shopping in the city with Juliet if I'd known Hayden was coming along. But there he was with his leather key chain dangling from his finger, heading for the truck, leaning in to clear the seat so there was room for both of us. I didn't want to be with them all day; I knew that much. His devotion made me feel lonely when I was with them, in a way it didn't when it was just the two of us. I didn't understand why people were always so devoted to Juliet. Instead of plain old love, she got absolute dedication; and instead of regular human anger, she got complete forgiveness. She gave so little back, too. Why was it that when we got crumbs from people who usually gave nothing, we were thrilled? A person's everyday abundant generosity, though—it could become ordinary and meaningless, the way you stop smelling perfume after the first few thrilling sniffs. A crumb from someone who gave nothing was a million dollars and a crumb from someone who *always* gave was just a crumb.

"I'm going off on my own when we get there, okay?" I said to Juliet in the ferry bathroom from my side of the stall. "I've got a lot of places I want to go, and it'll be faster."

"No problem," she said.

We each came out, stood at the sink, and washed our hands. "You want to come when we pick out the crib?"

"I thought you were shopping for clothes."

"That, too. But Mom gave us money to get a crib." She leaned toward the mirror, opened her purse, and took out her brush, combed her hair shiny and straight. I thought of them walking hand in hand in the baby aisles, a peachy glow around them like some sort of heaven-moment in the movies.

"The slats of the crib have to be really close together. If you can fit a soda can through, they're too far apart. The baby's head can get stuck."

"Thanks, Scarlet," she said, as if she already knew this even though I was sure she didn't. She studied her face for a moment, then closed her purse again and turned away from her image. "Well, I guess I'm still me, only pregnant."

I played a successful game of Dodge Juliet and Hayden in the mall, seeing them only once, at one of the iron tables in front of Joy Juice, sharing a large drink from one straw. We met up afterward and got back into the car, Juliet in the middle and me on the outside edge by the window, where it seemed I had always been and might always be. We'd timed the ferry just right so we didn't even have to wait in line. Juliet and Hayden both seemed happy. They held hands across the seat of Mom's car, and Hayden would bring their joined hands to his mouth for an occasional kiss. They were in love, and that was good. When you cared about someone, you wanted for them most what they themselves wanted, I reminded myself again. Juliet was calm and light and joking, and Hayden's eyes glowed with warmth and hope for all their future days together. Yeah, it all made me a little sick.

On the ferry, we sat on two bench seats across from each other. One of Juliet's legs was flung over Hayden's knee, and he rubbed it slowly. Juliet said something like, *Did you hear that airplane?* which made them both crack up in the annoying way of couples with their stupid inside jokes. I wanted them to be happy; it's what I hoped for most. I would have done anything for her to love him properly, I would. For him and for Jitter and for her, too. But the real truth was, you could want one thing and have a secret wish for its opposite.

I watched the rushing waters of the Sound outside my large window, but the scenery was making me think too much, like scenery does. So I put my back against the window instead and played the game I rarely but sometimes played in public places where there were lots of people, the Maybe My Father Is Here and I Don't Know It game. It wasn't some depressed, obsessed activity or anything—the game was more just curiosity and boredom, the way you looked for out of state license plates on long car rides. Maybe that was him in the suit and long overcoat, reading the fat Robert Ludlum book. Maybe that was him with two sticky kids and a wife with hair down to her waist like a prairie woman.

I was amusing myself in this manner, searching for men with Juliet's blond hair, when their laughter abruptly stopped. It was one of those times when you could feel the change in the room come suddenly. I looked over. Juliet's leg was off Hayden's; she was staring just behind me, her face pale, and he was looking at her and leaning forward a little, trying to understand.

"Juliet?"

I looked over my shoulder, and I saw them. Buddy Wilkes— and you'd never believe it, never—sweet, delicate Elizabeth Everly, walking down the aisle past the bench seats. He was saying something to her, but she wasn't listening, mocking him, maybe; it was something that caused her to shrug her shoulders in a way that meant his words were completely unimportant to her. And then it happened, as we all watched. Me and Juliet, but Hayden, too. Me and Juliet and Hayden and a previously limp, bored couple in my line of vision, and an old man standing by the candy machine, and a single woman drinking coffee and doing a crossword puzzle. We all saw, as Buddy, in his jeans and T-shirt with a dress shirt loose over it, grabbed the top of Elizabeth Everly's arms and practically shoved her against the door marked LIFE PRESERVERS. He thrust his face onto hers and moved his hands to her hair and kissed her so hard and long that the lady with the coffee stopped her cup just shy of her mouth.

Juliet made a small sound behind me. Buddy let Elizabeth Everly go. Her hair was stuck up in a funny way and her cheeks were red, but she looked beautiful. They'd obviously had practice at that. But maybe what was more shocking than the kiss itself was the way Buddy looked afterward, the way he stared into her eyes as softly as the kiss was hard. The thing was, Buddy Wilkes was in love with her. Really *in love*. You could see it. It was so plainly there, plain as Elizabeth's own hands reaching for a book to shelve at the Parrish Island Library.

They started walking forward again, and the woman went back to her crossword puzzle, and the old man dropped his coins into the snack machine slot, and the couple went back to ignoring each other. You could smell Elizabeth Everly's perfume as she walked past, light and clean, fresh enough to drown out the smell of cigarettes on Buddy's clothes. He was walking right past us, right past, maybe two feet from Juliet at the most.

"Buddy!" Juliet said. It sounded fake-light, fake-casual, the appropriate start to fake small talk, the kind that's actually heavy with history and meaning—*How've you been, fine, great to see you again*—but that didn't happen. If he even heard his name, he gave no indication. Buddy just walked right past, not even looking our way. Not even looking Juliet's way. He didn't even notice her. His name just hung there in the air until you weren't even sure Juliet had ever spoken it.

When we arrived home, Ally Pete-Robbins was heading up her driveway carrying one of the Martinellis' former Bundt pans, and that motorcyclist I'd seen on the street before was thumbing through their record albums and reading the back of one called *Boots: Nancy Sinatra*. Mr. Martinelli was snapping his fingers and dancing a little to some nonexistent music. Mrs. Martinelli was giving the hard sell to two middle-age women holding a pair of Christmas sweaters and a Joni Mitchell album.

Inside our own house, on the kitchen counter, was the Martinellis' old VCR and collection of videos in a box marked $2.00. Mom was always several entertainment devices behind the times. She was proud that her car had a tape player.

"Well?" Mom shouted down the stairs. You could tell she was having material-object thrill—a new VCR and a crib we must have bought, but Juliet was heading downstairs with her mood, not wanting to talk to anyone. Hayden followed her. I felt sorry for him, and for Mom, too. I felt sorry for everyone who'd ever been hurt by self-involved people.

Mom thumped down the stairs happily. She stopped when she saw me. Zeus sat down nearby, as if he was sticking with us.

"We saw Buddy on the ferry," I said.

Mom said nothing.

"With someone. *Really* with someone."

She sighed. "I don't get it," she said. "I don't get him. I never did."

I was wrong about Hayden following Juliet downstairs, because suddenly he was there too. "She says he makes her feel safe," he said.

We both looked over at him. I was sorry he'd heard us. His face was grim. "He makes her feel safe because he's badder than anything bad."

That night, I heard the doorknob handle turn. I wondered if I might hear the engine of Hayden's truck start up and leave forever, if I might hear it that night or another night. Instead, I only heard the frustrated, unsuccessful flicking of that lighter again.

That night, we didn't speak. I just tossed him the pack of matches and he caught them against his chest, as the pink light of morning showed over the horizon.

Chapter Eighteen

The note had three lines.

Steadiness and permanence, Juliet.
Those are the strongest words I know.
I will not leave you like you've been left before.

This, Hayden had wrong, I was sure. Who had ever left Juliet?
No one left Juliet.

The next morning, I caught Hayden just standing and staring at Jitter's black-and-white image stuck to the front of our refrigerator.

"Still trying to figure out if it's a boy or girl?" I said.

I'd startled him. He jumped. When I saw his face, it looked unbearably sad.

"Scarlet . . . ," he said. He held my eyes. He seemed to want to tell me something. I waited. He would speak, and I would be there to catch his words, whatever they were.

"Are you all right, Hayden?"

He shook his head.

"Hayden?"

"Shit, Scarlet," he said. "Shit." And that was all. Then he opened the refrigerator and took out the orange juice, as if that had been his plan all along.

During the summer, there was only one thing worse than going to the place where everyone from my school hung out, and that was going to the place where everyone from my school hung out while I was wearing a bathing suit. Summer was supposed to be a reprieve from school, I thought, not a two-month warmer version of it. Every time Nicole had asked me to go to the Parrish Island Community Pool, I had a lie handy. I told her I was working much more than I was, or that I was babysitting Jeffrey and Jacob, which you couldn't pay me enough to do. But it was becoming a lie traffic jam, and so I knew I had to agree, just once. Then I'd be free to start up the lies again. This was a clunky but workable system. You throw in a yes, and that allows you about five more no's in the future.

A bikini requires you to feel comfortable with a bikini, but a one-piece looks like what your mother would wear, so I compromised and wore my tank suit that's technically two pieces but looks like one. Even my bathing suit walked a line of dishonesty. When I went downstairs that morning, Juliet clicked the hang-up button of the phone fast and started one of those cover-up conversations that are the verbal equivalent of the dog kicking dirt backward after he's just pooped in the yard.

"Pool or the beach?" she asked. "Pool's so much nicer. No sand." Her hands were moving nervously, setting the phone exactly straight against the counter edge.

My stomach dropped. It was the fourth or fifth time in the four days since the ferry ride that I'd caught her with that phone in her hand, or against her ear, listening to something as if her life depended on it. I knew what was happening and where this was headed. Sometimes you just know before all the facts are in, the way rats are supposed to know to flee a ship before it's about to go down. I would never understand her and Buddy Wilkes. Never. "Who were you calling?" I asked.

"I wasn't calling anyone," she said.

"That's why you're holding the *tele*phone," I said.

She put her hand on her stomach then. It made me think of the cemetery, when Buddy Wilkes had put his hand there too. I hadn't wanted to think what I'd been thinking. I counted back the number of months since Juliet had visited us last. I remembered a weekend at home, a night she'd gone out with friends and didn't return until 2:00 a.m. No, it couldn't be. It just couldn't.

"My *hus*band. If it's any of your business."

"Will Quail's got a phone on his boat?"

"Cell phone, idiot," she said. "Hayden does have one, even if you've never seen it. He uses it for emergencies."

I remembered this from my psychology books. How to tell if someone was lying. They used too many details. They covered up their nose or mouth with their hand, which Juliet did just then.

"You're pretty mature for someone who's about to be a *mother*," I said. I slammed my way past her, grabbed some drinks out of the fridge, and left out the front door. I knew it was a hypocritical thing for a liar to feel, but I hated being lied to.

Every morning, I took Mom to work in case we needed her car, so I headed for her Honda Accord parked at the curb and that's when I saw Mr. Martinelli with the black-and-red FOR SALE sign gripped in his teeth, his hands holding two fat strips of silver duct tape. He had on jeans and a Hawaiian shirt. I don't think I'd ever seen Mr. Martinelli in something so festive before. He usually wore tan button-up sweaters and serious janitor-green pants. Maybe he had found it in the back of his closet during all the cleaning.

The set of silver stairs that allowed you to reach the door of the Pleasure Way was already set out, looking like a step-right-up welcome to future buyers. Mr. Martinelli took the sign out of his mouth and slapped it onto the side of the RV.

"You're selling it?" I shouted.

"It's a beauty," he said. But there wasn't anything like regret in his voice. In fact, it was as happy as a dozen cupcakes.

"I thought you were going to go to Montana this summer to see your daughter."

"Who wants to sit in that tank for twenty-two hours?" he said.

"I thought you guys loved the Pleasure Way," I said. Something was going on there. If I saw a sign on their house next, I'd really get worried.

"Love," he scoffed. "Maybe you want to take a tour? You know someone who might like all the comfort of home on wheels? Leather seats? It has more storage than you'd think." He reached over the front tire, where I knew he kept the key. He waved it around at me enticingly.

"I'll spread the word," I said.

"I'm going to get her shined up," he said. He patted her side. *Bamp bamp.*

I could hear the far-off cheerful, tinkling music of Joe the ice-cream man, at an hour when no one would yet want ice cream. When he passed, he looked morose and hungover and had a cigarette dangling from one corner of his mouth.

"Good luck," I said to Mr. Martinelli. I got into Mom's car. When I drove down the street, I saw Kevin Frink in his Volkswagen, a few doors down from the Saint George house. In the small dome of the car, I saw him lean forward and blow out a lit match. I felt a strange but strong uneasiness, a wrongness that seemed silly and paranoid. Information from our most important guide ever, our instinct, too often bumped up against our favorite belief that everything was fine and under control. I headed to Nicole's house. I put every warning sign of all that might happen right into the garbage can of my self-deceptive brain. Then, I turned the music up.

Nicole's mom, Theresa, dressed in more fashionable clothes than Nicole did. Short skirts, tight layered tops. You could tell she wanted to be seen as "the cool parent"—at least, cooler than Nicole's dad, whom she called Jack even though his name was Dennis. Jack, as in jackass. Nicole lived in dual-personality divorce land, where at one house (Theresa's) there was every junk food possible and lax rules and "fun," and in the other (Dennis's) there were rules for everything and an insistence on a "healthy" lifestyle, which meant you were a shameful, weak loser if a Dorito passed your lips. If Theresa wanted to be cool, Dennis wanted to be . . . a jackass.

"You girls going to hang out by the pool and check out all the cute guys?" Theresa asked. This was another box to check on Theresa's internal cool list—talking about "guys" and more specifically "cute guys." Maybe she thought this was a way to be one of us, even though it didn't work for me. I never really understood the general discussion of "cute guys" as if they were all interchangeable, as if their cuteness mattered more than any other quality. She didn't ask us if we were going to the pool to check out nice guys, or smart guys, or funny guys. It made you understand how she had ended up with "Jack," who looked a little like he had stepped out of a men's magazine, but whom you really didn't want to spend more than five minutes with. It made you also understand the shoes she herself had on—high narrow heels that looked good but that probably killed her feet.

"I only have eyes for one," Nicole said. "The sole and only reason I've spent half my summer at the pool when I don't even like to swim that much."

"You've given up on Jesse?" I asked. I was surprised and maybe a little relieved. I couldn't see him hanging out at the pool. If he didn't even want to stay in our cafeteria, he wasn't likely to be found straddling some deck chair next to Evan O'Donnell and Jake Tafferty as they flung their wet heads around trying to splash girls.

"Give up? Giving up is for pansies. At least that's what my father says."

Theresa snorted the snort she gave whenever Nicole's dad was mentioned. It was like in the psychology books, the way Pavlov's dogs salivated whenever they heard the bell ring. Theresa fingered one of the many stacks of legal documents on their dining room table, as if her fingers couldn't bear to be away from the conflict for long.

"Jesse doesn't go to the pool," I said. I was guessing.

"Doesn't *go*. He works there. He's a lifeguard."

Deb Caletti

"A lifeguard?" *A lifeguard?* I had one of those moments where your thoughts seem to freeze and race at the same time. A lifeguard. A rescuer of things maybe. Maybe even someone who apologized to dogs.

I didn't have time to think about this, because Jasmine arrived then, and after a flurry of lunch packing and towel finding, we all got into Mom's car and drove to the pool. It was pretty much what I pictured. Leo Snyder and Quentin York wrestled each other in the water and Caroline Dale sat on Renny Williams's lap on a deck chair and Melissa DeWhitt was putting lotion on Casey Chow's back as she held up her long hair with one hand. High school reunion, mixed with little kids in droopy bathing suits holding their mothers' hands and the slapping sounds of bare feet on wet cement. We found a spot to lay out our towels on a grassy slope near the shallow end, and I looked up at the lifeguard chair. No Jesse, only a senior girl who was in band whose name I didn't remember. She looked bored in her red bathing suit.

"He starts work at noon on Wednesdays," Nicole said. She'd been watching my eyes. Her words were sure and proprietary. She might as well have been some wife ordering for her husband in a restaurant. We watched two little girls on the pool steps play with their Barbies in miniature bathing suits and we had one of those conversations when no one was really listening to anyone else. Jasmine kept checking her phone for Christine Fhara (cello, second chair) to call, and Nicole kept watching that lifeguard chair, and I realized Jasmine and I were just props—we'd be the reason Nicole laughed loudly and shook her hair around and gestured dramatically. I guess it was just too hard to get someone to notice you when you were quiet and sitting alone and not performing in your own personal play.

Twelve o'clock came and went and Nicole "went to the bathroom" and came back too soon, meaning she'd just taken a lap to look for Jesse. I was feeling irritated, and things didn't improve when, a few moments later, Reilly Ogden showed up. He came over and stood in front of us while we sat, and this provided us with a clear and terrifying view of his mostly naked body. White, soft baby flesh; tight bathing suit with tropical flowers stretched over the cheerless triangle that was his pelvis. Just above eye level was the knuckle of flesh that was his outie belly button.

"I knew I'd find you here," he said. He had his glasses off, which gave his face an unfamiliar and empty look.

"You forgot your glasses," Jasmine said. She'd noticed too.

"Contacts," he said. This was not the movies, though, where Reilly would have gone through some transformation now that he was minus his eyewear. Get contacts, add some new hairstyle, and he's a stud in disguise—nope. Like most people, Reilly would always and forever be mostly just himself. In fact, the absence of glasses made things worse. There was less between him and you. His eyes made a direct hit, and it was somehow unsettling.

"Hello, Reilly," I said. Once again, I hoped my tone would say all it needed to. It was a disappointed hello. An oh-there-you-are-again-too-bad hello.

"I assume you've been thinking about my proposal?" He scratched the back of his calf, where there was the red lump of a mosquito bite.

"Proposal?" I didn't have a clue what he was talking about.

"Three months? Trial period? Never mind." He sighed, and then looked around and back to us again. "I've taken up photography."

"That's great, Reilly."

"I thought we could go out on a shoot together."

"I've given up photography," I said.

"I've just spent three hundred dollars on photographic equipment," he said.

"Good for you. Wow, look at the time," Nicole said. "Twelve thirty, time for you to move on."

"It's a free country. This is a public place."

"Personal conversation," Nicole said. "Vamoose."

"Summer becomes you," he said to me, and then walked off, his towel under his arm. He arranged himself on a stretch of bare cement at the other end of the pool not far from the diving board, a sure place to get continually splashed by anyone jumping in or kicked by fast-passing legs excited from the awesome dive they'd just made.

"We'll see him on the news someday. Fucking psycho," Jasmine said.

She was likely right, but watching him made me feel bad inside, as if I were somehow responsible for his bad luck in life, or at least responsible for changing it. We ate lunch, although the bad feeling stayed with me. Nicole lost her buzz of energy as the afternoon went on with no Jesse in sight. I wondered why we were still there, and I guess so did she.

"He must be sick or something," she said.

"I've got to meet Christine in an hour," Jasmine said.

We gathered up our towels and our lunch garbage and headed back to the parking lot. Nicole grabbed my arm.

"There he is. Look. In the ticket booth. Oh God oh God oh God. Well, that explains things."

I looked over, and sure enough, Jesse Waters was handing orange entrance tickets to a father and his two boys, one who was jumping around and holding his crotch like he had to pee. Jesse looked up and noticed us, smiled, and I gave a little wave. There—I hoped the trip was worth it to Nicole now.

"God," she breathed. "He's so cute."

I jingled my keys. Her comment annoyed me. She made him one-dimensional, and he wasn't. "Stalking time now officially over," I said.

"Ow, ow, ow," Jasmine said. She hadn't put her sandals back on. The asphalt was hot. "Jesus Christ, unlock the door already."

"Hey! Scarlet!" Jesse emerged from the ticket area behind us. He wore baggy red swim shorts and a towel around his neck. He gestured me over. I didn't even think. Or maybe that's a lie too. I did think, but I went anyway.

"Just a sec, guys," I said.

I trotted over to see Jesse. I was glad to see him. Maybe not in the two hundred percent way that I was glad to see Hayden, every day, every time, from the moment I'd see him making toast, to hearing his car drive up. It was more of a ninety-five percent happy, which was a pretty good happy anyway.

"Been to any garage sales lately?" I said.

"Every time I see a sign, I stop. Just hoping for a turquoise tie clip to match my cuff link."

"That would be so handsome," I said.

"Maybe you might want to come with me sometime. Look through people's old junk. Rusty garden stuff, playpens . . ."

"Creepy neckties," I said, but didn't answer him about going. He held the ends of his towel and looked at me with an open smile. I didn't want to give him the wrong idea, though. I could already feel Nicole's anger crawling under my skin from back where she stood or maybe that was my own guilt. And there was

Hayden, too. "Why is it that garage sales always make me want to wash my hands?" I said instead.

"I went to a Goodwill once and breathed through my mouth the whole time," he said.

I laughed. "A lifeguard," I said.

"I hate to see little kids drown. Ruins my day."

"I've got to go." I hooked my thumb in the direction of Nicole and Jasmine.

"See ya," he said. Two kids waited in line and were looking his way, but he still seemed to be waiting too. His question hung there between us.

"Back to work," I said.

"All right, then." He tugged on the ends of his towel twice and turned back. I rejoined Nicole and Jasmine. The air between Nicole and me was thick and jagged. Jasmine had put on her sandals, but the straps hung free.

"He speaks," Nicole said.

"An actual real person," I said. Maybe that was hard for her to understand.

We heard the gunning of an engine, the supposedly impressive rev of an engine as it sat still. Jasmine scanned the parking lot.

"Guess who?" she said. I saw the car. A BMW. I couldn't read the bumper sticker from where we stood, but I could see it. I knew what it said, anyway. I'M PROUD OF MY 4.0 STUDENT. Reilly Ogden. His parents' car.

"Oh God."

"He's telling you how big his engine is," Jasmine said.

I socked her arm. "I'm all his now."

Nicole didn't join in. She was silent the whole way home.

When we got to her house, she opened the car door. She turned and spit the words.

"I thought you were my friend."

She flung the door closed, and it slammed so hard that a pen on the tray of Mom's dashboard jumped out and hid on the floor. I felt that slam way down inside. Helping people, being good to them, was who I most was. It felt completely and utterly wrong to be anything but that person.

But behind the bad feeling sat something else. Anger. The part of me that looked after myself, only myself—it wanted to be heard. I could talk to whoever I wanted, be friends with whomever I wanted, even love whomever I wanted.

Right then, I realized that other people's "needs" were sometimes only big nasty demands, in a soft disguise. It was no different from those deer hunters in their camouflage outfits. *I'm a nice peaceful tree. Ignore the gun on my back.*

I thought it had worked for me, looking after everyone else. I thought it had. But it didn't. Not anymore.

"Don't ask me," Jasmine said.

Chapter Nineteen

They just can't fucking *do* this," Kevin Frink said. His big face was red. His eyes were squinched. He looked like he might cry.

"Jeez, Kevin. What?" Kevin Frink had rung our doorbell again and again. It was lucky I was the only one home. Zeus would have gone nuts.

"They want her to go to Yale. Those freaky parents of hers. She doesn't even want to go to Yale. She wants to go to art school. Here."

"She got into Yale?" I didn't even think Fiona Saint George ever went to class.

"She's brilliant, you hear me? *Brill*-iant. Smart enough to fucking know what she fucking wants to do with her life." It was a hot day, the kind of steamy hot that made it hard to breathe and he was sweating. Big dark rings under the arms of his T-shirt, drops gathering on his forehead.

"God, I'm sorry," I said. "She's not going to go, is she?"

He let out a sound. An exhale of protest that might have been the start of a sob. "Does she have a *choice?* Do you know what those people said? They won't help with her education at all unless she goes there. They used the biggest lie of all time. *For your own good.* WHOSE good? THEIR good. Not HER good. What kind of parents do that, huh? Tell me that." I'd always had the idea that Kevin's mother ignored him altogether. Certainly, she wasn't the parental role model who was part of his activities and interests, supporting his goals of blowing things up. Kevin hit the door frame with his palm. I should have invited him in, but something told me that was a bad idea. I didn't think we had enough room for that much anger in our house.

"Kevin," I said. "It's okay."

"There's nothing okay about this. Nothing."

"She'll work it out with them." I'm not sure if I believed that, but it seemed like the right thing to say.

"You know she can't do that on her own. You know how alone she is. She needs me to help her."

I remembered the dark hair over Fiona Saint George's eyes, the chalk paintings of vampire parents. Maybe he had a point. I had thought she needed that help too; it was dark in vampire land. "Yale," I said. I still couldn't believe she got in.

"*Would you stop going on about fucking Yale!*" he hissed.

It was the kind of anger that makes you shut up, fast. I felt an eerie, electric shiver go through me. I switched over to some voice I imagined that FBI agents used with kidnappers.

"It's okay, Kevin. Everything's going to be okay."

He looked at me, and right then as he stood sweating on our front porch, I saw the real him down in there. I saw way, way past that big head and angry eyes and tight fists. He seemed very small and scared. The small and scared that you are when you finally decide to hand your love over only to find out exactly how unsafe that leaves you.

"You're okay," I said.

I wasn't so sure about that at all.

I saw the letter because the mailbox was left open. When I saw it there and saw whom it was addressed to, I felt it was my duty to look further. Call it a fateful intervention by me, caught before the mailman arrived to pick it up and send it on its wrong way. I ripped it open on the spot.

Buddy—
Why are you ignoring me? Why did you change your e-mail address? I thought we promised never to do that, no matter what.
Buddy, why?

Anger lit in me as quickly as fire on dry wood. I let it fill me, maybe because I also felt something else, some sort of sadness I didn't want to feel. Some sense of her desperation, when she wasn't a person whom I truly thought could feel that. It wasn't just her bad behavior that was letting me down. She was being too human, and there are some people we don't want to see this in—mothers and older sisters, fathers, people we rely on for some sense of firm ground, because there aren't many places to go for that. Juliet always had everything, and shouldn't that mean you sat somewhere beyond despair? I brought the note inside, but she wasn't there. I wasn't going to let her off the hook this time.

"Scarlet, is that you?" Hayden called from the living room.

"Yep, it's me," I called back.

"Can you give me a hand?"

Hayden's voice was muffled, and when I went to him, he was hunched behind the TV cabinet; his butt clad in those cargo shorts was the only real visible part of him. I didn't mind this.

"What's going on?" I said.

"Behind the cabinet. Can you see this cord I'm wiggling?"

I looked. "Uh-huh."

"Grab it for me, would you?"

I reached back and caught it.

His head appeared. His hair was all tousled, and one curly lock fell over his forehead. "I thought that Dean was an engineer," he said. He took the wire from me. "Thanks."

"He is an engineer. Computer engineer."

"That's even worse. Dick wad can't even hook up a VCR properly. I can't stand that guy. 'I think Americans are so pompous and judgmental,'" he said in a high Dean-accented voice, with his cheek against the cabinet.

"You sort of sounded like the queen of England."

"You should hear my Nixon," he said.

"I can't understand what she sees in him. I just can't."

"Maybe he's one of those things people either love or hate, like beets," he said.

I laughed. "Ha. *You* are the one who notices life, remember, like you told me?"

"Yeah?"

"Yeah."

"I guess we're an awful lot alike," he said.

He leaned back behind the cabinet again, and I could hear the scritching of wires against wood. "There. That should do it. Hey, thanks. My trusty assistant there wasn't much help." Zeus was curled up in front of the couch, snoring. He snored like an old man.

"They always ask to go on their break, just when you need them," I said.

"Ever since he joined the dog union he's been impossible." Hayden reappeared again. "Okay, let's try it."

He sat down on the couch. I shouldn't have sat beside him because of how much I wanted to sit beside him, but I did anyway. He picked up the remote and pointed it toward the TV. One of Mrs. Martinelli's old exercise tapes started up. A dark-haired studly guy appeared; he was on a Hawaiian beach, surrounded by six women on round mats, all with their legs in the air.

"Let me hear you!" the stud said. "Seven, eight, nine, ten. Feel your buttocks burn!"

"No wonder Mrs. Martinelli watches so much TV," I said.

"I'm sure this got her heart rate up, all right." The muscled leader was now lunging side to side as if he were in a duel. Robin Hood and his merry Lycra-clad women.

"I'm sure Mom appreciates your help," I said.

"Take that, Dean Neuhaus," he said. "Sucker engineer."

Zeus began to dog-dream growl, accompanied by a half-suppressed dog-dream bark, a funny little *wuf* that made his lips flubber. "Zeus is chasing bad guys in his sleep," I said.

"He's a hero in his own mind."

We watched his furry butterscotch chest go up and down with sleep, as the exercisers on TV squatted down, their arms straight out in front of them.

"Maybe he's ripping Dean Neuhaus's pant legs to shreds," I said.

"Buddy Wilkes's neck," Hayden said.

He looked at me and I looked at him, and I couldn't help it. I took his hand. I held it and I rubbed the back of his hand with my thumb. It was probably the wrong thing to do, but I didn't care. I wanted to lean over, kiss him. I wanted that bad. I let that thought in, allowed it for just a moment, and it felt good. But for now, I just squeezed his hand. He squeezed back as if it were the most innocent thing in the world. My skin on his—it didn't feel innocent, not to me.

"It's really hard to understand," he said.

"It's going to be okay," I said again, and again the words felt echoey and vacant. I'd never wanted to help anyone like I wanted to help him. I could love him the way he deserved to be loved. I wanted to give him so much that it was an actual ache. My heart felt like it was taking up ninety-five percent of my body.

"You're going to love someone properly, Scarlet. I can tell that."

I couldn't speak. Any words I might say were caught in my throat. It seemed possible that my real voice would be locked inside forever.

"God, is it a million degrees in here, or is it just me? Jesus." He let go, wiped his forehead with the bottom of his T-shirt.

"I'll open some doors," I said.

Hayden turned his eyes to the tight bodies on the TV. "I bet that guy's about eighty now," he said.

I didn't wait to talk to Mom about Juliet this time. I would handle this myself, if no one else would. Hayden could get hurt. That baby could. And that baby wasn't just Juliet's baby, it was all of ours. I could feel him move under my hand. If you held very still, that baby rolled and turned against your palm. I imagined he was having the most peaceful underwater time he might ever have. No matter what I felt, at least, at the very, very least, he deserved to be born into a parental land that was not war torn. It seemed to be one of those simple human rights that was so basic that it became impossible, like equality or the pursuit of happiness.

I waited until Juliet got home, until Hayden had taken Zeus with him to do some work on Will Quail's boat. Juliet was in her old room, going through the clothes she still had in her closet. She wore a pair of shorts low down on her hips, and a T-shirt that stretched so tight that the bottom of her round belly showed underneath. There was a big pile of pants and blouses and skirts on the floor, which I assumed she was getting rid of. Any other time I might have liked to go through it, trying on things that were her but that maybe could be me with some effort. But now I didn't even want those things.

I flung the envelope her way. The corner of it hit the top, fleshy part of her bare arm and fell to the floor.

"Jesus, Scarlet," she said. "What are you doing?"

"Question better asked of *you*." I stood in her doorway. I didn't even want to be in her room.

"Do you want this?" she asked, before she bent down to see what I'd flung at her. It was a sweatshirt with our school emblem, a tiger, on the front. I'm surprised she was getting rid of it. I'd have thought she'd try to hang on to her glory days as long as possible. Glory days were a pretty simple thing on an island, and even simpler in the sub-island that was high school. They were a whole lot harder to come by out in the big world.

She looked at the envelope in her hand. Her face got red. She just kept staring down at it, at the jagged bits where I'd torn the paper.

"You had no right," she said softly.

"You have no right," I said.

"You butt into everyone's business."

"Only when I need to. Like now."

"Need to? Right. You do it because you don't have your own life. That's why. That, and a complete lack of confidence and self-esteem. What, the world won't turn without your help? People won't fall apart without you."

Her words stung. "You brought Hayden into our lives. You brought this baby. You made it our business. You can't just make a mess and think we're all going to sit around and clean it up."

"I'm not asking you to clean up anything."

"We have to watch people get hurt."

Her eyes blazed. Maybe with anger but maybe, too, with shame. "*We.*"

"Yeah, *we.* Mom and me. You're playing out your family drama right under our noses."

She threw the sweatshirt at the top of the pile. "Mom supports me. Mom supports my own decisions. Don't speak for Mom. You don't know. At least she remembers that I'm an *adult.* In your mind I'm not supposed to grow up. I'm not supposed to do anything I don't get *permission for.*"

"Adult? You've got to be kidding. It's the last thing you're acting like." I was breathing hard. I looked at her face, the face I'd known for years and years. She was selfish. A selfish person. I'd been second to her first place forever, but now she was making Hayden bow down to her: Hayden, a good person who didn't deserve it. He shouldn't have to follow behind her like she had

Deb Caletti

made me do when I was five, carrying the back of her nightgown like she was the princess. "You go on about growing up. You know what I think? You got pregnant so you didn't *have* to grow up. So people would take care of you. So you could stay in our childhood forever. You're *afraid* to grow up."

I hadn't even known I thought that. But it was clear then. This wasn't a great big move on her part. It was a way to come home.

Her mouth was slightly open; she didn't look like the strong person who got everything she wanted all of the time anymore. She wasn't the person who stood up on a stage while people sat below her and watched. Maybe that person had been too much for her. She had moved all of the pieces around, moved people and their feelings as if they were for her own use only, and now she had gotten herself backed into a corner.

"You don't know what you're talking about," she said. But her words lacked force. She sat on the edge of her bed and held that envelope.

"Buddy is going to somehow make this *better*?"

"Buddy understands me," she said.

She disgusted me then. I shook my head at her stupidity. Buddy wasn't anything true. He treated girls like shit. He was an idea more than a person.

"Buddy's an excuse not to have anything real," I said.

She looked pale. Unwell. She didn't say anything. She just looked at that envelope in her hands.

I had to ask her. I had to. "Buddy's not . . ." I didn't know if I could say it.

"Not what?"

"Buddy's not Jitter's father, or anything, is he?"

"Oh for God's sake, Scarlet," Juliet spat. "For God's sake. Just . . . get out of here, would you? Get."

And so I did. I got out of there. I left her alone with all the things she wanted and wanted and wanted.

I hadn't seen Clive Weaver for days. His house sat so quiet, it might as well have been boarded up. The newspapers gathered on his porch. I sniffed around the outside, hoping I didn't smell something bad like people always did in the crime books, when the neighbor's gone missing.

I wondered if I should deliver the Make Hope and Possibilities Happen for Clive Weaver project sooner than I'd planned. I had folded more than a hundred paper cranes and had twenty or thirty pieces of mail ready for his box. I wasn't anywhere near my goal yet, and when I closed my eyes I saw it playing the way I imagined, loads of mail, loads of it. Well then, something else had better be done now. A person ought to check up on him anyway.

I went downstairs and made a quick batch of brownies. Too much fat and sugar was bound to be bad for his heart, yet he needed it for his spirit. I licked the bowl as I waited for them to bake, drank a big glass of milk that chased away the bad feelings I had about Juliet and Hayden and Kevin Frink and about Nicole, too, who had been nothing but cold to me since that day at the pool. I had wanted to help all of them, but it seemed like I was failing miserably.

I felt the way you did when you had been swimming for a long time, or running, or working on an endless research paper. Like the end was too far away, the obstacles too great, like you wanted to lie down and rest. But you didn't rest, right? Or quit. You didn't do any of those things that meant giving up, because quitting was for losers and babies, for the weak and lazy, for people with no backbone. You persevered, even if there were setbacks and you were tired and didn't want to do any of it anymore. If you wanted some sort of triumph, you had to be persistent. You had to pay with all of your endless efforts. You had to stick with it. You just worked harder to make it happen, whatever "it" happened to be.

The chocolate was catching up to me.

I cut the brownies into squares and put them on a plate. I carried them outside, their warmth steaming up the Saran Wrap I had stretched over them. But it was true, wasn't it? It was practically un-American to not set goals and then do everything you could, everything, to reach them. *Quitting*—it was a dirty word in a place where pilgrims had endured harsh winters and where pioneers had struggled through death and disease to create new lives. Giving up or stepping back or setting aside something you thought you wanted—it was almost a shameful act. I wasn't one of those people who gave up easily. Sometimes it was confidence and not the lack of it that made me want to fix the bad I saw around me. I believed in the power a person had to change things.

Clive Weaver's blinds were drawn, and the house looked very still. I was surprised, then, when the front door opened and Ally Pete-Robbins stepped outside, holding an empty Bundt pan. She looked at my brownies, and I looked at that pan. I wondered if I could see my future in its curved Teflon surface.

"His condition is worsening," Ally Pete-Robbins said. But she sounded snippy. My brownies were invading her Bundt cake turf.

"Oh no," I said.

"He has dishes out from days ago," she said.

"Maybe somebody ought to wash them," I said.

"I already did." Her words closed the conversation. Her shoes clipped back down the sidewalk, sounding useful and efficient. I loved that sound, I had to admit, especially when my own heels were making it. Heels on sidewalks or shiny floors—the sound of important business.

But I wasn't so much in the mood for visiting anymore. The Saran Wrap was coming unstuck around the edges of the plate, and my stomach felt too full from uncooked batter. I rang the bell, though, and when Clive Weaver answered in his bathrobe, his old face unshaven, his breath smelling sour, some mix of coffee and soup in cans, I only handed him the plate and said a few words I can't remember now. Clive said, *That's mighty kind of you, mighty kind, goddamn,* and I swear his eyes started pooling up, the way old man eyes did after so many years of life piling up. I got out of there. I got out of there, but still I could feel some urgent sense of my decisions following me. The decisions I had made, the decisions I was about to make.

Later that afternoon, the big dark Mercedes pulled up in front of the Martinellis' house. The realtor lady with realtor lady hair and realtor lady shoes came out and rather forcefully dug a hole into the ground in front of the Martinellis' yard. She shoved the FOR SALE sign into it. I recognized her from all the calendars and magnets and notepads she'd sent in the mail over the years. Yvonne Yolanda, our Friend in the Real Estate Business.

Chapter Twenty

I waited for the Mercedes to leave. The doorbell sounded far away in the Martinellis' house. I looked into the glass by the door, waited until the bright flowers on Mrs. Martinelli's dress appeared. I pounded on the door then. She needed to understand the urgency of this. The moment I saw that sign, I knew what was going on. They were not moving to Arizona or Florida or even Montana, where their daughter lived. They had not bought some condo in the sun to live out their days playing golf and sipping "highballs," as Mr. Martinelli called the gin drinks he had every night at five thirty.

"Mrs. Martinelli, open up," I said.

She peeked around the door. She wore her reading glasses on a chain around her neck; her dress was a large shouting garden of sunflowers.

"Why, Scarlet," she said. She sounded like some old lady on television, which is not how Mrs. Martinelli ever talked.

"What have you done?" I said.

"Whatever do you mean?" she said. "Come in, dear." I rolled my eyes. Next she would be offering me Freshly Baked Cookies and telling me about The Good Old Days. It was the sweet old folks countermove. A cover-up.

"You know what I mean. The FOR SALE sign. Getting rid of all of your stuff. Where is Mr. Martinelli?"

I followed her into the kitchen. It looked empty, and so did the living room. Her collection of glass dogs that had lined the living room shelves was gone. So were the shelves themselves.

"Ginger!" I said. Oh God, what had they done with her? I could just see the small white dog sitting in the passenger seat of Mr. Martinelli's Buick, heading for the Great Pound in the Sky.

"Don't get your knickers in a twist; she's right here." Mrs. Martinelli whistled somewhere in the back of her teeth, and Ginger appeared, toenails clicking on the linoleum, her blank black eyes shiny behind her aging bimbo-fluff hair.

I put my hand to my chest. "Thank God."

"Her kidneys are bad, but Mr. Martinelli said if we'd put *him* down when his kidneys got bad, it would have been years ago."

A tea kettle started to whine in high-pitched need. Mrs. Martinelli removed the kettle from the stove, opened a cupboard to reveal shelves vacant except for four lonely cups. She took two down, set them on the counter.

"Cocoa?" she asked. She ripped open a package of Swiss Miss.

"I knew it," I said.

"It has the little marshmallows," she said.

"They are scam artists, Mrs. Martinelli. I don't know where you're going, but you're not going to find any cocoa plantation when you get there."

"Don't be ridiculous. We've talked to Morin Jude herself. We wouldn't have just gone and sent that kind of money unless we knew she was a real person. They're getting the house ready for us on the Ivory Coast. Herb has been reading up on cocoa. You would be surprised how involved it all is." She poured steaming water into the cups. "The seed is actually green when ripe, not red. Isn't that interesting?"

"We've got to call someone and get your money back." I looked around. The place was so empty, I'd have bet even the phone was gone.

She opened a drawer, a mostly empty drawer, except for the accumulated bread crumbs and toothpicks still clinging for dear life to their old home. She took out a spoon, stirred the brown dust and unnaturally small white bits that were supposedly marshmallows.

She handed me a cup, which I held but ignored. Mrs. Martinelli sipped. "An inferior product," she said. Her top lip was spotted with dampened chocolate dust. Ginger still sat at her feet like one waiting slipper. She was apparently still hoping for food, the only thrill of her little day. I always thought it was sort of sad, how thrilled dogs were to have their two meals. Then again, I'd had days where there'd been less excitement.

"Mrs. Martinelli. What you've done . . ." How to get this through to her? "You've maybe given away everything. *Everything*, okay? For *nothing*. These people have sold their 'plantation' countless times, all right? Countless. We've got to contact some authorities. You've got to get your money back somehow. Get that sign out of the yard. . . ."

"You don't understand. Poor Morin Jude. Her father was *murdered* on that business trip to France. By his own *business partners.*" She drew her finger against her neck to demonstrate. Poor Morin Jude, all right. Thousands upon thousands of dollars richer.

I sighed. I rubbed my forehead the way Mom always did when there was nothing else to be done. This was a disaster. "You're going to get hurt here. Please. I care about you; can't you hear me?"

She put on her glasses, read the ingredients of the box, sighed, then put it back down. "Scarlet, should we stay in this house and just move one day closer and another day closer to being dead?"

I looked into her eyes. I saw that same small, vulnerable person I had seen in Kevin Frink's. Maybe we all just wanted someone to believe in. That's all each of us wanted, and it should be so simple, but it never was simple.

"You gave away things to people who don't have your best interests at heart, Mrs. Martinelli. We can't give away things to people like that. Your money—you may never see it again."

"You wouldn't believe what this has done for our sex life," she said. She snapped her fingers.

I wanted to clap my hands over my ears. "Oh God."

"Oh, don't be a prude, Scarlet. Birds do it, bees do it, even old ladies do it." She rolled something in her cheek. "They call this a marshmallow?"

"Maybe I should talk to Mr. Martinelli," I said.

"He's not here," she said. "He's at the consulate picking up our passports. Then he's dropping off the Buick at Bill Rogers's house. He paid more than what it was worth. The minute this house sells, we're outta here."

I had to get on the phone. There must be something that

Deb Caletti

could be done. It was wrong; that was all. People just couldn't be taken advantage of like that.

"Swiss Miss," Mrs. Martinelli scoffed.

"I don't know what to say," Mom said. Shoes were strewn all over the rug in my mother's room, and blouses were tossed onto the bed in small mountains of rejection. I had those moments, too, when nothing, *nothing* looked right or felt right. "I think you have to let other people have their own disasters."

"Juliet talked to you," I said. Her words weren't just about the Martinellis; that was obvious.

"You can't fix it all, Scarlet. A person can't hold that much in their own hands. I wish you could."

"Why can't a person? I'm sorry; I don't get that."

"Why?" She looked at herself in the long mirror on the back of her door. "It's just, you've got to . . ." She turned back to me. "I don't know, the idea that we can control things is wishful thinking. Sometimes, there's nothing that can be done. You can let go; that's all. Maybe that's the most important thing to do."

"That's chicken shit," I said. "When something bad is happening, you don't just give up and let it happen! We know that. We're *taught* that. Can you imagine a movie where there's this big war between good and evil and the fighters of good just say, 'Oh well, there's nothing that can be done.' Film over."

She gave her outfit a dissatisfied glance in the mirror, turned, and looked at me dead-on. "A different film would start. Maybe a more real one. Bad guys do win. Things aren't fair. There isn't always some great big terrific something that happens to make everything turn out right."

"I know that," I said. It came out sounding sarcastic and

childish. Maybe I didn't really know that or, at least, completely believe it.

"Sweetie," Mom said. She sighed. She sat down on the edge of her bed. I looked at her in her confused clothes. She seemed very tired. She had only one shoe on. "We don't always get what we want."

This scared me. The one shoe, the sighing, the discarded clothes—it looked like defeat. But what scared me even more was the change in her message—the message we'd heard from the time we were small. You *can* have anything you want. If you thought positively and set your mind to it, *anything was possible.*

"Mom," I said. "Do you hear yourself? You have to believe in your own power to make things different. You told us that! What about conviction? There's *proof*, I've read about it—thinking positively, setting goals, believing in yourself—people can cure their own *cancers!* You're the one who said we could do anything we set our mind to . . . we could have what we wanted if we *believed* and *worked hard.*"

"Optimism can get you into a lot of trouble. You can put your belief in places it doesn't belong. You can work hard to fix things that you can't fix. I'm not sure that kind of optimism is always the best thing. Positive thinking, hope—it needs better guidelines. It needs *rules.*"

Something had changed in her, and I wasn't sure what it was or when it had happened. But I didn't like where this was going, not at all. Hope and belief were the *good guys.* Weren't they? If you went to the other side, if you left persistence and optimism in the dust, what could happen? Could Dean Neuhaus happen? What would fate do, what would *you* do, if you set down those Laws of the Universe, the capital *T* Truths? Because maybe in the old days you weren't supposed to say the world was round, but now you didn't mess with determination and willpower and reaching goals and thinking positively. What she had said—it was a modern sort of burned-at-the-stake heresy. Everyone knew that those things were the *right things*.

"God, Mom. *Cynical*."

"Maybe I'm getting my period," she said. "Or having an epiphany. Does this look awful?"

"You're only wearing one shoe."

"You're right."

"What is this? Big date?"

"Dean's taking me out to dinner. He has something important to ask me."

My stomach dropped. It was beginning to make sense, the clothes, the strange talk, the resignation. Please, no. It wasn't possible, was it? Was she giving up hope of something better? She wouldn't do that. She wouldn't *marry* him, would she? She couldn't. Maybe I'd been watching the wrong disaster in the making. Maybe it was Mom I should have been saving all along. "*What* does he want to ask you?"

"I don't know, Scarlet. It could be anything." But when she looked at me, I saw the lie on her face. It sat there plainly. It was as obvious as spilled red wine on a white tablecloth.

I didn't know what to say. Dean Neuhaus would shatter us. When she finally spoke, it was more to herself than to me.

"Oh, the power of imminent loss," she said.

I went to my room, folded about eight paper cranes, fast. Four for me, four for Clive Weaver. It was sort of like praying, only in origami. The ceiling of my room was getting full, a purple and red and yellow and green sky of swaying paper birds. I stood on my bed, taped these up with the others. Let that keep all of the badness out.

If Dean Neuhaus moved in with us, I would move out. I would find my father, maybe. I imagined this—a phone call, an invitation. Or else, Hayden would appear in my doorway. He'd look straight at me. He'd say something simple, but charged. *Let's get out of here.* I'd grab a few things, follow him out to his truck. The fantasy got a little hazy after that, except for a long highway and the feel of his jeans under my hands. It was stupid the way a fantasy could actually make you feel better for a while, even if it wasn't real. You had a few minutes when you could really just feel it, and it was actually terrific.

The paper sky was crowded. Like the rain forest canopy that protected all of the delicate living things underneath. We needed protection. Right then, we had no canopy, no ozone, no anything. There were only the straight, hot, poisonous rays of the sun beaming down.

My phone rang. Nicole.

I stared at her name on the screen until the very last possible moment when I finally answered. A part of me was ready for just one more thing to go wrong. It was that sick piece of me that says, go ahead. Bring it on. You feel disaster building and you push things a little further.

"Do you have a minute?" Nicole said. Her voice was everything cold. Icicles and the arctic and vast, empty polar regions.

"Go ahead. You might as well get mad at me too, since everything else is turning to crap now."

She ignored this. But of course she ignored this. When did she ever actually listen to *me*? When did she hear my stories or support my problems or *give*? We'd been best friends since the fifth grade, when she had had that operation to fix the bones in her knees. Or something like that, the details escaped me—we were eleven. She was in a wheelchair for months, and then on crutches, and it was me who wheeled her around and fetched her lunch tray and carried her books and kept her company at recess when everyone else played. I was the one who for years afterward listened to her problems and helped her out of situations and into other ones—I even wrote that note she gave to Geoff Standish in middle school, declaring her love. Maybe I should have charged an hourly rate. Minimum wage times all of the hours I'd been her friend. People like me were made for people like her. Maybe I was having an epiphany too.

I could hear Nicole breathing. "I just want to say, any person who would do what you did is not what I would consider a friend."

"And what did I do? What exactly did I do?"

She let out a disgusted sigh, the one that's somewhere between a cough and a choke, when it sounds like you've got a revolting thought caught in your throat. "I think you know full well, Scarlet."

"I talked to someone who wanted to talk to me. I don't think you have a relationship with Jesse that requires actual loyalty."

"I have one with *you* that requires loyalty."

I stumbled. For a moment I had no idea if she was right or not. But something was building in me, too, my own momentum. Hayden and Juliet, and Ally Pete-Robbins and Clive Weaver, and the Martinellis', and now the threat of Dean Neuhaus, of Mom and Dean Neuhaus forever and ever . . . Anger was there, suddenly, sitting right at the surface. The kind of anger that explodes things. "You have a relationship with him in your mind. That's all. It's not even real."

"It's real to me. My feelings are real."

"You think he should like you simply because you *want* him to. You want him to, big deal. It doesn't work like that. Other people get a *say*. You can't just force your way onto someone else."

She started to cry. Great. *Great!* I didn't have a chance now. So much for anger! So much for speaking your mind! "I can't believe how mean you're being."

My will and my fury were shoved aside by guilt. It was that easy. I could feel the anger there, turned down to a sudden simmer, but the guilt had gotten bigger and louder. "I'm sorry, Nicole." I wasn't a mean person. Hurting anyone was the last thing I ever wanted.

I tried again. "It'd be like saying *I* have to hate who *you* hate, or . . ." Wait. I *did* have to hate whom she hated. We stopped being friends with Ashley Brazlen when Ashley didn't invite Nicole to her sleepover when we were fourteen.

"I just, I think . . ." She was crying hard now. I felt like shit. "I'm sorry, okay?"

"I talked it over with my mom, and I think we need to stop doing things together for a while. You can't just let people think they can stomp all over your feelings."

"What?"

"I think our friendship is over," she said.

I was stunned. "Nicole, wait . . ." I mean, we'd been friends for years, no matter what. It was practically like your sister saying she wouldn't be your sister anymore, or your mother or your *father* . . .

I felt a little panicky. I didn't want her to just go off and leave.

It seemed suddenly very, very important that she not. All of my earlier bravery turned to dust. "Please," I said.

But I heard only dead air—no breathing, no fuzzy telephone background noise of traffic or televisions. Only the quiet that meant that someone was gone.

That night, I called Jasmine. I wouldn't ordinarily have called Jasmine, but I did. I was unsure and abandoned and my conscience was bothering me, and if Jasmine was on my side, it might mean that none of those feelings was necessary. Jasmine didn't answer—I got her chirpy voice mail and I didn't leave a message. I called Kiley. No answer. And then I did something else. I called Erin Redfly, this girl I used to be friends with in the sixth grade. We had nothing in common anymore—she was a volleyball player and was always traveling to far-off cities for some kind of tournament that would get written about in the *Parrish Island Courier*. Her picture would be there sometimes, her body extended and her arm raised as she reached to spike the ball. My only experience with volleyball was in ninth grade PE, when I was yelled at *en masse* by my team whenever the ball would splat right at my feet.

She answered the phone. I told her I'd been thinking about her, which was a lie. I never thought about her. She told me about a tournament they'd just come back from in Bellevue. There was an awkward empty pause that I finally filled by asking how her mother was. Her mother had given me a ride home once when I felt sick during the sixth grade Valentine's Day party. She said we ought to get together sometime, which made me immediately regret calling.

I stayed in my room most of the night. I usually liked being in

my room—I liked the cave comfort of being tucked away, knowing that Mom's knock or the phone ringing were the only possible intrusions. But that night, my room felt too much like me,
and it was me I needed an escape from. I sat in the living room,
and then in the backyard in the cool night, and then went back
to my room. No matter where I went, there I was. I was lonely
but didn't want company. Everyone was out, anyway. Hayden
and Juliet had gone to Long Time No See, a small movie theater
downtown with creaky rubbed-bare red velvet seats. They showed
only old movies—*Kramer vs. Kramer* had been showing for almost
a month and before that, *Zorro*.

I wasn't even in the mood for Zeus's companionship—he
would have been too kind and warm and soft, loving me when I
didn't feel deserving of it. Instead, he slept right up against my
door, as close as he could to the only other creature in the house.
I could hear his elbows and knees banging against the wood as
he shifted around and his sighs through his nose, which sounded
world-weary. He couldn't have the actual me, so he took what he
could and tried to be satisfied.

I heard Juliet and Hayden come in. Or rather, I heard Zeus's
toenails scrambling and scurrying like crazy against the wall—
sometimes he had trouble getting all of his parts going in the
right direction. Finally, he was up and barking even when he
wasn't supposed to and there was the sound of the front door and
coats coming off and then silence except for a little stern crooning
to Zeus from Hayden. Juliet said something sharp, *I can get it!*
and I knew they were fighting again. The tension came right up
the stairs. It was clear to me that when Buddy Wilkes was in her
thoughts, they fought, and when he wasn't, they didn't. He was a
wall between them, and Juliet didn't always mind walls.

The hollow hum of voices downstairs went on and on and finally stopped. At 12:00 a.m., my mother arrived home, the exact time she always did when she went out with Dean Neuhaus. Maybe she set her own curfew and she'd be in big trouble if she broke it. I heard her car, and then the engine turn off, and the key in the door. I heard her clink down her purse on the counter, her steps sounding tired on the way to her room, the click of her door as it shut.

I had a hard time sleeping that night. My feelings seemed hard to grasp and name, except for some sort of guilt and grief, which curled inside like ignited paper. It wasn't that I actually felt I had done something bad to Nicole. I wasn't even really sorry for what I did. But her going away had left me with this aloneness, an alarming aloneness, an abrupt, scary empty-something, like the time when I was four and I lost my mother's hand in the crowd at the Parrish Island Fourth of July parade. I'd been so scared. It was alone-forever-and-ever scared.

This time it was me who got up and put on a sweatshirt over my tank top and pajama shorts. Maybe I was hoping that if I went outside and stood with my confusion out by Hayden's truck that he would also come, the same as I had when he stood there with his. Kevin Frink's Volkswagen was parked down the street, sitting cold and dark, and I wondered if he had sneaked into Fiona Saint George's room. The streetlights made the Martinellis' FOR SALE sign look as bright and white as the moon. By then I was honestly and completely hoping for Hayden's appearance, his toe kicking the ground, his eyes looking up to the sky, his cigarette, even. There were no maybes about that hope, except for one: Maybe it would be for the best if he didn't appear right then. I wasn't sure I could be trusted.

I was hoping so hard that I was shocked when it was actually Juliet who appeared. She came out through the side fence and started heading down the driveway without seeing me. She wore one of Hayden's jackets, his denim one, over a tossed-on dress. I hadn't realized how big she had gotten—*they* had gotten—her and Jitter. The streetlights and the night shadows showed her solid roundness and curve of her back in some way that the daylight never did. Her hands were shoved into the pockets of Hayden's jacket. She walked fast; she knew where she was going.

"It's one a.m.," I said.

She froze, her hand to her chest. She spun around. "Jesus, you scared me," she said.

"It's one a.m.," I said again.

"What are you doing, spying on me?"

Only a guilty person would have thought so. The psychology books have a word for it. "*Projection*," I said, knowing she wouldn't know what I meant. "Not everything is about you, anyway."

"I was just going for a walk," she said.

"Right," I said.

"Scarlet . . ."

"How about if I come along?" I said. That anger—it was back. I heard it in my own voice and felt it pushing against my chest.

She rubbed her arms as if she were cold. I bet Jitter would have preferred to be tucked into a nice warm bed, instead of out there in the night, staying up too late, heading to places he shouldn't be heading.

"You know, you used to be nice. I liked you back then. What happened to the nice person that used to live here?"

"Oh," I said. "I see. I've got it figured out now. You're nice as long as you go along with what other people want. You do or say something people don't like for once, somehow you're not nice anymore."

She wasn't looking at me, more at a point down the street, somewhere she was wishing she was. But then, she did look. "Are you going to tell anybody about this?" she said.

"Anybody? Like who? Like our mailman? Like your second-grade teacher? Oh, you must mean your *husband*."

"Goddamnit." She shook her head as if she couldn't believe how unreasonable I was being.

"You get pregnant so you . . . what, have some sort of answer. Maybe so you don't have to *be* all these things you were supposed to be. Right? Okay, I got that much figured out. You wanted some sort of rescue and you got it, but you picked a really fabulous rescuer. Really. It's, like, the smartest thing you did in all this. Probably, the smartest thing you've ever done." She turned away from me, but she didn't leave. She just stood there and took it. Maybe she was relieved someone had a conscience, even if it wasn't her.

"But now . . . Buddy Wilkes? That's what comes between you? High school loser boyfriend who doesn't even *want* you?"

"God!" she cried. She put her hands up to her face. I wanted to feel bad for her, but I couldn't. I was so angry with her, maybe seventeen-years' angry. But especially-now angry. For having everything and for everything not being enough.

"Just . . . *why?*" I said.

The night was quiet. Just some crickets, the shimmery shush of trees in the night wind. A man's faraway cough on a faraway porch.

She looked at me and her face was wet with tears. A strand of her hair stuck to her cheek. And then she said something I didn't expect her to say. It was so unexpected that it stopped me right there. "What would happen if I let go and loved him, huh? What."

My breath caught. Before I knew what was happening, my own throat closed up, tears rushed forward. I swallowed hard. I felt some deep loss and recognition at those words—*let go*. The words seemed so large and impossible and dangerous. I wanted to run to her and hold on, the same as I used to when I was little and scared. I'd get in her bed and she would be the big sister and everything would feel safe, but this time, maybe we'd just hold on to each other. We'd both hold on against big dark things of the night that snatched away what you most needed.

"What would happen?" My voice shook. I could barely say the words. I didn't want to say them, but they were the ones that most needed to be spoken. "Maybe you'd be happy."

She looked at me for a while. And then she turned back the way she had come, back to her basement bedroom and to the sleeping body of her husband.

Chapter Twenty-one

That night, I had one of those dreams where you try and make a phone call but can't, no matter what you do. There was an emergency and I needed to call Mom, but I couldn't remember her number and every time I tried to dial, something interfered. It's the dream equivalent of the moment in the horror movies when someone's car won't start.

Kevin Frink's Volkswagen was still parked by the curb in the morning, its rounded top shiny and wet with dew. He was asking for it; I'm sure he knew. Everyone in my life was asking for it. Maybe even me.

Downstairs, Mom looked like hell. She was blowing her nose like she had the start of a cold, and her eyes were flat and tired. Her hair was shoved up in the back like it had been forced against its will to participate in morning. I looked at her hand— no ring. But I saw it there on the counter. A small black velvet box. Funny how a small black velvet box can have the power of a loaded gun.

"So, the new Mrs. Neuhaus?" I said.

She gave a little shudder.

"That's a good sign," I said.

"What," she said into her coffee cup. The word was as flat as her eyes.

"You just shuddered," I said.

"I didn't shudder." But it sounded like a question.

"Yes, you did."

"I didn't shudder."

I let this drop. No one was making pancakes or eggs or some great breakfast this Sunday morning. A big breakfast required optimism. Our house seemed to be lacking that. No, this would be a Shredded Wheat morning, something punishing like that, a spiky bird's nest rectangle with milk on top.

"You know, my first date with Dean? We went out to this little café. He said, 'I'll have what you're having,' and I said, 'I'm just having coffee.' And he said, 'I don't want just coffee.'"

"Uh-huh," I said. I barely dared to speak. The truth seemed to be sitting there right at the end of my tongue, but I wasn't sure I was ready to let it out and about. I had done that last night with Juliet, spoken the truth, and all I had gotten from it was the feeling I still had—my heart exposed and hurting. No wonder people stayed hidden.

"The second date, he told me I held my fork wrong. He showed me the proper way. Upside down, like the British. The way I did it looked *lower class*."

"*We're* all lower class too," I said. "Look." I swigged out of the orange juice carton without a glass.

"Scarlet," she said.

I tried to burp loudly too, but it didn't happen. It was quiet and unimpressive. I was never very good at that.

"Use a glass," she said in her mother voice, but it was her amused one.

"Does this mean Dean's not my new daddy?"

"I thought *I* was in a bad mood," she said. She eyed the little box as if it were one of Kevin Frink's explosive devices. "I told him I would think about it."

"Think about it? Isn't that one of those things you either know or you don't?"

"There's a lot to consider."

What was there to consider, just how completely destroyed and unhappy we all would be? The actual degree of destruction? Is that what needed to be considered? And, wasn't this supposed to be one of those blissful moments of celebration? When the man you supposedly loved asked you to be his wife? She looked horrible. She looked like her personal world had been bombed.

"Well, I can see how overjoyed you are," I said. It seemed obvious to me, if not so obvious to anyone else. Happiness shouldn't make you so miserable.

"It's complicated. Dean has a lot of great qualities. He can offer us a lot."

Right—he could offer us the chance to feel like crap about ourselves on a twenty-four-hour basis. If there was a time for honesty, right then was it, no matter what the consequences. This wasn't just her life anyway. "Like what? What can he offer us?" I said, but she didn't answer. We were interrupted by the sound of Juliet coming up from the basement, the thud of her feet on the stairs. For such a frail-looking person, Juliet had a heavy step, she'd always had. She actually looked pretty great, after last night. She wore a sweet white nightgown and a soft pink robe untied over her belly.

"Oh, I feel like a sea lion," she moaned, as if she were in distress. But she didn't look distressed. Her cheeks were pink and her eyes sugar-crystal bright. "Coffee . . ."

"You're not supposed to drink coffee," I said. "The baby ingests whatever you do. His system is too delicate for caffeine."

"In moderation it's okay," she said. "I looked it up."

"You looked it up?" I was surprised.

"Bring that baby over here," Mom said. She put her hands on each side of Juliet, rubbed, bent down, and gave that tummy a kiss. "Good morning, baby."

"Okay, enough," Juliet said. But she was smiling.

"Love that baby," Mom said. "*Love* that baby."

"That's what Hayden says every morning," she said. She was practically glowing.

If happiness shouldn't make you so miserable, misery shouldn't make you so happy.

That Sunday morning, I tried to call Nicole, but she didn't answer. I tried again. I was beginning to act as desperate as Juliet with Buddy Wilkes.

We stayed in our robes too long that day, past the point of luxury and into the territory of self-disgust. We were all restless and edgy until finally everyone found a place to settle—Juliet took a nap, and Mom got out her scrapbook materials, something she hadn't done in a long while. She sat cross-legged on the floor and spread out images of Beijing and Darjeeling and Trinidad on our

Deb Caletti

coffee table, studying them with her head tilted to one side as she drank a cold beer. Even Clive Weaver had decided on something—he had taken Corky on a rare walk, letting Corky lead, as always, meaning they were then unwinding themselves around one of Mr. Martinelli's rosebushes where they had become tangled.

Hayden had taken over my job and mowed the lawn, and as I laid on my bed and read, I had the full summer experience through my window—the sweet new odor of cut grass mixed with warm sun and the smoky, rich smells from someone else's barbecue, set against the background music of a baseball game in the field a few blocks over and the tinkling notes of "The Entertainer," coming from psycho Joe's ice-cream truck.

The lawn mower stopped and started up again in the back. I wished we were having whatever those people were barbecuing. The construction men weren't working on the weekend so there were no construction sounds, no radio *Old black water, keep on rollin', Mississippi moon won't you keep on shining on meeee*. I did hear the lumbering of a big vehicle out front and a bit later, Mr. Martinelli's voice talking to another man. I couldn't see either of them, just heard two voices and saw two old RVs parked next to each other, the Pleasure Way and some other big prehistoric beast, with a license plate that read CAPTAIN ED. Mr. Martinelli boasted about the GPS System and the Ample Storage but Captain Ed must not have been impressed enough, because he drove off a few moments later, leaving Mr. Martinelli silent.

That's when the blast came. It was an explosive shot, a fierce crack and crash and shatter that I felt through my whole body. There was the clattering of glass, raining down like hail. A few pieces landed right next to me on my bed, one on the very page of *Psychological Diagnosis* by Dr. Gerald Drinksmore. I flew to my feet. My heart was pounding hard, hard, hard. Jesus, what had *happened?* There was a jagged hole in my window, right in my own *window*, glittering glass everywhere, a plastic rocket on my floor.

"Scarlet!" Mom yelled. I heard her racing up the stairs.

"I'm okay," I yelled back.

I looked outside. I could see Jeffrey and Jacob there, staring back up at me. "Dad said to *wait*," Jeffrey said.

Ally Pete-Robbins dashed into the street, her blouse buttoned wrong. "What have you done?" she yelled. She looked up, saw me standing there. "Are you all right?"

"Everyone's fine," I called down.

"Dear Lord, you could have hurt someone! You're lucky no one was hurt!"

Mr. Pete-Robbins came running out next. His hair was messed up, and he was shirtless. "Boys!" he said in a father voice.

"You coulda poked someone's eye out, Jacob," Jeffrey said.

Hayden covered the broken window with cardboard and duct tape until it could be repaired, but you could still feel a draft of cool air from the opening. It reminded me of the dreams I had sometimes, when a puncture would appear in the side of an airplane I was in, sucking things out.

I could hear everything outside as if there were no barrier between me and anyone else, none. I shot awake when the milk truck came the next morning—it sounded like it was driving right up to my bed, and while I was getting dressed later on, the voices of a couple and their small children and Yvonne Yolanda barged right in and made me cover up, fast. I hadn't understood the importance of that sheet of glass before, or even the screen, how necessary a barrier was. Even the thinnest and most breakable boundary was better than none. But now, with only cardboard, I was open and exposed to whatever might happen.

I worked the cash register at Quill while Mom helped customers. I was glad to be there, away from that hole in the glass. It disturbed me. At Quill, I was inside four undamaged walls and large unbroken windows. Joe Nevins from the ferry dock picked out a birthday card for his mother in Florida. Then an hour later, his brother, Jim, came in and did the same, but forgot his wallet. A bunch of tourists came and wandered around but didn't buy anything. Bonnie Randall from the bookstore next door came and bought a fountain pen, and my teacher, Ms. Cassaday, chose a beautiful leather notebook stamped with shells and scrolls.

Mom let me go a little early; it was a quiet day in the store in spite of the hordes of summer tourists. I headed out with my purse over my shoulder, wondering what I should do with myself, when I heard bells jangle and bash hard against the door of Randall and Stein Booksellers next door. There was Jesse Waters—he rushed out with one of their green bags in his hand.

"Wait!" he called.

I stopped. "Jesse. Hey." I was both surprised and suddenly guilty. I was sure he was only thinking about what I was: how I'd shoved him away in that strange, unclear way the last time I'd seen him. I was sure what I had done sat between us like a huge animal, and that it would always sit between us, gigantic and unforgivable. "What about all the drowning children?" I said.

"Four until close today. I was actually coming to see you. I saw that you were working. . . . I saw you here a couple of times. . . ." He sounded friendly, happy even. He didn't seem to even remember the large, terrible thing I had last done, and so the beast wandered off. It was a relief to be so easily forgiven. "Anyway, I thought I'd bring you something."

"Me?" He handed me the bag. There was a little flurry as he grabbed it back and snatched out the receipt. He was giving me a present? I'm not sure anyone had ever done that before. Family, sure, and maybe friends. But a boy, and for no reason? Never.

"It's a book," he said. "Well, of course. Bookstore . . ."

"I can't believe you got this for me," I said.

"Maybe you better wait until you see it," he said. "Before you get excited. I don't know."

I took out the book. There was no mistaking the bearded guy on the cover with the serious eyes. "*The Interpretations of Dreams*," I read.

His words rushed forward. "I've always seen you with a psychology book. So I thought . . . I didn't really know what to get. I figured, Freud, psychology. Too . . . stupid? Obvious?"

I was stunned. "This is so nice of you."

"It's okay?"

"Yeah! Great. I'm not exactly used to people doing nice things like this for me."

"You're kidding," he said. He laughed. He looked relieved. He had his jacket on, and I noticed Mr. Martinelli's cuff link still pinned there.

I just stood there on the sidewalk. Bonnie Randall's dog was looking at us out of the window. "I can't believe you even noticed my books."

"No one else reads stuff like that, if they even read at all," he said.

"This looks really good," I said. I looked at the back cover, although the words there did not reach my actual brain.

"I'd have thought people did nice things for you all the time. They should." He looked at me from under his bangs. It seemed like he really meant it.

"Thanks, Jesse, really. It means a lot."

"Okay," he said. "I've got to run. I'm glad I caught you before you left."

"Me too," I said.

He picked up his bike, set down on its side by the front of the store. He got on, and I watched him cruise down the street, one arm waving good-bye just as he rounded the corner.

I felt some high, zapping energy buzz, a mix of pleasure and confusion. It was the mental equivalent of what your body does after one of the lattes at Java Java.

I couldn't go home yet. I decided to take Mom's car to Point Perpetua, not exactly where you went for calm and quiet during the summer months, but better than nothing. Tourists were *everywhere* in the summer months. People who lived near the beaches would steal the park entrance signs and hide them, just to have a little peace. You'd see some couple in matching T-shirts by the roadside, holding one of the island maps and looking perplexed, and you knew just what had happened. Someone like Otto Perkins had snitched the sign and put it in his backyard with the ten or twelve others he'd stolen over the years.

I was lucky to even find a parking space. People came in droves to "whale watch," but whale watching was no different from fishing—a lot of waiting, little or no outcome usually, and the hours the whales appeared were the ones when visitors from Michigan or California were having cocktails at the Lighthouse or sleeping in their down beds at Asher House B & B, dreaming of raspberry scones. I didn't think whales liked to be watched. They liked their privacy. Their appearance was a favor, and they gave that favor to only a few.

I grabbed my camera from underneath the seat of Mom's car, headed down the windy path to the beach. God, I loved that smell— the briny water and the tang of salt, odd ropes of slick seaweed thick with the odor of the oldest and deepest parts of the ocean.

Some stupid kid in cartoon swim trunks was throwing rocks at bored seagulls, and two teen boys I didn't recognize were swimming where they shouldn't be. A young woman with short, short hair picked her way along the rocks, looking for treasures. I wished I lived right there on the beach. Every day, you could see what the ocean brought you. I made my own way, my palm finding familiar flat places on which to balance. I climbed up my favorite rock and sat.

I lifted my camera to my eye, played around with different shots, took a few that weren't really any good. The book from Jesse sat in the bag beside me, and I thought about opening it, cracking the shiny cover of that book and sniffing deeply, exploring its contents. But instead, I took a breath and let Point Perpetua settle inside me, and when I did, it was Hayden I kept seeing—sitting beside me that day, his head tilted up to the sun, his eyes closed, wearing his favorite green T-shirt. The way he rested his forearms on his knees, the ease he had with his body, the strength you sensed in his man hands and in his shoulders . . . A man seemed a fine thing to curl up against. A man could seem like shelter.

It felt like a decision, to keep that bag closed, with the book tucked forever inside. And I guess it was.

Chapter Twenty-two

The Martinellis' house sold in two weeks. On the second Saturday in July, Yvonne Yolanda came back with her real estate lady hair and real estate lady high heels and tacked a SOLD sign on, placing it at a triumphant diagonal. We didn't know who had bought the house, but I did see a motorcycle there a couple of times, the same one, I was almost sure, that belonged to the driver who had so loved Jeffrey and Jacob's purse trick. I also saw an old pea-soup-green Chevy Nova parked behind the Pleasure Way once or twice. A woman with long black-gray hair and a long skirt and beaded bracelets got out and spent some time looking around the backyard. She looked like the woman who sold her hand-made jam at the Sunday market.

I didn't see Mr. or Mrs. Martinelli to ask, but I did see Kevin Frink. It was a hot, hot day. I was in the backyard on the lawn chair reading *The Psychology of Love*, when I heard my name called. I jumped—saw Kevin Frink's face from the nose up, looking over our back fence.

"Kevin!"

He'd surprised me. I clutched my beach towel to my chest, covered up my body in my bathing suit. Good thing Zeus was with Hayden, or he'd have gone nuts. Zeus could be a good guard dog, even if his alarm buttons were sometimes hard to understand. He'd snarl at a large package but sometimes ignore the doorbell. He disliked certain people for his own reasons.

"I need your help," Kevin said.

I tossed on my T-shirt, unlatched the gate, and let him in. I'd thought he looked bad the last time I saw him, but now he looked worse. The weight that he seemed to have lost was back on, and a roll of stomach pushed against his T-shirt. You could almost see the frantic shoving of potato chips and ice cream and melting cheese that lay there, the impossible, anxious hunger. A small gathering of chin hairs had been allowed to grow too, an uncontrolled faction, a splinter group maybe; if he ignored them, they might attempt takeover. His skin looked white and fleshy, an underground kind of pale. It made you think of night creatures with scared pink eyes.

"What's going on?" I said. "Wait, do you want something to drink, maybe? Lemonade? Something?" It was strange to have Kevin Frink in my backyard. I thought of the crime books, a killer disguised as a delivery man. Maybe I shouldn't have offered to get him lemonade. Kevin Frink didn't belong there with Mom's pots of tomatoes and the bird feeder (which needed filling) and the pile of our sandals next to the back door. He brought the pieces of a different life. His mom drove a hearse and they lived in a house where the curtains were never open and the roof was green with a thick layer of moss. He had body odor. We had lotions that smelled like pomegranate.

His eyes shot to our tree, to the noise of a squirrel scratching along a branch. Then, they were back to mine again. "We've got to break her out of there," he said. "You go over, okay? Pretend to ask her somewhere. Shopping. Coffee. Who gives a shit. She goes with you . . ."

"What do you mean, break her out of there?" He seemed to think I was following along with him inside his head.

"She's not supposed to leave. Fiona. Especially not to see me. It's bullshit. She's *eighteen*."

"They can't keep her prisoner."

"Exactly. Jesus, it's hot."

He wiped the sweat from his face with the back of his arm. I pictured Mr. and Mrs. Saint George keeping Fiona locked in her room until she agreed to go to Yale, bringing her sparse meals on metal plates. I had a vision of stone walls, like in medieval prison movies. Then again, they didn't seem that horrible. Mr. Saint George would bring in Clive Weaver's garbage cans for him. Mrs. Saint George grew geraniums. They both were scientists over at the Marine Science Center. I doubted you could be too cruel if you studied sea life. "So, why did they ground her exactly?"

Kevin Frink picked at the plastic around the edge of our table. "It was dumb."

I waited.

"You don't need to look at me like that," he said. "Big deal. My mom caught us in the back of the hearse."

I'd never seen the back of a hearse, but my mind flashed a series of pictures. Maroon carpeting, quilted satin, a single creepy, curtained window. The slick bottom of a casket, slid inside. Kevin Frink's big white whale flesh. I shuddered.

He stared at me. "For God's sake, no one was *in* there," he said. "It's just a *car*."

I didn't want to help him and Fiona, not at all. Not anymore. I felt a little sick, from the sun and hot heavy air and from my intentions, which seemed right then stupid and innocent. They had gotten away from me, had become something else. All of my intentions had. The thing is, you open doors, but you never necessarily know what will come through them.

I wanted to back out of my actions, to sneak away in guilt, the same as that time I once knocked over a container of yogurt in the grocery store when I was maybe ten, leaving a splotch of white on the linoleum floor that I didn't tell even my mother about. "I can't do what you want," I said.

"We just need to get her out of the house. That's all. That's all I'm asking."

"What then?" I was afraid to know.

"She doesn't want to go to Yale. She said she wasn't even sure." The high whine of a saw started over the back fence, and Kevin pulled at his ear distractedly as if the pitch bothered him. The radio started up. *Do you re-mem-ber . . . The twenty-first night of Septem-ber . . .* "Fucking Earth, Wind & Fire," he said. "My *mom* listens to that shit." He flicked the nail of his middle finger with his thumb over and over again. *Click, click, click.*

I wanted to say that not being sure about Yale wasn't the same as not wanting to go at all. I wanted to say that I was sorry for leading him into a place he wasn't really ready to be in. And that I was sorry too for abandoning him now in that place. But I didn't say any of those things. "I can't, Kevin."

"You're kidding, right? I thought you were my friend. I thought I could count on you." He kept flicking that nail. It was making me nervous. I wanted out of there. No, I wanted him out of there. This was my place.

I was quiet. I felt that thick curl of guilt again, the one that got in the way whenever there was something I most needed to say. "I *am* your friend," I said finally.

"Whatever." He headed for the gate. He stopped the nail thing, but he was shaking his head.

"Kevin."

"What*ever*."

The gate slammed behind him, and the latch shut with a clatter. The smell of him hung around a while until it, too, decided to go.

I stood there in the backyard among cheerful things—Mom's watering can, the doormat with the sunflowers on it—and I listened to Kevin Frink step on the gas of his Volkswagen, listened to the screech and scream of his tires as they rounded the corner of our street.

I could tell the night would bring bad things the moment I heard Juliet's voice. I had never known a world without Juliet in it, and so when she was angry I could tell before she even said a word. When she was happy or guilty or planning something terrible, I could read it in her gestures and the spaces between her breath, and in the way she held her shoulders. When we gathered in the kitchen that early evening for our own various reasons, and when her voice sounded like bells—sweet and unreal—there was no question in my mind that whatever commitment she had promised Hayden the night before was about to be snatched back and destroyed. She was holding the bomb in one hand and the matches in the other, I knew.

And, I knew, too, because I had seen Hayden's latest note. It held the kind of relief and certainty Juliet was destined to crush, was crushing right then as we stood there.

Juliet—

Commitment.

When you said the word to me last night, I became sure of one thing: I'm the luckiest man alive.

Juliet's hair was up from the heat. She wore the lightest dress, white, as thin as a curtain. She smelled like perfume. "I'll be so glad to see Melissa again. She's only here for two days. . . ."

"I don't remember Melissa," Mom said. "Melissa who?" But she was distracted. She was looking for something in her purse. You'd have thought she would have heard the bells in Juliet's voice too, but she didn't. She never heard those things. She always seemed to listen with hope instead, the hope that everything was just fine.

"Melissa Beene?"

"You were never really friends with her," I said. "You didn't even *like* her. You shared a locker one year, that was *all*."

Juliet ignored me. I noticed that she had painted her toenails, too. They had gone from a chipped pale state to a shiny pink, some statement of intention that shouted more loudly to me, even, than her own voice. "She came over that time when we were working on our senior project, remember?" she said to Mom. "Went on to college in California? Brown hair? We used to go over before school to that bakery that went under."

"Once!" I said. "If that." I felt anxiety building inside, felt it pacing somewhere in the area of my chest. You feel joy in your

Deb Caletti

heart and fear in your stomach, but your chest is the place you feel things going wrong.

"Right," Mom said. "Right. You don't try to compete with Honey B's. You just don't. Ahh, I can't believe this heat." She looked up as if there were a cool breeze to be found high up somewhere.

"Anyway, she said she'd buy me dinner, and God knows, I eat like a horse lately." Juliet smiled. Hayden was getting a beer out of the fridge. He twisted off the top and took a long swallow.

"Okay, so where is this Honey B's? I love a good cinnamon roll," he said. Hayden was always game when it came to food or talk of food. His shirt was loose, and he was barefoot.

"Oh, they're *huge*," Juliet said. "Even you couldn't finish one."

"I take that as a challenge," Hayden said. He didn't hear the bells in Juliet's voice either. He and Mom *both* listened with hope. He was at ease, just holding that cool beer, and he didn't know he shouldn't have been. It was unfair to let him think everything was fine, to not even *warn* him. That seemed particularly cruel of Juliet. I wanted to say something, something that would stop all this right here, but nothing came. I could think only about Juliet and Buddy and Juliet and Buddy and Juliet and Buddy, and something I'd been trying not to think about at all. That day I'd asked Juliet about Buddy and Jitter. How she'd never actually given me an answer.

"You're on your own for dinner, then," Mom said to me. "I'm going out myself." She finally found what she was looking for in her purse—a wad of bills, which she handed to me over the table where I sat.

I didn't want those bills. I didn't want anything from Mom

then, because she sounded guilty too. Both of them were guilty, already guilty, and they hadn't even left our kitchen. I knew exactly where Juliet was going—that skanky apartment Buddy Wilkes lived in above the Friedmans' garage, less than a mile away. And I knew where Mom was going—toward some future involving that black velvet box. I understood something else, too—that premeditated acts were always the worst ones.

"I don't need money," I said. "I'll eat something here. Actually, I'm not feeling too well. I think I'm sick."

Mom put a distracted hand up to my forehead. "You feel fine," she said. "It's the heat. Take some vitamins. Go to bed early."

"I might be *really* sick. I might need you," I said.

She rolled her eyes. "You?" She laughed. "You're fine." She was right. I wasn't the sort who needed things. Even when I was sick, I felt a pride about getting my own ginger ale and Kleenex.

"Hot date, huh," Hayden said to Mom. He caught my eye, tightened his jaw in fellow Dean hatred. He had no idea. I noticed that the ring box was missing from the counter where it had sat for weeks. It was in her purse, I guessed. Her fingers had probably touched it as she had rummaged inside. By the end of this night, she'd be wearing that ring.

"Dean and I are having dinner," Mom said. I could smell her perfume. Her hair looked stiff from hair spray and was high off her neck like Juliet's. She wore a slinky black sleeveless blouse. It wasn't the kind of blouse you wanted your mother to wear. It was a blouse with ideas.

"When you recover from your sudden illness, you and Hayden can order a pizza," Juliet said. Of course—you made plans for other people only when you wanted them busy and out of your way.

Deb Caletti

"Yeah, come on, sister-in-law. We can watch some stupid television. Distract ourselves from the fact that it's a hundred degrees out." Hayden tipped the last of the beer into his throat.

"Mom's got a huge collection of old videos now," Juliet said.

It was the second time she had used the word *huge*. If there was a time to believe in the subconscious, maybe this was it. *Huge* described what she was about to do. Enormous, disastrous, monumental. Buddy Wilkes must have changed his mind about Elizabeth Everly. Juliet and his history together, whatever it had been, and whatever it still was—I guess it was just too powerful to let go of.

Mom was right—sometimes the bad guys did win. Sometimes, even if you tried your whole life to keep things going in their best direction, to hold things in their truest places by your sheer will, rightness could slide through your fingers so fast, you could feel the actual *strength* of badness. You could stand there in your own kitchen one summer night and find that all of your control had suddenly run out, the way a car with a broken gauge suddenly runs out of gas in the middle of some dark nowhere.

Hayden and I were alone for the night, then. It was hard not to be aware, aware, aware of this. The heat made sweat gather at the base of my neck, behind my legs. I worked on the Clive Weaver project, made my nightly, unanswered call to Nicole, but I felt restless. I looked for Kevin Frink's Volkswagen, which was not out by the curb or anywhere on the street, as far as I could tell. My window had been repaired from Jeffrey and Jacob's rocket, but with all the windows in the house open, I could know if he was driving up. It seemed important to hear Kevin Frink coming.

"Scarlet!" Hayden called up the stairs. "Come on, let's get out of here. It's too hot to stay inside."

I was no different, maybe, from my mother or sister, who had walked right into something destructive to themselves or others. I didn't do the responsible thing and mentally argue the pros and cons of going with him on that night in particular. I knew where my sister was, that she was taking something that wasn't hers, or giving away something of hers that she couldn't or shouldn't give away twice.

"One sec!" I called back to him. I actually hurried. So fast that I caught the toe of my sandal on the carpet and nearly lunged forward. The edge of the bed caught me; I did not catch myself. I rushed on a swipe of lipstick. Mascara. A clean-smelling perfume I had snitched from Juliet's drawer a long time ago, when she was still living here.

"You look great," he said when he saw me. Both he and Zeus looked up at me from the bottom of the stairs. I flushed. "You're going out with a piece of crap." He pointed to himself, in his ragged shorts and T-shirt.

"No worries," I said. I thought he looked great too. He was one of those guys who looked even better the messier he got. After he mowed the lawn and he was unshaven and his hair was damp with sweat . . . You didn't mind the smell of outside and motor oil and grass that he brought back in. You wanted it.

"I'm not even in the mood for pizza," he said.

"Neither am I," I said, although I didn't care what we had. I wasn't hungry. Maybe it was the heat, but more likely it was the moment, which filled every bit of me, even my stomach. My body was humming oddly, more awake than awake, conscious of every one of his movements. He put down the back of his truck for Zeus to get in, and Zeus leaped up.

"Careful. Hot," he said to me of the vinyl truck seat, and he was right. I could feel the sear of heat through my dress on my thighs and back.

"Ouch," I said.

"Here." He tossed me a towel, and then leaned over to hold it against the seat so that I could set my back against it. His face was right near mine. I could see the places where the stubble grew from his cheeks. "That'll help," he said.

"Thanks."

"What do you want to eat? Burgers? Fish?"

"Anything is fine."

"There's that great burger place by the docks."

"Pirate's Plunder," I said.

"Annoying treasure boxes on the napkins?"

I nodded. "Sounds great."

We rode with the windows down. I felt uneasy, but it was stupid because feeling easy with him was one of the things I liked best. No one else was feeling guilty tonight. He turned on the radio, some cowboy song that he knew the words to, and he sang loudly, a show for me. He kept looking at me sideways, to make sure I was appreciating the fineness of his terrible voice.

"So, why do you think dogs can't see themselves in a mirror?" His voice was raised over the wind and the radio.

"Or feel music," I said.

"Right. That, too."

"The eternal questions."

"And maybe they *can* talk, but they just choose not to." He was grinning.

"Messing with us."

"They talk to each other behind our backs," he said.

"So that's what that noise was."

"I crack jokes to him all the time, but . . . no answer."

"Maybe it's the jokes," I said.

He laughed. "Do you know this is our second meaningful conversation about dogs talking?"

He remembered. Of course I did, but now I knew that he did too.

We got our food, wrapped in foil, sat out on that same bench in front of the Hotel Delgado, which overlooked the marina. The water off the straits cooled the air, and finally you could take a breath that went all the way through you. The metal rings on the tops of the sailboats clanged against their masts, and you could hear the flap of the flag on the hotel and, on the boats—a couple of guys joking, who later appeared and called out Zeus's name as if they were old friends. Zeus went over for his own visit and the guys waved to Hayden and then disappeared again. It reminded me that Hayden had his own life outside of us, and this thought took me by surprise even though it shouldn't have. He had a life and experiences and a past and his own private thoughts and it could be a scary realization, that one. It meant a person had options. It meant they had chances, maybe, to leave.

"Larry and Gavin," he said. He leaned over and took a man bite out of that burger. Zeus was back again and sitting politely for food, his *Please notice, please notice* look on his face, sitting as straight as the second-grader who wants so badly to be excused for recess first.

"Your friends," I said.

"Not exactly. I haven't seen my actual friends in a couple of months. These guys sailed in from the Keys. I would bet money that Gavin's running from the law or something. What do you think? Drugs?"

"White collar crime. He used to be a banker," I said. God, those fries were so good.

"You gotta wonder about guys like that who just disappear." He froze his burger halfway to his mouth. "Christ, I'm sorry. I can be such an idiot."

I didn't know what he was talking about. If he thought he was offending me, he wasn't. Then I realized. "Oh, you mean our *father?*"

"You sound surprised. Okay, great. You didn't even care. Now I should apologize for apologizing." He took another bite, chewed with appreciation.

"It's just, we don't even really think about that. Him. It was a long time ago. I don't have a single memory of him. Not one. So, nonissue, you know? I don't exactly cry over it every morning."

"I thought maybe it bothered you like it does Juliet. Zeus, quit it. Back off. Those are not your business." He leaned down, lifted our Cokes from the ground where Zeus had been sniffing their lids.

"It doesn't bother Juliet," I said.

He looked at me, perplexed. "I think it does. I *know* it does. A lot."

Now we stared at each other. We each had a person in our mind that the other didn't know, not at all. I didn't know how I could make him see.

"Juliet is invincible," I said.

He laughed.

"Juliet gets what she wants."

He shook his head, the sort of shake that means you think someone is sadly mistaken. He didn't understand. Wouldn't. Maybe even refused to. And if he didn't understand, if he didn't *see*, how could he be warned? How could he ever protect himself?

He didn't see what was coming, what was happening right then at that very moment. Juliet, with her fingers in the belt loops of Buddy's pants, pulling them down past his thin hips. I could see into Hayden's future as he sat there on the bench with his soft eyes, and it made me feel like my heart was being crushed.

He put his burger down in his lap. Set down that food and looked at me hard. "Scarlet," Hayden said softly. If he was calling me, I wanted to go, wherever he was leading. "If you lose someone like that . . ."

Inside me, there were a pair of doors, and right then something was shoving up against them. Shoving and pressing, but I could not open them, even if he was asking me to. There was too much behind those doors. Too much, enough to spill out and over me; I could feel the press against my chest at only the thought.

"That's not the way it is," I said. But my voice was hoarse. Something was squeezing me inside.

There was the scrunch of a paper bag and then the feel of his body as he scooted next to me. He put his arm around my shoulders, and I laid my head against his chest, the soft T-shirt beneath my cheek. I was supposed to be saving him, helping him, leading him to a safer place. But instead, it was me who was feeling the shelter of someone stronger.

"It's okay, Scarlet. Huh? A lot of life is just about surviving what happens."

I lifted my cheek from his chest. I was so close to him. He was smiling, and then he wasn't. His eyes had a seriousness I had never seen before. I could smell the tang of his sweat. I looked into his face and he looked into mine. He swallowed hard.

I leaned in and I kissed him then. His lips were soft and sudden and somehow familiar. I breathed in his smell. I could have

Deb Caletti

wanted more, much, much more; I believed and held on to that belief, I knew what I desired and why; I wanted to go, go—but he pulled away, there was a firm shove on my shoulder.

"Scarlet, stop," he said. "No." He looked sad. He looked so sad that shame and embarrassment instantly filled me. I wanted to run. I wanted to run so far away from there.

"Don't say anything," I said. "Just don't."

"I'm sorry, Scarlet."

"Don't."

"I'm really sorry." I wouldn't look at him. "Listen," he said. "Hey listen."

"Oh my God. I can't believe I did that. Oh God. Oh God, I'm so sorry."

"Scarlet, it's okay, okay? We're good friends. We're good friends and that's a great thing."

"I'm so sorry."

I was too ashamed to look at him, to move, to walk back and sit beside him in that car again. Ashamed, but if he had changed his mind then and kissed me back I'd have forgotten that. He was nervous, rubbing his palms on the bare skin of his legs, running his hands through his hair. We didn't move or look at each other. We just sat on that bench for a long while, not saying anything. We sat there longer than I even realized, because the sun and sky turned orange-yellow and the night shadow started to fall, and it got cool enough for me to shiver.

"Let's just go back," Hayden said finally.

Those words were so simple, you could almost forget how impossible going back truly was.

Chapter Twenty-three

When we came home, the house was still empty, emptier than empty, the way it is when you can hear a ticking clock and the rooms almost echo. Zeus made two victorious laps around the living room, but the furniture seemed to be sitting ever so still, and you could hear the sound of crickets coming through the back screen door we'd left open.

Every movement of mine felt full of shame and humiliation and wrongness. I didn't speak, because I knew my own voice would be bad and horrible. We, Hayden and me, did not settle onto the couch in the living room to watch the Martinellis' old movies that had been popular in the 1970s, as he had suggested before. Instead, Hayden said he was going to bed. He walked down the stairs to the basement, but Zeus stayed behind, by my side. He knew when a person needed comfort. He would never know what a fool I was. "Velvet head," I whispered to him.

Finally, I went upstairs. My room felt like a display of my wrong love, still blazing, blazing right then at that moment—the paper cranes, that photo, all the hours I had spent there with feelings that were mine and mine alone. I could feel Hayden's presence downstairs, awake and waiting for Juliet. I heard him walking around, heard him come upstairs again, heard the worry in his footsteps.

In my mind I kept seeing Buddy Wilkes, the times he had been at our house. The way he had showed his right to be there—by stretching his legs on the couch, his arm on Juliet's leg as if to hold her down. And the other times I saw him too. His skin glowing green from the TV left on without any sound, his bare ass leaping into jeans as Mom's car came down the street. Juliet hooking her bra with one arm behind her back. Nothing tender or romantic or permanent, just zippers and hooks and body parts with other body parts and Juliet seeming distant and preoccupied in the morning. Buddy Wilkes's cigarette butt in our garden the next day.

I put on my long T-shirt, but kept the light off; I lay on my bed in the dark, propped up against my pillows. The light from the streetlamp shined in and illuminated my room in an eerie glow. The paper cranes rustled and swayed in a small breeze. I heard someone's wind chime outside.

I watched my clock with growing unease. I heard the television go on and then off again. I waited for Hayden to go outside to smoke, a place I might never join him again, but this never happened. The basement toilet flushed. The house was giving away the secret of his restlessness. I got up and looked down the street for a car—Buddy Wilkes's, Mom's, anyone's—same as I used to when I was small and Mom was late coming home.

I would watch and watch and beg silently for her car to appear, equally sure as not that it would, relief filling me and being replaced with joy as soon as it did. She always seemed surprised how happy we were when she got home. She'd put Neil Diamond on the stereo, and we'd dance.

But that night, the street was so dark and so still, absent of any cars or people or animals coming or going. The heat had tired people. The SOLD sign on the Martinellis' house looked very white under the moon; it looked bold, defying the darkness with only pressboard and a declaration.

I could hear every tick of my clock. It was getting close to midnight, and Mom would be home soon, I was sure.

But then, midnight came and went. Serious worry was shoving out shame for my attention. Mom always came home at midnight, always. I kept getting up every few minutes to look out at the empty street. My worry turned to anger. Maybe they just had too much to celebrate. Mom in her slinky black blouse and Dean Neuhaus with his clean fingernails. Mom's new diamond on her own finger, her hands not belonging to herself anymore. Maybe she was sleeping off a bottle of champagne beside him.

I wondered if I should call. I imagined her cell phone on his bed stand in a house we'd never even visited. He had children we had never even met. I could call and embarrass myself, intrude when it would no longer do any good. I was good at shoving myself into places where I didn't belong. There was nothing I could do about any of it, anyway. Helping hadn't kept me safe. It had been an illusion. *It had done no good, none,* I thought, and it was at that moment, that exact one, that I was thrown back against my bed and to the floor. There was a soul-shattering clash, an explosion, a blast so deep I felt it in my cells, glass raining down, nothing like the toy rocket, although the toy rocket was my first thought. I was on the floor, and glass was falling around like stars. The sky seemed to open. My window was gone, and the black night was there at my fingertips.

I heard shouting. There seemed to be some sort of fire outside through the frame of my window now absent of glass.

Hayden was shouting. Other people too. I didn't understand what was happening. Nothing made sense. My window was gone and I was sitting in glass and there seemed to be a fire and people were shouting and that's all I knew.

"Scarlet!" Hayden was there in the doorway. He was still in his shorts, without his shirt. His hands were on either side of the doorframe, as if the frame itself had just stopped him before he fell in.

"I don't know what happened," I said.

"There was a blast across the street," Hayden said.

This didn't make sense to me, not yet. Glass was in my hair.

"Your window again," he said. "Are you okay?"

He lifted me up. He set me on my feet. He looked me over. "You're okay," he said.

He saw my shock. He put his arms around me. I felt the skin of his chest against my cheek. "It's okay, sweetie," he said. I could feel his care. Real and true care. I wanted to stay there, with him holding me. I was scared. It felt safe with his arms around me.

"What happened?" I said.

"Something exploded across the street," he said again. He gestured toward the window. "I'm going to go see, okay? If everyone's all right? Maybe there was some kind of gas explosion. God, we need to see if everyone's all right."

I felt dizzy and confused, like I was waking from a dream or maybe was still in one. Maybe this was another dream that had a deeper meaning, a blast, my life as I knew it exploding and destroyed. But it seemed to be the present moment after all. I could feel Hayden's fingers grasping mine. I saw my clock, still ticking; saw that nothing that most immediately needed changing—Mom coming home, Juliet, too—had changed. This disaster had happened and they were still gone and we were still waiting even as we ran down the stairs together to the front door.

Zeus was turning circles of excitement and anxiety. Trotting with wild eyes around the coffee table, muscles tensed in fear for what had already gone wrong.

"You stay here, boy," Hayden said. He tried to make his voice calm, but if I could hear the alarm there then Zeus heard it a hundredfold. Hayden was putting a T-shirt over his head, and I was following him in my bathrobe, although I don't remember ever putting it on.

He opened the door, and Zeus was there, and I saw him put one hand on Zeus's forehead to keep him back, but the front door was always a barrier Zeus wanted to get past, always, even when there was nothing urgent beyond it. The beyond was urgent enough for him, but that night even more so, and he pushed with all his force and broke free.

"Goddamnit, Zeus! Not now! Scarlet . . ."

"I've got him," I said, even as Zeus's large butterscotch self raced across the street where I could now see a fire burning in some gaping hole where the Saint Georges' garage had once been. The walls looked frail and papery and blackened, and you could see Mr. Saint George's few tools on a pegboard just beyond the fire, and a lawn mower, too, ready to be swallowed by flames. I knew what had happened then, knew that Kevin Frink had found a way to what he most wanted, a way that he was most familiar with, matches and detonators and explosions, the destructive reordering of his own and our own universe.

It hit me, the same as the force that had thrown me across my room, what I had done, what I had contributed to, how this was in good part my fault. Good intentions didn't even make this forgivable. I had gone where I didn't belong and set the wrong things in motion. I had tried to give what wasn't wanted. And I had done it all to make myself feel better, not them. Myself—because it felt better to have a little control over a situation, to feel some power, to move things around for a better outcome. To have fate in your hands instead of the other way around.

Hayden was running and shouting and Clive Weaver was on the lawn in his underwear holding Corky in his protective arms, and Mrs. Saint George was out on her lawn sobbing with Mr. Saint George's arms around her, as Buster looked worried at their feet. Fiona and Kevin Frink were nowhere in sight. Ally Pete-Robbins held her boys around their shoulders, their eyes wide and blinking as they stood barefoot in their spaceship pajamas, as their father, too, ran across the street to see if he could help. Mrs. Martinelli was in her bathrobe in the driveway, her arm against her eyes from the brightness and growing heat of the flames, and Mr. Martinelli was saying, *"Get back, get back; I used to be a firefighter!"* People were shielding their loved ones, and my loved ones were missing, except for Hayden, running, and Zeus, running across the street as I called after him.

I went after Zeus, who was racing in mad circles around the yards, crazy from everyone else's fear and his own sudden release. His people were going fast, and so, he too, needed to go fast. He crossed the street and crossed back again, dashed through the

Martinellis' junipers around the Pete-Robbins's Acura; he flew past Ally Pete-Robbins, and Jacob made an unsuccessful dive for his collar.

He stopped on the sidewalk across the street. I didn't want him going near that fire. You could feel the heat of it on your face. I tried to command his stillness with my voice, calling him sternly. He was panting. I had a chance. But then, his head turned suddenly toward the wide street beyond that fire, beyond the licking flames and the crackles and pops and the ash floating in the air. He ran.

You could hear the sound of sirens coming. All I could do was the one thing I'd been asked to do by the man I loved, to help the one good dog I was responsible for, and I went after him.

"Zeus!" I clapped madly. I could hear sirens coming closer now. I imagined a night of deception and of fleeing—Kevin Frink and Fiona Saint George heading off to some unreachable place in his Volkswagen, Juliet fleeing her marriage in Buddy Wilkes's El Camino, Mom fleeing the stagnation of her life in Dean Neuhaus's arms. And me fleeing, too, leaving my mistakes behind, mistakes now up in flames, running after Zeus as he rounded the corner far beyond the Pete-Robbins's house.

"Zeus, PLEASE!" I felt frantic now. I couldn't get to him—he was always just beyond my grasp. I was worried he would be hit by one of the fire trucks or the ambulance, which I could hear approaching. Zeus had abandoned everything in his fear; his anxiety propelled him forward, forward, around, anywhere, in wild motion. We weren't on our street anymore. I was in my robe in a stranger's yard. My voice was hoarse from calling. Lights of houses went on, porch lights, too. I ran through the new bark and freshly seeded lawn of the house where the construction had been going on all summer. My chest was full of fire from running. Zeus was in another backyard and I didn't know if I could keep up with him much longer.

"Boy!" I pleaded. "Zeus!" The commotion on our street sounded like a dim roar, but I could smell the destruction in the air, some dark blend of damage and charcoal and melting plastic. Zeus stopped and looked at me, too far for me to catch him, and when I started toward him, he took off again. I was crying now. "Zeus!" He ran two blocks over and disappeared. I called and called him.

I was desperate for the sight of his butterscotch fur, his triangle ears. I was crying his name and could only see him gone forever, gone, could feel the loss of him, and my own failed responsibility to the man who loved him, whom I loved.

The street was empty, just streetlights, and the faraway sound of the place where I lived, the moon so still and forever. He had vanished. No dog in sight. No beloved dog. Just a neighborhood at night.

I bent over. All of it, the whole night, Hayden, that wrong kiss, my sister gone, my mother, Kevin Frink, and Zeus, Zeus, Zeus—it filled me and crushed down hard and I sobbed. Sobbed and sobbed, my chest wracking; I held my stomach. Mom had been so right. Control was just wishful thinking, and you controlled things to hedge your bets, to be safe, to guard against loss. But safety called its own shots, and now I had destroyed things. The things that mattered most to me.

Zeus was gone, and the loss of him felt like the worst thing, the worst. We hadn't been careful enough. I hadn't been. You have to be careful with the people you love. It's the least they deserve.

I wanted to look up and see him there, but that didn't happen. There was just the gone-ness of him, and the empty street.

I knelt on the sidewalk in my robe under the streetlight, my head in my hands, crying. That's when I saw the big lumbering form of the Pleasure Way drive up. That's when Mr. Martinelli opened the door and held out his hand and that's when I got in. I sat down in the real leather seat and rode with Mr. Martinelli up and down our streets, calling Zeus's name through our open windows.

Chapter Twenty-four

Juliet

Just that, on a crumpled piece of paper. I smoothed it with my hand. I had the same longing, the desire to call a name and have whom you most wanted to see appear. Zeus had been gone for three days, Juliet, too. Hayden looked like a ghost, his skin white and his eyes hollow, and I felt like a ghost, everything of meaning gone and over with.

I watched the street every day, put Zeus's food bowl in the front yard, his water bowl, too, called his name again and again and listened for the jangling of his tags. I made flyers with a picture I had taken of him, his face eager and looking straight into the camera so that he looked right into your eyes from the page. People needed to see what a good dog he was. I walked our neighborhood, putting up the flyers and calling to him, looking for some movement in the bushes or trees. Every time the phone rang, my heart leaped in hope. Every time I remembered that he was gone, it was like getting the bad news for the first time—the hurt and realization hit with a force that felt forever new.

I imagined him being taken in by someone, his collar gone, maybe, ripped off on a tree branch. He would be sitting with some new family as they had dinner, wondering where we had gone. Why had we not come and gotten him? Or I imagined him running still, or exhausted, or the worst imagining, scared and alone. He was innocent and vulnerable out there by himself. He could be hungry or tired or thirsty or hurt, and he had no voice to ask for what he needed.

I couldn't stand that he wouldn't know how hard we were trying to find him. What if he thought we didn't care anymore? He might think we had stopped loving him, when we would never, ever be the kind of people, person, who would stop loving him, who would abandon someone who needed us.

"I know she's fine," Mom said. She misread my agony, my inability to rest, my ceaseless watching through our living room windows. We *did* know Juliet was fine. She had called from a phone booth and given no explanation other than she needed to be away for a while. As for Mom herself, we didn't discuss her own disappearance, her arrival at 4:00 a.m. that morning, when she finally came back to the shattered pieces of her neighborhood and her own home, her makeup off and her hair disheveled. She still wasn't wearing that ring on her hand, though I didn't care anymore. Fine, go ahead and marry Dean Neuhaus. It didn't matter anyway. It mattered less who came than who was gone, Hayden most of all.

And Hayden was gone, even if he was still there in our basement room. He was sullen and didn't eat with us or talk much—

his reason and justification for being with us had disappeared, and so he made himself as scarce as possible too, as he waited for Juliet to return. For Zeus to return too. He talked to Mom downstairs in the kitchen and I listened in. The conversation had only big empty spaces where answers should have been. Mom didn't know what to do. Hayden didn't know what to do. We avoided each other, like my kiss was a bad part of town we needed to stay away from. He would stand outside and shake the box of treats Zeus liked. He had lost everything.

"Scarlet!" Mom yelled up the stairs. In Jasmine's house, no one yelled, there was a rule against it, but not at ours. Mom would call out from wherever she was—the backyard even—when she needed something. Dean Neuhaus would hate that.

I poked my head down the stairwell.

"Honey, I need you to get some stuff for dinner. Unless we want milk with a side of milk." In spite of everything that had been going on, she looked good. Calm, maybe even happy. Marriage proposals were obviously uplifting. "I told Hayden to be ready in five minutes. I know you're perfectly capable of doing this yourself, but he's driving me crazy. Get him out of here for a while? I need some time away from the black cloud that we're living in. One hour, to *breathe*. Me and Neil Diamond need some time together."

"Mom . . ."

"Please, Scarlet. He needs to get out. I need him to get out. I worry about him being alone so much."

I wanted to protest, to find a way to escape, but I heard the basement door close, his footsteps on the kitchen floor.

"Bus is leaving," he called.

We didn't talk in his truck. The windows were down and the radio was on, but there were no jokes and no laughter and no ease. Our pain and the ways my family had let him down sat right between us. He looked in the rearview mirror as he always did to check on Zeus. I couldn't even speak about his absence. I couldn't even speak about my own part in everything that happened. There was an equation—the degree to which you hoped and wished for a good outcome multiplied by how wrong it all went equaled the amount of despair.

We walked across the parking lot of Johnny's Market, with its jarring sounds of clanging carts and small children and into the store itself with its jarring bright lights and jarring music and jarring bodies reaching for containers of yogurt and plastic bags to put broccoli in. Every color felt too bright and every sound too loud. Bad things make the regular world too much to bear. It's too simple then. Its simplicity shouts. A tube of toothpaste is so regular it makes your heart break. A cereal box does.

We were there in the international foods aisle, with its mundane assortment of the no longer exotic—refried beans, soy sauce, Thai food in a box. Hayden reached for a bag of rice and added it to the basket he carried in one hand.

"Onion," he read off the list, and we continued down the aisle, and that's when I saw him, the lean coyote body, the thin angular face capable of destroying our lives. Buddy Wilkes just walking past the aisle, fast, too, like he had places he needed to get to.

It hadn't occurred to me that she was right here somewhere, still on Parrish Island. I'd have guessed they would have had the decency to at least go away for a while to some stupid motel, some loser house on the mainland rented by one of Buddy Wilkes's loser friends. But I never imagined her here, her head on a pillow not five minutes away from Hayden's agony, sleeping in some pull-out bed in Buddy Wilkes's apartment over the Friedmans' garage as Hayden lay awake under our own roof.

My heart stopped—I hoped Hayden hadn't seen him. I would veer us away, steer us toward the frozen foods, something, just not where he was or maybe, God, her, too. Would she be that cruel to appear in public like that? Could she be right here, picking out some pack of cinnamon gum? She had been cruel enough to leave; that was the thing.

Maybe Juliet had some stupid craving Buddy was now responsible for, or maybe he came to get more cigarettes, I didn't know. *He'd better be fast*, I thought, and I grabbed Hayden's sleeve to steer him left instead of right. I hadn't looked at Hayden's face, though, until that moment. He was looking down the way Buddy Wilkes had gone, eyes fixed. His face looked much older than I had ever seen. He lifted the basket and renewed his grip on it in a way that made the contents clatter against each other. He cleared his throat as if he were about to speak.

"Come on," I said.

We just stood there at the front of the store, where the lines formed, where people read the fronts of the magazines and plucked containers of mints to add to their loot on the rolling black mat. A toddler tried to stand in a cart, and his mother shoved him down. Mrs. Sheen, the attendance lady at our school, said a brisk *Excuse me* to us to indicate we stood between her and the tortilla chip display that was the priority of her life right then.

"Hayden, come on," I said again, as Mrs. Sheen's arm reached pointedly around us.

"I think I saw . . . ," he said. His voice was husky.

"Let's get out of here."

But Hayden didn't listen. Instead, he set down our basket right there, right in the center of the aisle, and he strode toward the bakery department where Buddy Wilkes was headed. *God, oh God,* I thought. We were going to have a scene, a scene in Johnny's Market, right near the croissants and freshly baked pies. I didn't know what Hayden was capable of, and if I'd have imagined a situation like this, I'd have guessed him to return to his truck and start it up and drive home. I wouldn't have guessed his angry stride, his tense jaw. I thought of what he had said about his father—a bad man. I wondered about the places in him we didn't know, in him or in anyone, that stayed undiscovered until what was most precious had been taken.

"Hey!" he called. His voice, which had been flat and emotionless for days, seemed full and roaring, like that fire in the Saint George garage. "Hey!"

I followed. He was walking fast enough that up ahead I could see the back of Buddy Wilkes, who looked so suddenly less of everything that Hayden was. Less strong, less intelligent with his pale face and stupid grin, less attractive, less of a man in all ways. Buddy Wilkes turned to the sound of Hayden's voice. He held a box of doughnuts in his hand, just doughnuts. The kind that came in a row, all dressed up in powdered sugar.

"Where is she?" Hayden said. "That's all I want to know."

"Who the fuck are you?" Buddy Wilkes said. He looked honestly surprised. Maybe even a little scared.

"Her *husband.*"

"Her husband?" He squinted. "Look, man, I don't know who—"

"Don't play games with—"

Hayden stepped toward him. We were right there in the bakery department, where you could get your name put on a birthday cake underneath frosting balloons.

"Juliet *Ellis's* husband?" Buddy's face cleared in understanding. The threat that made his body tense was gone, and he held his free hand out as a stop sign instead. "Look," he said. "Keep that chick away from me, understand? I don't want anything to do with your problems."

"What?" Hayden said. He looked a little unsteady. The fight drained out of him too. It looked possible for him to fall right into that table of cookies in plastic containers.

"Tell her to stop calling me, okay? It's not my problem."

I didn't understand, and then I did. I understood when Elizabeth Everly appeared with a container of milk. She looked at all of us with uncertainty, leaned into Buddy, and whispered something to him. He put his arm around her, guided her away from where we stood.

I took Hayden's elbow. I knew, as he did, that this was worse somehow, worse than if Juliet had been in that garage apartment with Buddy Wilkes. Buddy Wilkes would have been a simple reason for leaving. Hayden could have brought her back, maybe. He could have forgiven some stupid misguided act with some rival who was in no way his equal. But that she had wanted to break her vows and didn't and had left anyway—it meant that her reasons were rivers of need too deep and treacherous to cross. You couldn't see those rivers and still have hope.

That night, Mom and I were alone for dinner. We had been alone for dinner a lot before Juliet had come home. I had been used to the feeling, Mom and me like an old married couple, the two of us talking about our day and asking the other to pass the butter. But now there was the sort of vast space and stretching time between us that made the clank of the silverware the chosen sound of loneliness. The space was as ragged and confused as the hole in the Saint Georges' garage, covered in plastic, as ragged and confused as the empty places created in the absence of those you loved, people who had left you that you cared about—Zeus and Hayden, Juliet and Jitter, Fiona Saint George and Kevin Frink, driving and driving and driving God knows where in that Volkswagen. Each time my knife scraped my plate or the tip of Mom's fork hit hers, I felt like it was possible to go on and on forever feeling alone.

I felt too many things, and they were crashing against each other until I could not tell which feeling was which. Aching loneliness, despair, worry, but something else pushing to be heard too—something maybe even more honest than the rest.

"People shouldn't just go abandoning other people," I said.

"That's true," Mom said.

"What about the baby?" I said. "Is she just going to stay away and we'll never see it?"

"I don't think that will happen," she said.

"Maybe we should take care of it. She should have the baby and you and me and Hayden will take care of it."

Mom stopped moving her food around with the tines of her fork. "I think Juliet's going to be an excellent mother."

I could have spit my milk. The feelings were shuffling and rearranging themselves into some order. "Look what she's doing now."

"She's scared now. You can be scared and still be a good mother when the time comes."

Truth was funny, because it was an insistent thing, maybe as powerful and insistent as some force of nature, the push of water or wind. You could keep it out only so long, but it had its own will and its own needs, and maybe you could keep it at bay with lies, but not for long, not for always.

Too many things had happened in the last few days, and those things shoved me hard then so that everything I had held up for so long tipped easily, just like that. You don't realize all that's been eroded sometimes, all the damage that's been done, until the moment when the water rushes through and everything is finally and thoroughly destroyed.

"This is so old," I said. And it was, it felt a million years old, her watching so carefully over this strong person, my sister. Her giving and giving and giving to Juliet, who took and took and took. The words were out and the anger, too—the truth of how angry I felt was right there for her to see. It filled me up, beyond what my body could hold. It could have picked me up, overcome me, like a big swell of the sea, taken me far, far out from what I knew. That's how big it seemed.

"Here you go, defending her again. No matter what she does, you're there to show your endless support." I sounded like a small and jealous child. I felt like one.

Her face turned red. I'm sure she was wishing she were any-where else, now. Whenever there was a talk radio show that got too heated, even, she'd snap it off. "I would do the same for you. You know that."

My face was red too. I could feel its heat rise up my neck and flame in my cheeks. "Maybe I don't know that," I said. "Juliet uses up both our rations of love and understanding. That seems pretty clear."

Mom threw her napkin down as if she'd had enough.

"Scarlet, that's ridiculous." She shook her head back and forth. "Do you think I need this at this moment? This whole little sudden outburst?"

It didn't feel sudden; it felt years and years old too, an outburst that had grown layers like the crust of the earth, now forced to move. It was so old that I knew all the lines from hearing them so long in my head. The words came swiftly and easily. "What would happen if I were Juliet right now? You'd argue and you'd spend hours together crying and talking alone on her bed. While I sat and did my *homework* or something. Juliet has always gotten everything. From you and from everyone else."

"That's unfair, Scarlet. You never seemed to need the same things Juliet did. You didn't want them. You were always . . ." She searched around for a word. Her face looked lost.

"Forgettable?" I said.

I might have thrown a dagger, that's how wounded she looked, a surprise attack with an arrow from an assailant hidden behind a tree. Her eyes filled with tears. "Why would you think this about yourself? Or me? Why?"

I remembered shut doors, laughter, voices, raised or quiet, on the other side. "Like anything else. You just come to conclusions. You just see things and you come to conclusions and then it's fact in your mind."

"I think you've come to some very wrong conclusions. About yourself and me and even Juliet."

"It's always the two of you."

"Oh honey," she said. She reached out to me, took me in her arms even though I didn't want her arms. "Oh honey, I'm so sorry you feel that way."

I didn't want to fold into her right then, I felt too angry, but anger sits right there next to grief, so, so close that you lean just so slightly and you're there, in this other place that feels like another country, but is the same country, with different customs and a different language but with the same shared ground. I started to cry. Your own sense of being shut out was huge and powerful. It meant it was just you, by yourself, in this big space of loss, with its depth and endlessness and lack of boundaries. You stand in front of a deep, dark sky and feel your own smallness, and you stand in front of loss or the possibility of it and feel even smaller than that. Loss is what you'd do anything to avoid.

"Oh, if you had any idea how much I love you and treasure you. You." She kissed the side of my head. I could feel her chest heave against mine and mine against hers. "If you don't already know that—I blame myself."

"Just, Juliet . . . You two are always . . ." I crossed my fingers where they lay on her shoulder.

She broke away from me, took my shoulders. "Oh honey. I got this so wrong. Since . . ." She put her hands up to her eyes. "Since . . ." It was funny—I didn't know what she was going to say before she said it. That's how far I kept it from my own self. "Since your *father* left . . ." The word *father* sounded funny coming from her. "Juliet had a hard time. More than you—you were younger. You were *resilient*. She remembered. There's this thing Juliet has, about going and staying. Keeping people away, she keeps people away, maybe even me, the way you keep people close. You keep people close by looking after them. It's what I do too. I hold tight. Even what I've done with Juliet. See. Scarlet? You and I have always been the similar ones. You and I are."

I took this in. I had to listen hard. It was a new way of seeing things, and I had held fast for a very long time to my old way. But it made sense to me, the simplest sort. It was possible, maybe, to have facts in your mind that weren't facts at all. You could build a whole life's story on false assumptions. You could make truths out of untruths and untruths out of truths. Until you spoke them, really said them out loud or checked for sure, you may not have known which were which.

"Oh sweetheart, I am so, so sorry. I didn't know. You were just so *capable*."

"You're going to marry Dean," I said.

"No, honey. I broke up with Dean. I was so late that night because I was telling Dean I didn't want to see him again."

"You broke up with him?"

"I kept wishing it would be different. Trying to make it something it would never be. I always hated giving up. But giving up isn't always the worst thing. It isn't. It's gotten a bad name. Giving up can be *good*. There are better places for my hope. Much better places."

"Mom . . ." The word was relief and pleading and understanding and a million other things. I wasn't capable right then. I set my capability down, and she held me. She patted my back like a baby but I didn't mind. I felt exhausted from too much emotion. From having the ways I had seen things detonated and shattered. I would have to look again. You could try and understand people, you could read books and understand words and concepts and ideas, but you could never understand enough or have enough knowledge to keep away the surprises that both fate and human beings had in store. This was too bad, I thought, but this was good, too.

We were both exhausted, we agreed. And so Mom and I did the thing that we did sometimes—our own thing—we turned on a movie and she made popcorn, and we ate it and watched, sitting beside each other.

"It's funny," she said. The psycho killer in the movie had been finally brought down by the young girl and her kid brother. "No one is ever quite as strong or as weak as you'd think."

Chapter Twenty-five

Kevin Frink and Fiona Saint George were somewhere in California when Kevin Frink's Volkswagen broke down. My mother heard this from Mrs. Martinelli, who heard this from Mrs. Saint George. I could imagine Kevin Frink sweating then, somewhere in the heat and dry air, unfamiliar yellow hills around them. Fiona would have used her family plan cell phone to call her parents for help. Fiona Saint George and Kevin Frink were on their way home now, in a rental car with air-conditioning and room to recline their seats. Mr. Saint George had wired her money, because that's what you did when you loved, right or wrong. When you were gentle, loving people who studied ocean creatures, or who created scrapbooks of faraway places, or who wrote notes that were really poetry, or who folded paper cranes and more paper cranes, you gave when maybe you shouldn't give, gave even when your very house had been blown to a million pieces.

Or else, you gave until you finally couldn't anymore.

It had been five days since the blast, five days that Juliet had been gone with Jitter, and five days since I'd last seen the back of Zeus disappear around that corner. I can't tell you how badly I wanted to see him, to see his funny face, his person-not-person self looking back at me with eager eyes that seemed to wonder what great thing was coming his way next. I would have given anything to see him again. Anything.

You were supposed to have hope, right? You were supposed to respect its power and hold on. And so I did. I held, and held, and let hope fill me. But as the days went on, it seemed I could be holding for a long, long time. Hope could be the most powerful thing or the most useless.

The Salvation Army truck came and got the last of the Martinellis' belongings. They didn't even need a moving van. Rob's Taxi (basically Rob Millencamp in Rob Millencamp's Ford Taurus) came and picked them up to go to the airport; Rob waited patiently at the curb reading *How to Win at Poker* as Mrs. Martinelli rolled her luggage down the walk. Mr. Martinelli wore that Hawaiian shirt again, and he was beaming and bouncing all over the place, pinching Mrs. Martinelli on the butt. She got teary for a moment as she shut the door, but only for a moment. Maybe it was even my imagination.

Mom and I both said good-bye. Mrs. Martinelli had taught her how to prune rosebushes and had given her recipes and advice, and Mr. Martinelli had unclogged our sink and fixed our furnace and repaired our bathroom light switch. They were as close to parents as Mom had, hers being long dead. I saw her watch Mr. Martinelli when he got up on the roof to clean his gutters or when he was on a ladder putting up the Christmas lights. She had always kept a firm eye on him until he was safely down.

"We'll write you and tell you all about the plantation," Mrs. Martinelli said.

"You better do that," I said. I felt choked up suddenly. It was the way she grasped her purse tightly. It was how his hair was combed so straightly across his head and how he smelled of cologne. The vulnerability of that made my throat close. It was the thought of them out in the big, big world, flying across continents, and the disappointment and heartache that would surely await them. That, and the fact that I rather loved Mr. and Mrs. Martinelli.

"Come and see us! We'll send you the address when we get settled!" Mr. Martinelli said. He slapped the hood of Rob's Taxi, the same as he used to slap the Pleasure Way, which now was also owned by the people who had bought the house, the motorcyclist and his partner, Jayne, who sold her homemade jam at the Sunday market. I took the Martinellis' picture, standing close together with their arms around the other's waist.

Jeffrey and Jacob played with a half-pumped basketball in the street. One would toss it and it would fall with a splat at the other's feet, causing them both to break into laughter.

"*Pffft*," Jacob said, making a farting noise with his mouth.

"*Pflll*," Jeffrey said, making a farting noise with his.

We hugged good-bye. I gave Mrs. Martinelli a kiss on her soft old cheek. Mr. Martinelli gave me a firm, hearty hug.

"Take care of the old neighborhood," he said to me.

"Take care of each other," I said.

The glass had been replaced in my window again, but I heard the sound through the screen as loudly as if the glass weren't there at all. My mind must have been waiting for it, even in sleep. I looked at the clock—1:30 a.m. Hayden, and those matches.

I looked at him through my blinds, his solitary figure leaning against his truck door in the streetlight. The trees were whooshing around as if we might see a storm after days of dry heat. Purple clouds were inching across the sky. The air smelled as if it were thickening with rain.

The shame of that kiss kept me right where I was, behind the wall we'd built. Maybe he needed to be alone anyway.

I watched him for a moment as the wind picked up. It loosened some small leaves from the Martinellis' tree, leaves that spun and tossed in the air, most landing on the ground, but one landing unnoticed in Hayden's hair. It was cheery and sad and hopeful sitting there on his head, waiting to be seen and yet not being seen. The thing was, no matter what, I loved Hayden.

I tossed on my sweatshirt. I stepped carefully and quietly down the path to where he stood.

"The midnight hour," he said to me.

"Yeah," I said. "A leaf . . ." I took it from his hair and handed it to him and he looked at it as if I'd given him something important.

"Thank you for coming," he said. "I've missed my friend Scarlet."

I thought I could cry. I leaned my own back against the truck beside him. I was glad to give him something, a leaf rescue, comfort, looking after—maybe just the presence of another person on a summer night when your heart was broken.

He blew smoke out upward to the sky. We both looked at the stars which were out and then gone as a cloud moved past.

I heard the flapping of the black plastic that covered the hole of the Saint Georges' garage. I heard Clive Weaver's television, keeping time with the flickering images behind his living room curtain. And then I heard something else. I thought I heard something else.

Hayden stood straight.

"Did you hear that too?" I said.

He nodded.

I didn't want my heart to soar. I knew what would happen if we were wrong. It had been five days. We all knew what the likelihood was as each day passed, even though no one spoke it.

"Zeus?" Hayden called.

We listened. I strained my ears to hear again, please hear, *please*, what I thought I had. The jingling of tags.

"Zeus! Come here, boy!" Hayden was looking around, and so was I. Corky might have gotten loose. Clive Weaver might have left his back door open.

"Zeus!" Hayden cried. We heard it again; we did. "Zeus!" Hayden's voice pleaded too.

"Zeus! Over here. Come here!" I called.

Please.

And then, like in a dream, like your best dream possible, like every hope you've ever had finally coming true, there he was. With his butterscotch fur and triangle ears, there he was, trotting around over by our back fence. Trotting around like it was any other day and he was any other dog.

"Zeus!"

I did start to cry then. I did. Hayden laughed out loud. I cried, and tears just streamed. Every piece of me was flying—with relief, with happiness. Something a hundred steps beyond happiness.

"Oh, thank God," Hayden said. "Thank God he's okay. Damn

you, boy. Damn you for doing that bad thing. You stupid dog! Come here, you idiot."

And Zeus did. He looked thin and scruffy and mangled, but he came right back to us with the weary joy of homecoming.

I was surprised to hear her voice.

"Reilly Ogden has been calling me endlessly," Nicole said.

I didn't answer. Our friendship seemed like something from a long time ago. Maybe it was me who wasn't sure I wanted to be friends anymore.

"Are you there?" she said.

"Yeah."

"He says he keeps having this bad feeling that something is wrong with you. He's worried. He even went to your house."

"He did?"

"*Is* something wrong with you?"

"Reilly Ogden has no business worrying about me."

"He's a freak, but that doesn't mean he's wrong."

"I'm fine."

"Kevin Frink blew up your neighbors' garage. That's reason to worry right there."

She waited. But I didn't do what I had done for the last weeks or the last years. I didn't give, explain, plead, ask her to talk, or apologize. "Do you want to get together or something?" she said.

Images flashed—me carrying around her books all those months while she was in those casts. Me listening to every feeling she had had since the sixth grade, staying with her on the phone while she cried, even when I was tired, or when I had my own problems, or when there were other things I wanted to do. Giving, without any end point or boundaries or even the giving back that might make my own constant generosity justifiable. Maybe I should have just let her come into my house, my room, and take everything that belonged to me. That's what I'd basically said—I'd said, *Here. Take it all.* "I don't know, Nicole. I'm rethinking a lot of things right now."

"Oh," she said.

I stayed silent. I didn't feel like giving anything anymore, even words. That's what happens when you give too much. Suddenly you reach a point of *over.* You don't even necessarily know that point is coming. It just arrives. It's a long overdue passenger on a long overdue train, but finally it's there.

"I saw Shy at the pool. He asked about you too. Everyone's asking about you since you sort of . . . disappeared. He said I should tell you to give him a call if I saw you."

Jesse, I thought. He had a name. "Great," I said.

"You can't make someone love you if they don't."

"Yeah. It's too bad, the thing about people having their own free will," I said.

She didn't speak, and neither did I. There was only the infinite dark universe sound of open phone lines minus voices. I didn't mind this. I hoped she felt a little of my pain, as un-nice as that was. That was the truth, *is* the truth, of nice people pressed too far. We could start to feel a little mean. A little angry. A lot angry. Anger stores up in there, whether you know it or not.

"Well, I guess I better go," Nicole said.

"Yep," I said, and I hung up without saying good-bye.

A week and a half had passed since the explosion, ten days. Kevin Frink and Fiona Saint George arrived back home in the rental car. I saw them go inside the Saint George house, and a few moments later, Officer Beaker showed up. Kevin Frink walked out beside him, Officer Beaker's hand firmly on his arm. There were no handcuffs or sirens or any of the excitement you might see if it were a movie. In the true crime books, too, it was always more exciting. But Kevin Frink just walked out and got into the car, and that was that. Somewhere along the trip, we learned later, Fiona had told Kevin what she had told her parents from a phone booth in California. She hadn't wanted any of this. She hadn't wanted to go to California. She wanted to go to Yale. She hadn't wanted to tell Kevin before; she'd been afraid to hurt his feelings.

Jitter was twenty-eight weeks old. He was two and a half pounds, and his head was likely down now, getting ready for the trip into the world. He could hiccup and blink and maybe even dream. He was doing all of these new things somewhere else, away from us. I missed Jitter, even if I didn't miss Juliet.

I could tell something was in the air, change—I could feel it. It wasn't just the clouds, although they had stayed around and then got heavier, bringing cool air and occasional drizzles from the waters of the straits. You heard people shutting their windows. Clive Weaver had a sweater on when he went to check his mail; he stood out on the street for a long time before Ally Pete-Robbins reminded him that it was Sunday.

There wasn't any banging and clattering of moving and packing, but then again, he had come with very little. His boundless hope would have filled a thousand moving trucks, but Hayden's actual belongings took up only the backpack that sat by the front door. The sonogram picture was missing from the refrigerator.

"What's happening," I said when I saw it was gone.

Mom sighed.

"I want to know what's happening."

"I think you know."

Hayden himself appeared then. "Scarlet," he said.

"You can't leave."

"Come on and walk me out." He slung his bag over his shoulder. He hugged my mom and thanked her.

"This is wrong," I said. I was getting more used to speaking my mind. I was ready for honesty in my life, because the lies had done no good. *"Wrong."*

"Come on," he said to me.

I walked outside with him. Zeus followed, as if this were a regular day and he was going off to work with Hayden at the docks. "You can't do this," I said.

Hayden called Zeus, kept one hand on his collar, led him to the car where he jumped into the passenger seat. Hayden shut Zeus safely inside. "After what we just went through with him . . . You lose something important once, and you're so afraid it's going to happen again."

"We need you here," I said. He came back around to his side of the truck. I stood in front of him. You could smell the rain coming again.

"A person can't just keep trying," he said.

"You're supposed to have hope. Everyone knows that. You *know* that."

"I'm going to give you something," he said. "Okay? It's one of the most important things I have."

I didn't want something. I wanted him. I wanted him not to go. Ever.

He reached into his back pocket and took out his wallet. There, in a careful place, separated from the messy bills shoved inside, was a frail piece of lined white paper. He unfolded it carefully. He handed it to me.

Deb Caletti

But he did turn that key. Over the sound of the truck's engine, he said, "Tell that fucking ice-cream man to get another *job* already," but his voice was cracked and his eyes teary.

Hayden's truck wasn't going to go, wouldn't, couldn't back out of that driveway, but it did. It did; it backed out and drove forward down our street. Hayden gave a wave of good-bye out the window, and a loss so great overtook me, sucked me up; I could feel something ripping inside me—grief, loosening its tight hold. The loss was so huge it was bigger than Hayden even, bigger than one human could account for, bigger than every disappointment and every separation, big enough for my father, finally, because at its center was the most hollow and lonely abandonment—long, empty stretches of it, of aloneness, of being left behind by someone bigger than you who filled you, whom you had hoped, hoped, hoped was solid enough to make you feel safe.

I saw Zeus's sweet head in the passenger seat disappear as they turned the corner. We didn't even get to say good-bye.

Chapter Twenty-six

*J*uliet returned that very afternoon, as soon as she had called home and found out from our mother that Hayden was gone. She'd used up the last part of her last check from the Grosvenor Hotel, staying in the Tide Away Inn in Anacortes, just on the other side of the ferry.

I didn't want to look at her shiny blond hair and her large stomach where she was supposed to be keeping our baby safe. She moved back up to her old room, where I could hear her moving around, settling clothes into her old drawers, putting things back on the dresser where they'd always been. We would sleep right next door to each other, pass each other on the way to and from breakfast and dinner, but I would avoid her. Her presence reminded me of what, who, wasn't there. It reminded me of what she'd already taken from Jitter. If Hayden was goodness, she was badness and the reason goodness was gone. Juliet felt like the worst kind of intruder, like the one we had let in instead of Hayden, the one who had finally decided to set a match to our house.

Mom seemed to go on like she had before, working and tending to Juliet, making sure she ate and napped, putting her hands on either side of Juliet's great belly and watching the rolls of Jitter's round heel or elbow. But something had changed. Mom was more wary with Juliet; she kept her distance and watched, the way you watch something that you're unsure of from a slight way off.

The neighborhood felt colorless, and my sadness made everything feel slow and heavy and without purpose. We didn't see much of the new neighbors; we only heard the motorcycle rev up and leave to go to work and only smelled the smell of blackberries cooking on a stove and warm wax. I didn't call Jesse or Nicole or Jasmine or anyone else, and I worked at Quill only two days out of those weeks. I was in the self-imposed exile of sorrow and didn't feel the energy for anything but the back lawn chair and magazines. I didn't take pictures, didn't want to capture anything. My psychology books seemed too much, even—too much understanding and no understanding, too many answers and no real answers.

I went to Point Perpetua one afternoon. I sat on my rock with the clouds lying low over the sea in front of me. I opened the green bag from Jesse, took out the book with its shiny cover and new-book smell. I opened it to the center and stuck my nose in and took a long sniff. I looked at the words at random. It felt thick and complicated and maybe more like the sort of book you think you should like more than you actually do.

I started the first chapter.

> In the following pages, I shall demonstrate that
> there is a psychological technique which makes it
> possible to interpret dreams. . . .

I liked the idea of a technique, a process, a series of steps for figuring out things and people. I needed some answer to all of the loose puzzle pieces in my mind and heart. I would have to try to put more faith in the idea of a subconscious, though, that supposedly murky land that existed behind a secret door of the mind. Maybe I just didn't *want* to believe that there were things I kept even from myself.

I read for a while, and then I rested and watched the beach that I loved. A man was trying to surf on a white board; there was a family made up of two couples, an assortment of kids, and grandma with her jeans rolled up. There was a father on his knees in the sand too, with a large sand castle taking shape in front of him. His back was curved with effort, and his arms reached to pat and build as his little daughter in a frilly bottomed bathing suit ran to fetch more seawater. The grandma in jeans bent down to choose a rock; a few seagulls on a blank stretch of sand were having a seagull conference with poor attendance. In all of it I could only feel Hayden's absence.

That night, Mom tried to barbecue hamburgers for us all; she was terrible at barbecuing, she always had been. We always teased her about the time she had cremated a pack of hot dogs. I watched her humming and trying her best with the smoke swirling around her. I pictured Hayden there with us, doing the job Mom wasn't so good at, wearing one of Mom's old striped aprons over his favorite green shirt and cargo shorts. I pictured him as a father, his and Juliet's baby, all of our baby, tucked in a front pack next to him, but never, ever near the smoke or the fire. I pictured him holding the baby in the crook of his arm, pictured him warning a small child away from the hot metal. He would cut the meat into tiny bits. He would make sure she did not sit too close to the tipping end of the lawn chair.

That night I dreamed again, with the cool air coming through my screen. I was small, and I was at the beach. I held a bucket of water in sandy hands. I was running toward a sand castle and caught my toe on a hump of driftwood. I started to fling forward, but was caught by the strong hand of my father. He was wearing a soft green T-shirt.

I woke up in shock. Even if you didn't believe in the subconscious, maybe it still believed in you.

I sat upright in my bed, and right then I felt like everyone all at once—me right now; me a long time ago; my mother years ago, losing the man she loved; Jitter, even, adrift and fatherless. *Know what you desire but, more importantly, why you desire it.* That *why* was where the trick lay, I realized. *Why* was a land of trapdoors and hidden places, trees and rocks that looked like one thing, but were actually another.

I was taking out the garbage when I saw Ally Pete-Robbins's Acura driving up our street with Clive Weaver in the passenger seat. She stopped in front of our house and rolled down the window.

"I found him at the ferry terminal, sitting on the bench," she said. "I thought he had a suitcase on his knees, but it was an old clarinet case."

"Mary played the clarinet in the high school band," Clive Weaver told me from the next seat. "She was very good, too. She had a gift, you might say."

"I would have liked to hear her play," I said. I still cared very much about Clive Weaver. That was one thing that did matter to me, and I remembered that then.

"We're going to get settled back in," Ally Pete-Robbins said. The window slid back up and they drove home, but that evening, I collected credit card applications and catalog and discount oil change flyers from the recycling bin. I got serious about it. It would take him days and days to open all the mail. I changed the recipients' addresses from ours to Clive Weaver's. I wrote more letters on pieces of perfumed stationery that Mom had gotten from Quill.

Dear Mr. Weaver—
I hope this finds you well. My husband, Roger
Woodruff, and I have returned from the South of
France, where we lived for several months. The mail
service there was dreadful. I had to write and tell you,
as I recalled then your fine service to our home every
day for twenty-five years. You are an inspiration, and
the French have a lot to learn from the US Post Office
and the respected members within it.
Sincerely,
Doris Woodruff

Dear Mr. Weaver—
I am writing to thank you for the example you set while
being our mail carrier while we lived on your route. My
son, John Roberts, has decided to join your profession,
and I have no doubt it was because of the role model
you were without even being aware of it.
Deepest Gratitude,
Charlotte Roberts

Deb Caletti

Mr. Weaver—

I am sorry you have been sad. I want you to know,
though, that I think you are a fine man, and having
you as a neighbor all these years has been really great.
Corky, too.

Love,

Scarlet Ellis

Our own first letter from the Martinellis arrived at the beginning of August. Mom waved the envelope at me.

"You'll never guess who this is from," she said.

I took it from her, looked at the stamps. "Africa," I said.

"I'm afraid to look," she said.

"They need money. They're stranded."

"I can't stand it. Open it," she said.

I tore open the thin airmail envelope. Mrs. Martinelli's brittle-
thin handwriting filled two pages. I read a little. "Oh God," I said.

Mom sat beside me on the lawn chair. "Come on! What?"

I laughed. "Oh my God. You're never going to believe this."

Dear Annabeth and Scarlet,

Although it has been an eventful few weeks, Mr.
Martinelli and I are finally getting settled at our cocoa
plantation, which we have named La Nouvelle Vie,
or, new life, in French, the official language here.
Our journey was a long one—Mr. Martinelli had his
luggage stolen in Marrakech by two thieves posing as
rug merchants. We set out after them in a speeding taxi
and a ruckus ensued, and this series of events led us to
be escorted out of the city by our new friend, the chief

constable Mumbao Reynaulds, who we have come to call fondly Burt Reynolds, at his kind suggestion.

The letter went on. Morin Jude must have met a terrible fate—she never showed at their meeting in Abidjan. No one seemed to have heard of her, until Mr. Martinelli bribed two government officials to speak. They were then put in contact with an individual from a remote village. A hundred dollars exchanged hands, and that's when they were finally brought to an abandoned plantation and left, holding only the keys to their new home.

"Can you imagine how much a hundred dollars is to a village like that?" Mom said.

"They traveled across the world to buy an abandoned plantation for a hundred bucks. Do they know?"

"Does it matter?" Mom said. Her eyes danced.

"Not at all," I said. It was the happiest I'd felt in a long time.

"What a thrill, huh, Scarlet? What a thrill."

The day that the Martinellis' first letter arrived, construction began on the Saint Georges' garage. I recognized the voices of the men and their music. Hits of the seventies. *Midnight at the o-a-sis . . . Send your camel to be-ed. . . .* There was always reconstruction going on somewhere. Things that came apart were put together again, never exactly the same.

I had another dream that night. I dreamed Juliet and I were rolling down a grass hill, rolling and laughing, and when we got to the bottom, there were two sets of hands to lift us up, Mom's hands, and a man's, too. There was ice cream, and then things went bad. Juliet was crying and reaching out her arms and Mom was crying and there was a red car driving away, and we stood huddled together and Mom was calling and calling a name.

That next morning, I felt a sadness so pure I could almost hold it in my hands. It had risen to the surface sharp and clear enough that it felt real. I remembered Juliet beside me in the dream. A feeling of us bonded, sisters, the two of us against all things, against the bad stuff around us. Juliet and me, together.

She was still sleeping when I went into her room. There was no butterfly candleholder on her night stand anymore, no trace of Buddy Wilkes. She'd been reading my book *What to Expect When You're Expecting*, which she'd snitched back from my room and now lay on her floor. One of Hayden's notes stuck out from the end, used as a bookmark. I shook her shoulder.

She sighed awake, rubbed her eyes. "What time is it?" she said.

"Just eight," I said.

"For God's sake, Scarlet. I need my *rest*." She rolled away from me. I spoke to the back of her head and the curve of her shoulders. I told her about the dream.

"Am I remembering this or not?" I said.

"You're remembering this," she said. Her voice was tired.

I thought of Hayden's note. *I will not leave you like you've been left before.* I had thought he meant some boyfriend I didn't know about. Maybe Hayden had been more right about Juliet all long. "Our father is the one who left you," I said.

She didn't know what I meant. "He left *you*, too."

"I didn't think I remembered anything," I said. I was still talking to her shoulders.

"It's too deep in to ever forget," she said.

"What do I do now?" I said. "I liked it better when I didn't know I knew. When I just thought it was something forgotten."

"I think you're asking the wrong person for advice," she said.

I stayed there, kneeling beside her bed. I didn't know exactly what I wanted from her, or even if she could give it. Finally, she rolled over again and looked at me. "Look, Scarlet, you'll go on doing what you've always done—you'll make yourself so necessary that no one'll ever leave you. Or else, you'll stop. And I'll keep making sure no one'll ever leave me by keeping people away. Or else, *I'll* stop. Pretty much, that's all we've got as far as choices. You do what you do until you don't do it anymore."

It took me a moment to take this in. When it settled inside and found its place, I realized that she was right. Things can look suddenly different, things you've seen every day of your life, like when there's a snowfall and everything that had always been there before looks new. Or when someone who's been only thinking things finally speaks them. I could give you my theories on everyone—on why my mother was with Dean Neuhaus, on why my sister wanted Buddy Wilkes or why she ended up pregnant. I could tell you why Nicole had self-esteem issues, or why Kevin Frink blew up that garage. But I never could have explained why I kept so close to other people's business and so far from my own. Not the reason at the heart of things.

The truth struck.

"You love Hayden," I said.

"It's that simple," she said. "And that complicated."

"Jitter is yours and Hayden's and you love them both."

"More than I know what to do with."

I leaned over and hugged her then, and she pulled me toward her, up beside her on the bed, her round belly against my back, and we lay like that for a while, sisters together, just like a long time ago.

Chapter Twenty-seven

The second letter came from the Martinellis.

> Dear Annabeth and Scarlet—
> The cocoa plants were not cocoa plants at all, and the villa was in terrible disrepair, but neither of us has ever been afraid of hard work. . . .

And then a third. . . .

> Dear Annabeth and Scarlet—
> We love it here. We hope you'll come and visit. . . .

I spent more time with Juliet. I went with her and Mom to see Dr. Crosby, to hear the baby's heartbeat for myself, to see how Jitter was coming along. As the weather got hotter and she got rounder, she craved lemons and lemonade, and I would bring her frosty glasses and we would sit and talk about baby names and about the time when I was three and stuck a LEGO up my nose, and about the time Juliet was six and locked us and our babysitter outside the house. I learned things about her. She was afraid she wouldn't be able to stand the pain of labor or wouldn't be able to soothe the baby, and she hated that she looked like our father and not our mother, and she once had tried to get Gregory Hawthorne, our middle school algebra teacher, to kiss her. I would put my face right close to Jitter and I would say things like, "Listen, you stay in there until you're good and ready" and "We can't wait to kiss your baby neck." I took Juliet's picture sideways, and she would hold her dress down as flat as possible to show off Jitter in his best light.

Something else happened during those weeks, as summer started to close up shop and pull out fall, turning the edges of leaves orange, turning down the night temperatures, getting the display ready same as the drugstore dragging out all of the stuff for the next holiday. My love for Hayden turned into another kind of love, pieces that were there all along though I hadn't recognized it. A love for Jitter. The desire for Jitter to have something important that I never had. Hayden was right—the list was harder than it seemed. To know why you wanted something, why you desired a person, the real reasons why, the behind-the-reasons reasons . . . It could be thorny and layered, the answers hiding in the shadows, submerged even, in some depths too far out of your view. Every night I wished for it under the sky of paper cranes. *Let Jitter have Hayden. Let Jitter have this good father.*

"You don't want to keep doing what you're doing? Change something. Change one thing," Juliet said.

Deb Caletti

"Reilly Ogden," I said.

She drove me over to Reilly's house in Mom's car. *You've got to say what you mean and mean what you say*, she had said. *Doubt in your voice is an open door people will shove right through.* She waited in the driver's seat and I saw that she was keeping her eye on me as I stood on his porch and rang the bell.

Reilly's mother answered. She was a thick woman with tightly wound hair and she did not meet my eyes. She invited me in, but it wasn't a real invitation. Reilly was her boy, you could tell.

"Well, it's about time," Reilly said.

"Reilly . . . ," I said. I remembered Juliet's words. *Nice is shitty self-protection, Scarlet. You've got a right to say who you want and don't want in your life. Selfishness isn't always a bad thing, in spite of what you think.*

"You didn't mention my new contacts. They're blue," he said. He opened his eyes wide for me to peer into.

"I have something to say to you."

"Come in," he said. "We can talk in my room. My mother won't mind." He opened the door wider and I could see the edge of a recliner with a remote control on the arm. The sound of some war program from the History channel coming from the living room.

"No," I said. "Here."

He ignored me, stepped aside as if I'd come in anyway. He thought I'd do what he wanted because I'd never given him reason to think otherwise. *You can collude with people like that*, Juliet had said, *whether you know it or not. Just by not saying no.* "She'll make us sandwiches if I ask."

"Reilly, I want you to hear me. I want you to leave me alone. I don't want you to talk to me or follow me or come near me at all. I don't want to have anything to do with you and I never will. Never."

"Scarlet," he said, as if I were being unreasonable.

"Never. *Leave me alone.*"

A bad thing like selfishness could be a good one, and a good one, like kindness, could be bad. I needed both of those things, I understood, in careful measure. So I turned and went back to the car. I left the fried food smells and the recliner and the creepy basement and those blue contacts and I left the ways all of that might make me feel sorry for him. I turned my back on it, so that, finally, finally, I could look after myself.

The bedroom door was closed again, with just the two of them shut away behind it. I could hear intense, muffled voices, the sound of Juliet pleading her case. I thought I heard the word, but maybe I just hoped I had: *Hayden.*

I watched Mom when she came out. She didn't see me, just went downstairs for the rest of the evening; she sat cross-legged on the floor in front of our coffee table, her scrapbook supplies in front of her. When I went downstairs myself, I saw her there. She had her scissors in her hand and a paper image, which she turned in a careful circle as she cut. She looked at the page, thought, glued. And then she set down her scissors and shut the book.

"Juliet's leaving," Mom told me the next morning. I stopped my spoon halfway to my mouth.

"What?"

Mom poured coffee into a cup. "I told her she needed to go back to Portland."

I'd wanted her to lay down the law with Juliet for as long as

I could remember. But not *now*. *This* wasn't the time. This was the worst time possible. "You can't do that," I said. Juliet couldn't leave now. She just couldn't. We needed her. I needed her. Jitter, our Jitter, was going to be born in ten weeks. "She can't *leave*."

"It's not okay to hide," Mom said. "She's got a husband she needs to face. Hayden loves her and that baby. The baby needs a father."

"Why can't he come back here?"

"We need to let them work this out on their own. Without us."

I thought of Hayden, with his kind eyes and strong hands. I thought of his handwriting on a page and his firm grip on Zeus's collar. I thought of him with that sonogram image; I imagined it tacked up nearby him somewhere, wherever he was now. I thought of Juliet, and Jitter. If letting go, if letting people and things work themselves out in the way that they needed to without your help was the most important thing, then it was also the hardest.

"I need to let her grow up," Mom said.

Juliet was set to leave the next morning. I figured it was time, as good a time as any, for the end of the Make Hope and Possibilities Happen for Clive Weaver project.

I waited until it was dark. I gathered all of my supplies in a big garbage bag and went out the front door. I laid the bag on the sidewalk, let the treasures pour out.

I stuffed the mailbox first. I crammed so many letters in there, he'd have trouble getting them all out. I left the mailbox door open, let the letters pile up on the door itself, and then gather on the ground underneath in an enormous mound.

And then I went to his big tree. I tied crane upon crane—

blue and yellow and pink and white, cranes made out of Yvonne Yolanda's real estate flyers and clothing catalog, cranes made out of tire ads and mattress sales and coupons for extra-larges with everything. A dog barked and the Pete-Robbins's light went on. I imagined Ally Pete-Robbins peeking at me through the slats in her blinds. But I didn't care. I just filled that tree so that when he woke up, it would look like every good thing possible had happened.

I thought the cry I heard the next morning was one of pain, the sound of a heart ripping from a body, a howl of deep despair. Sobs, after that. The cries came from the front yard. I didn't even have time to open my eyes and look before Mom yelled from downstairs. "Scarlet? Scarlet, come down! What did you do?"

My heart stopped. No, please, please, no. I imagined the worst, some disaster again, some terrible thing happening because I had wanted to do something good. I ran downstairs without looking out my window. Oh God, what now? Didn't I ever learn? I heard Mom's and Juliet's excited voices. He was dead maybe. The shock had given him a heart attack and he was naked and dead on his lawn.

But when I got downstairs I saw Juliet at the front window in her robe and her sleepy face, and I saw Mom standing in the open front door. I heard the sound again, but the noise wasn't what I thought.

"Look," she said.

Mom pointed to what I already knew was there—the tree, full and bright and glorious in the morning light, shimmery with color and surprise, the mail pile as big as an enormous snowfall—and to what I didn't know was there, Clive Weaver, bent in half, laughing. Laughing so, so hard. He stood straight, looked over at us, his hand in the air to indicate he couldn't take the slightest bit more humor just yet. His feet were bare in the wet grass, and Corky ran back and forth in high-strung uncertainty.

I put my hand to my mouth. "Surprise, Clive Weaver!" I shouted. "Surprise for you!" My heart felt so big and wide. You could give and give until it hurt you, give without boundaries or self-protection or reciprocation, give out of fear, and it could leave you empty and depleted and even used. But you could also give out of something very simple—a pure desire—to be kind, and it could double and triple your own joy.

"It's Christmas, Scarlet," he said. "It's goddamn Christmas!"

And that was the best possible outcome, I thought. Because if it was Christmas when you didn't expect it, it was possible, just maybe possible, that it might be Christmas any day at all.

Chapter Twenty-eight

We would take Juliet to the ferry; that was the plan. She would get on, and Hayden would meet her on the other side. The reunion would be their business, and so would the car ride to Portland and their eventual settling into married student housing at the university. All of the letters he would write her from then on would be their business too. We hugged for a long time before Juliet walked onto the ferry. The four of us. Mom and me and Juliet and Jitter.

We watched her back disappear through the terminal doors.

"Well," Mom said. That's what a person said, after all, when there was a big wide range of possibilities in their view, none of which they could truly do much about.

"Well," I said.

Joe and Jim Nevins lifted the thick ropes from the dock pilings, and the huge white ferry eased away. Cars of tourists were already lined up for the next sailing out. That's how it was in the summer on Parrish Island. People coming and then leaving. But there were always those few who would look around at the beauty of what we had and who would decide to stay always.

"I've got an idea," Mom said. She had gotten a little too much sun the day before, and her shoulders were the kind of pink that stings a little.

"What kind of an idea?" I said. The ferry was getting smaller and smaller, almost toy boat–size. Seagulls were standing around looking aloof or were busy picking at dropped french fries or cigarette butts. The waters of the Sound were laid out in front of us, glittery in a way that was both mischievous and knowing. Mom looked a little that way herself.

"This is going to sound crazy, but I've been giving it some thought." She stopped, as if she'd told me already and was waiting for my reaction. I wondered if this was the sort of news that people in the movies would have to sit down for.

"Okay," I said.

"I thought we could visit the Martinellis in Africa. The two of us."

I wanted to laugh. I did laugh. The thought of Mom and me in Africa seemed as silly as the idea of Mr. and Mrs. Martinelli there.

"I'm not kidding," she said.

I thought about it, but I could only bring up some image of Mom and me in twin safari hats riding camels, which wasn't even the right country.

"Listen, Scarlet. It'd be good for us. I've been here since I was a girl. I've spent my *whole life* here. I've got money saved. I've wished for things and never really had the chance. . . . It's time to stop dreaming and do something about it. You've got to know what you want, then . . . go."

I remembered the rule, number two. The paper was folded in my pocket. I had kept it near me since Hayden had put it in my hand. I remembered the last rule, too. Rule six. You let go, and then you start again.

I changed the image in my mind—Mom and me, in our regular clothes, walking down the wide shiny floor of an airport, boarding a huge plane that would take us somewhere with different smells and sounds and sights. Real postcards to Clive Weaver this time. I would need to read up on the Ivory Coast.

"Okay," I said. I smiled.

"I really want to do this, Scarlet," she said. "I always talk about it. . . ."

"So now we stop doing what we've always done," I said.

The frame had been built for the Saint Georges' garage, and the smell of sweet fresh-cut wood filled our street. The sounds of the construction workers' radio, too. *Well, I keep on thinkin' 'bout you, sister golden hair surprise.* . . . The motorcyclist next door was named Dennis, and Jeffrey and Jacob followed him around like he was God. It reminded me of the time the guy from the Grateful Dead, Jerry Garcia, came to the island, and all of the dads started wearing tie-dye and hanging around Hank's—where Garcia had eaten lunch once—grabbing each other's arms like fourteen-year-old girls whenever they saw him around town. Jacob found one of Ally Pete-Robbins's bandannas and wore it tied around his head like Dennis did, and Jeffrey tied a shoelace around his neck with a silver gum wrapper hanging from it in some lame attempt to replicate the leather strand with a metal medallion that Dennis wore. I took their picture, arms around each other's shoulders like tough guys, hung it on my wall with the others.

Nicole called me again, and I answered.

"I'm really sorry, Scarlet," she said. "I was a shitty friend."

"I'm sorry too."

"I was wrong about Jesse."

"Maybe we can start over," I said.

"I hope so."

"I cut my bangs too short a full month ago, and they still look horrible," I said.

"You told me that cutting your own bangs was an act of self-loathing."

"I did?"

"I'm sure they look way better than you think. You've got great hair, no matter what," she said.

"I'm going to stop wearing the bag, then."

"I've hated it without you," Nicole said. "Things are going to be different from now on." This was how it felt when you didn't try so hard. When you didn't control everything. Sometimes maybe it meant people came to you. It wasn't only Nicole's fault that she had taken and taken. It was mine that I hadn't stopped it. I was the willing hostage, the same as Fiona Saint George.

At the end of August, Fiona Saint George left for school, giving me a shy wave through the car window. I heard Kevin Frink was moving away to be with his father somewhere in Florida after he was required to pay the Saint Georges a huge fine. Joe, the ice-cream man, came around less and less during that last week. Things were ending. The sun seemed different in a way you don't have words for, and I knew that summer was really over. Things could slip away, I realized, and that's when I went to Randall and Stein and picked out a book on Roman history and carried it in its green bag to the Parrish Island Pool.

Jesse Waters was right there in the ticket booth, not in the high lifeguard chair where I had imagined this scene taking place. So I got in line. I watched him. It was a moment that sat between *before* and *after* again; but when he looked up and saw me and he broke into a wide smile, *after* was right there, right then.

"Can you wait a couple of minutes?" he said. I nodded. I sat out on the hill of grass by the ticket booth, watching the little kids with towels around their necks and girl babies in frilly suits sitting in the crooks of their mothers' arms. When Jesse came out, I gave him the book.

"You noticed?" he said. I nodded. I was the one who felt shy. We sat together and talked. I felt the crackle of energy between us. This was my own life, not Juliet's, done in my own way, and I went toward it.

The conversation stopped. I didn't want it to. *What was your most embarrassing moment?* I remembered Hayden that night, smoke lifting skyward. I tried again. I said it aloud. Jesse laughed.

"Oh God," he groaned. "I don't know if I can tell you this."

"I promise I won't tell anyone but a few thousand of my closest friends," I said.

"Okay, but you've got to promise," he said. I waited. He took my hand, turned it over, and traced my palm as if he were Bea Martinsen who read fortunes at the Sunday market. "Middle school," he said.

"Oh no," I said. Everyone knew that was the worst time for an embarrassing moment.

Deb Caletti

"Uh-huh. We had to write a poem."

"Oh no." I started to giggle.

"Had to hand it to a partner to read aloud to the entire class."

"Oh God," I said. I was giggling pretty hard.

He paused. "Instead of *huge beast*, I had written *huge breast*."

"No!" I laughed loud and hard. He put an arm around my neck, pulled me close. It felt so good. Part of me lifted right up, like those dreams where you fly.

"You promised, right? Only a few thousand?"

We laughed together until we weren't laughing anymore. I felt his warm breath on my face. He leaned in to kiss me. It was my own kiss, a right and truthful one. Soft and sweet and long—I couldn't believe it and then I could. Just like that; it was easy.

On October sixteenth, at 2:35 in the morning, Tess Elizabeth Renfrew was born in a Portland hospital, with her father there to catch her. Mom and I arrived in Portland later that morning. It was the first time I had seen Hayden since he had left in his truck, and none of us could look at one another without our eyes filling. Jitter, now Tess, slept in a tight bundle in a plastic bed on wheels near Juliet. She had rosebud lips. When Hayden unwrapped her so that we could look, we saw her scrawny little chicken legs and tiny, tiny fingernails and arms that flailed at the sudden freedom. She wore a knit hat on her head, which Hayden pulled off carefully so that we could see her funny sweet head with dark hair like Hayden's.

"Beautiful, beautiful baby Tess," he sang to her as he wrapped her back up tight. She made gritchy little sounds, and he beamed at us to see if we heard them too. Juliet looked tired, her tummy still round but deflated. She lay her head back on the pillows and smiled.

"Zeus is a big brother dog now," I said. I still missed him.

"He can teach Tess her first words," he said, caught my eye, and grinned. "We *know* he can actually talk. We *know* it."

"Yeah, we do," I said. "He can probably play the piano, too."

Hayden laughed. "Sneaky canine bastard." Tess—she was lucky to have him. Juliet, too. All of us were.

We held the baby package and smelled the top of her head and handed her back to Juliet, who seemed suddenly to know what to do. She held her baby like she was a Tess expert. She would hand the baby back to Hayden and he would take her. They were working it out, the two of them.

Mom and I rode back down the elevator a few hours later and found our car in the hospital parking garage. I didn't want to leave Tess yet. The million pictures I took didn't seem enough. I wanted to sneak her out the back door, hold her and hold her and hold her. But Mom said they needed time alone. We would come back again soon to visit. And we would come back again after our trip to the Ivory Coast, that we'd be taking during my mid-winter break. We had already gone to the passport office, filled out our forms, and had our photos taken. Every day we checked the mail for the small blue books with the gold seal that meant we could go anywhere.

We got into the car. It was evening, and an October evening too. That summer—a summer of love and detonations and leavings—I had learned that you could be so afraid of loss that you let hope take over, or else, made sure that it never saw the light of day. You had to manage hope. But that night the sky was clear and we had a new baby in our lives and the world had

Deb Caletti

more hope than you had ever known it could hold. It was time for all the optimism in the universe then. All of it. So Mom did the only thing you can do, when you feel that full. When there is so much hope and so many possibilities. She rolled down the windows and turned the music up, loud. It was Neil Diamond, and we both sang along.

About the Author

DEB CALETTI is the author of *The Queen of Everything*; *Honey, Baby, Sweetheart* (a National Book Award finalist); *Wild Roses*; *The Nature of Jade*; *The Fortunes of Indigo Skye*; *The Secret Life of Prince Charming*; and *The Six Rules of Maybe*. She lives with her family in Seattle. You can visit her at www.debcaletti.com and become a fan on Facebook.